MYTHS

MYTHS

TALES OF THE GREEK AND ROMAN GODS

LUCIA IMPELLUSO

ABRAMS, NEW YORK

Cover illustration: The Birth of Venus, Sandro Botticelli, 1484–86, Gallerie degli Uffizi, Florence

Page 2: Jean-Marc Nattier,
Perseus Turns Phineus into Stone (detail), 1718, Musée des Beaux-Arts, Tours

Right: Francesco Primaticcio, *Ulysses and Penelope* (detail), *c.* 1552, Museum of Art, Toledo (Ohio)

Art Director Giorgio Seppi

Editorial direction Lidia Maurizi

Graphic design Chiara Forte

Picture research Paola Bacuzzi, Alice Fermi

Editing Giacomo Ambrosi, Marta Falco, Cinzia Mascheroni, AGMedia s.r.l., Milan

Layout Massimo De Carli, AGMedia s.r.l., Milan

English translation Rosanna M. Giammanco Frongia, Ph.D.

English-language typesetting William Schultz

Library of Congress Control Number: -
2008926919
ISBN 978-0-8109-7144-8

© 2007 Mondadori Electa S.p.A., Milano
English translation © 2008 Mondadori Electa S.p.A.
All rights reserved.
Originally published in 2007 by Mondadori Electa
    S.p.A., Milan

Published in 2008 by Abrams, an imprint of
    Harry N. Abrams, Inc.

Printed and bound in Spain
10 9 8 7 6 5 4 3 2 1

HNA ▮▮▮▮▮
harry n. abrams, inc.
a subsidiary of La Martinière Groupe

115 West 18th Street
New York, NY 10011
www.hnabooks.com

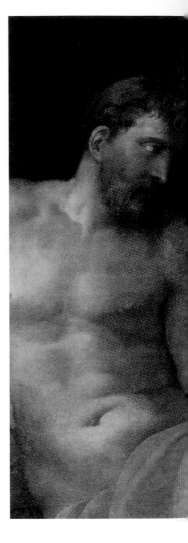

Contents

Introduction   6

The Beginning   9
The Olympian Gods   29
The Deities of Fate   313
The Sea and
Water Deities   321
The Earth Deities   333
The Infernal Deities   437
Monsters   463
The Dawn of Humankind   483
Heroes   511
The Great Exploits   595
The Trojan War   619
The Return after the War   707

Primary Sources   766
Index of Episodes   769
Index of Names   771
Photographic Credits   779

Introduction

Since the dawn of civilization, most cultures have described the world through tales that explain natural phenomena. These mostly oral legends were transmitted from generation to generation, modified and enriched with new details until they came to constitute a powerful intellectual heritage.

Western civilization, in particular, inherited its body of myths from the Greeks (later assimilated into Roman tradition), whose fertile imagination interpreted natural and spiritual phenomena in terms of animism and anthropomorphism. Plato, the celebrated Greek philosopher, spoke of the *mythos* as "a tale about gods and divine beings, heroes, and journeys to the underworld," and contrasted it with *logos*, the rational, demonstrable reasoning that forms the structure of philosophical speculation.

In the final analysis, mythology is a string of stories that have survived to our day, sometimes in fragmentary fashion, collected by scholars into a unified body. Over time, these fable narratives found direct correspondence in poetry, literature, and the arts. The many legends that tell of heroes, mortal men and women, gods, and divinities, far from turning to dust in the narrow field of archaeological treatises read only by specialists, have resisted time and survived through the centuries, and are still deeply rooted in the memory of modern man, where they have maintained unchanged their spellbinding power.

During the Middle Ages, barbarian invasions and the later hostility of Christianity could not totally erase and uproot pagan antiquity, which survived by adapting to meanings and forms that were more consonant with the succeeding ages. In the Renaissance, classical civilization, which had never been forgotten, regained its role as the exemplar of the highest creative values to which man should aspire. Soon, the myths came back to life in the fine arts and in the great Renaissance and Baroque frescoes that decorated the walls and ceilings of aristocratic palaces. In this period, several treatises on mythology were written, which were useful to the artists who painted fresco cycles or canvases with mythological subjects. This art often had moral, educational, or celebratory content. Being deeply rooted in the popular culture, the myths also became a source of inspiration to nineteenth- and twentieth-century artists.

This book offers a panoramic view of the best-known Greek and Roman mythological tales and how they have been interpreted in the visual arts. We tried to follow the narratives, avoiding abrupt historical gaps. Since time immemorial, artists have drawn inspiration from legends, giving them figured representation, from the earliest vase paintings to the sculptures that decorate public buildings and private homes.

Each mythological figure is illustrated by a number of images depicting episodes from the figure's life. Starting from classical antiquity, the images illuminate how artists' portrayals of a divinity, a hero, or a myth may have changed over time, and how sometimes artists deviated from the events of the tale in favor of a personal adaptation or reworking of the subject matter. This book is divided into two basic themes: legends about gods and goddesses from the first generation, born of the primordial Chaos; and legends about heroes, their great deeds, and the adventures they confronted and conquered.

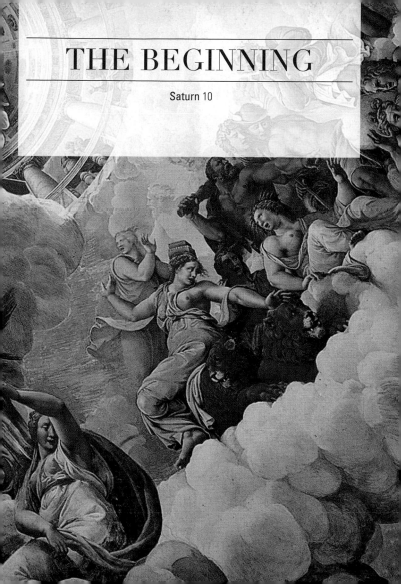

THE BEGINNING

Saturn 10

SATURN

▶▶

Saturn is one of the earliest Roman divinities. His cult is associated with agriculture, and he is considered its founder and guardian god. According to one legend, the god reached Italy after being driven from Olympus by his son Jupiter (see p. 20) and settled on Rome's Capitoline Hill, at the base of which a temple dedicated to him was erected. Here, the god began to teach the principles of farming to men, thereby shedding older, wild, barbarian customs, and introducing a lifestyle more suited to civic and moral order.

Later, when the principles of Greek mythology were Romanized, Saturn was assimilated with Cronus, the Hellenic god who devoured his children and became lord of the universe by expelling his father, Uranus. Born in an agricultural context, over the centuries the image of Saturn took on the role of the god of time and gained new attributes, such as the hourglass or the ouroboros, a snake biting its own tail that symbolizes eternity.

Greek name: Cronus

Attributes: reaping hook, hourglass, ouroburos

SATURN
Fresco from the House of the Dioscuri,
Pompeii
early 1st century CE
Museo Archeologico Nazionale, Naples

☐ In this Pompeiian fresco, a standing, bearded Saturn, his head covered by a veil and reaping hook in hand, is portrayed in his classical role as the god of agriculture.

SATURN

☐ In the late Middle Ages, images of Saturn, Venus, or Jupiter came to be identified with a planet and also appeared in illustrations of astrological texts. Saturn was considered the most unfavorable of the planetary powers and associated with a gloomy character. Also, as the slowest and most arid of the planets, he personified old age, poverty, and death. In the astrological imagination, therefore, Saturn was associated with unfavorable situations. In most cases, such as in this miniature, the god was represented as a stern, melancholy old man. Instead of the reaping hook, he holds a spade, which evokes his early role of god of agriculture, although here he is rendered as a king crowned and enthroned.

SATURN
Miniature
c. 1403

Saturnus · H ·

SATURN

☐ In the Middle Ages, the role of god of time was added to the image of Saturn, already assimilated to the Greek god Cronus. This identity was born from superimposing two similar terms: Cronus (Saturn) and *chronos*, the Greek word for time. The two terms came to be seen as identical, and Cronus and Saturn became the same god. The reaping hook used in harvesting became a symbol of time, which reaps human life.

In this painting by Jacopo del Sellaio, the personification of Time includes several iconographic elements: From the ancient Roman Saturn, only the image of the elderly white-haired man is left; superimposed on it is the medieval god as a winged figure (time "flying away") holding an hourglass (time's irreversible flow). Finally, the god leans on a crutch to remind us that time is infinite. With a golden wand, he moves the mechanism of the clock below him, pointing to the passing of the day and night.

To the left and right of the cart are, respectively, a group of young men and women and a group of middle-aged figures: All pay homage to time, which triumphs inexorably over human existence.

THE TRIUMPH OF TIME
Jacopo del Sellaio
c. 1480–90
14 | Museo Bandini, Fiesole

SATURN

☐ This painting by Poussin describes the allegory of human life constantly passing under the auspices of Time. In the center of the composition, four young women—the Seasons—dance in a circle, evoking their perpetual rotation. To the right is Saturn, an old, winged man ("time flies"). He plays a kithara to mark the progress of earthly life. To the right, one putto holds an hourglass while another, in the foreground at left, makes soap bubbles, alluding to the transience of human existence and the passage of time. Behind the putto on the left is a two-headed herm of Janus, an image of the past and the future, but also a reminder that this god is the origin of all events. High in the sky, Apollo, the Sun god, rides his chariot escorted by the Hours and preceded by Aurora (Dawn), the first light of the day: She is scattering rose petals, tingeing the early-morning vault of the sky with its distinctive color.

THE DANCE TO THE MUSIC OF TIME
Nicolas Poussin
1638–40

Wallace Collection, London

Saturn devours his children

The son of Uranus (the Sky) and Gaea (the Earth), Saturn belongs to the first generation of gods, the Uranids. The youngest of his siblings, he helped his mother take revenge against his father and succeeded him as the ruler of the universe.

The reign of Saturn was neither long nor happy. He married his sister Rhea and was wont to devour his infant children to forestall the fulfillment of a prophecy that one of them would dethrone him. Thus he sired and devoured Vesta, Ceres, Juno, Pluto, and Neptune. But Rhea was able to save the lastborn, Jupiter, secretly giving birth to him on the island of Crete and handing to Saturn, instead of the infant, a stone wrapped in swaddling clothes, which the god devoured without noticing.

☐ Goya portrays Saturn in all his savage, ruthless power, his crazed eyes wide open, as he pounces on one of his children. Unlike traditional images of this god, he is not devouring a newborn baby but an adult man, his body already atrociously mutilated.

SATURN DEVOURING HIS SON
Francisco Goya
1820–23
Museo del Prado, Madrid

The fall of the kingdom of Saturn

Hidden from his father, Saturn, Jupiter was the only sibling to survive. Once he reached adulthood, the prophecy was fulfilled (see p. 18): He gave his father a potion that caused him to regurgitate the stone he had swallowed instead of his lastborn, and all the children he had previously eaten. Then Jupiter chased him from Olympus and took over the kingdom.

☐ The theme of this painting is inspired by the Roman poet Ovid's *Metamorphoses:* Saturn is hurled into Tartarus, the dark region below the netherworld, while Jupiter takes over the throne. A figure in the left foreground introduces the viewer to the scene. Reaping hook in hand—his distinctive attribute—Saturn is knocked down by Fame personified, identifiable by the trumpet she holds in her hand. The third figure seen from the back could be Rhea, while on the far right, another divinity, most probably Pluto, is about to be sucked into the whirlpool. Above, high in the sky, Truth and Justice turn toward the new light, paying tribute to the imminent rule of Jupiter.

THE FALL OF SATURN
Giovanni Contarini
c. 1588
Art Collections, Castle, Prague

The fall of the Titans

The union between Gaea (the Earth) and Uranus (the Sky) brought forth the Cyclopes, the Hecatonchires (or Centimani), and the Titans. According to the more common tradition, there were twelve Titans: six males (Oceanus, Coeus, Hyperion, Crius, Iapetus, and Cronus–Saturn) and six females (Tethys, Rhea, Themis, Mnemosyne, Phoebe, and Theia). Afraid he might lose his kingdom, Uranus had confined the Cyclopes and the Hecatonchires to dark Tartarus. Gaea tried to convince the Titans to revolt against their father, but only the youngest, Saturn, dared to attack Uranus, castrating him with a reaping hook his mother had provided; he then took his place in ruling the world.

Later, Saturn was dethroned by his own son, Jupiter. The war waged by Jupiter and his brothers to oust him is known as the War of the Titans; it lasted more than ten years and took place in Thessaly.

☐ The artist has portrayed Jupiter with his fellow gods as he strikes the Titans with the thunderbolts he received from the Cyclopes and hurls them into Tartarus. The War of the Titans is sometimes conflated with that of the Giants, so that "Titans" and "Giants" have been used interchangeably.

JUPITER STRIKES THE TITANS
WITH THUNDERBOLTS
Charles Lamy
early 18th century
Musée du Louvre, Paris

22

The War of the Giants

▶▶

Wounded by Saturn, Uranus fell to the ground and his blood fertilized the Earth, bringing forth the Giants; hence, Gaea is their mother. The Giants were huge, terrifying creatures whose strength was invincible. Although their father was a god, they were also mortal in the sense that they only be killed by a god with the assistance of a mortal. Since birth, the Giants had threatened Jupiter's kingdom: They tried to reach the sky with boulders and tree trunks, even moving Mount Ossa to the Pelion with their brute force.

The great war that followed saw the participation of all the gods, aided by Hercules, the mortal whose help turned out to be decisive in wiping out the Giants once and for all, in accordance with the rules of war. The War of the Giants ended with the victory of the Olympian gods and the definitive establishment of Jupiter as the new monarch.

JUPITER AND THE GIANTS
Cameo
c. 150 BCE
Museo Archeologico Nazionale, Naples

☐ This cameo depicts Jupiter riding a quadriga, a chariot drawn by four beassts. In his right hand, the king of the gods holds the thunderbolts he is about to hurl at the Giants standing below him. In his left hand, he holds the scepter. In keeping with the most common iconography, the Giants have bushy hair, shaggy beards, and snakelike lower limbs. One Giant strikes back with a torch.

◀◀

The War of the Giants

☐ This fresco is divided horizontally into two parts. In the upper part of the composition, the Olympian gods, still shaken, witness the Giants' defeat, while Jupiter and Juno prepare to strike them with bundles of thunderbolts. In the lower part, the enormous Giants, their faces grotesquely deformed, are struck by the thunderbolts and crushed by the very boulders they had piled up in their attempt to reach Olympus.

THE FALL OF THE GIANTS
(detail)
Giulio Romano
1532–34
Palazzo del Te, Mantua

THE OLYMPIAN GODS

Olympus 30 • Jupiter 32 • Juno 78 • Minerva 88 • Apollo 102
Diana 128 • Mars 144 • Vulcan 150 • Mercury 156 • Venus 166
Vesta and the Vestals 196 • Janus 202 • Sibyls 206

SECONDARY DEITIES

Sol (Sun) 214 • Luna (Moon) 226 • Aurora (Dawn) 230 • Winds 234
The Muses 236 • Graces 254 • Victoria (Victory) 258 • Hebe 262
Ganymede 264 • Cupid (Eros) 268

OLYMPUS

After ousting the Titans (see p. 22), Jupiter became ruler
of the universe; thus began the third generation of gods, the
Olympians, so called because they lived on top of Mount
Olympus in northern Greece on the border between Thessaly
and Macedonia. The ancients described it as a place never
struck by wind or rain, where the sky is always blue and the
light shines brightly. On the upper reaches of the mountain,
whose peaks almost reach heaven, Vulcan built the palaces of
the gods and goddesses. The gates of Olympus, hidden from
mortal eyes by a blanket of clouds, were guarded by the
Hours. On the mountain, the divinities met at banquets to
discuss human and divine affairs, though their fates, ultimately,
always rested upon Jupiter's final dictum. Later, poets moved
the abode of the gods to the summit of heaven.

□ This fresco depicts the divine
council called after the trials of
Cupid and Psyche (see p. 292).
Standing on the far left, Psyche
receives the cup of immortality,
filled with ambrosia, from Mercury.
On the opposite side Jupiter listens
to Cupid. All around them, the
gods await his decision on whether
the young couple should be
united forever.

THE COUNCIL OF THE GODS
Raffaello Sanzio, known as Raphael
1515–17
Villa Farnesina, Rome

JUPITER

The son of Saturn and Rhea, Jupiter is the supreme god, the lord of the skies; he is also called the father of the gods. He rules wisely, guaranteeing authority, order, and the law, and commanding men as well as gods. Of all the gods, he is the only one with full freedom of action, the only restriction on his will being the power of Fate (the Parcae).

Called by the Greek poet Homer the "thundering one," Jupiter can unleash deadly storms or dissolve the clouds with thunderbolts. The latter he received from the Cyclopes when he freed them from Tartarus, where Saturn had confined them.

It is possible that the image of Jupiter was originally linked to a specific aspect of the natural world, a theory that rests, above all, on the belief that still existed in the Classical Age—in the literature of the time especially—that rain and the rotation of the seasons rested directly on this god. In any case, his Greek name, Zeus, means "sky" or "day."

Greek name: Zeus

Attributes: thunderbolt, eagle, scepter

JUPITER WITH THUNDERBOLT
late 2nd–early 3rd century CE
Antiquarium della Villa dei Quintili, Rome

☐ Jupiter is presented as an august, majestic figure in this statue. Enthroned, he holds a thunderbolt in his right hand.

JUPITER

☐ Jupiter appears with his distinctive attributes, the thunder-bolts in his left hand and the eagle at his side. Sitting on a cloud, he listens to Iris, the personification of the rainbow that connects sky and Earth, gods and men. Charged with transmitting orders and messages to the deities, Iris is at the service of Jupiter and especially of Juno.

IRIS AND JUPITER
Michel Corneille
1701
Palace of Versailles, Versailles

Jupiter's childhood

Saved in extremis from his cruel father Saturn, who devoured all his children (see p. 18), according to the most common version of the myth, Jupiter was raised on Mount Ida on the island of Crete by nymphs who fed him honey and the milk of the she-goat Amalthea. (In other versions, Amalthaea was a nymph.) After the goat died, Jupiter took its skin and made it into armor, the famous aegis whose strength he tested for the first time in the war against the Titans. When he became an adult, the king of the gods confronted his father and, after several battles, brought order back to the universe.

☐ The artist has painted an infant Jupiter being nursed by Amalthea while another nymph in the middle ground gathers wild honey from a hollow tree. In the middle ground at right, the seated goddess holding an urn, from which water flows, is a spring nymph.

CHILDHOOD OF JUPITER
Nicolas Poussin
c. 1636
36 | Dulwich Picture Gallery, London

Leda and the Swan

Leda was the daughter of Thestius, king of Aetolia, and Eurythemis. When Tyndareus, king of Sparta, was ousted from his kingdom together with his brother, Thestius gave him shelter and the hand of his daughter in marriage. According to the myth, Jupiter took a fancy to Leda when he saw her bathing by the Eurotas River, and he materialized before her in the guise of a swan, seducing her. That same night, she also lay with her husband. From this double union and two different eggs were born Pollux and Helen (children of Jupiter), and Castor and Clytemnestra (from Tyndareus). In another version of the myth, a shepherd presented Leda with an egg, born of the love between Jupiter and Nemesis, the goddess of vengeance who had transformed herself into a goose to escape his clutches—but the king of the gods had turned into a swan and seduced her. Upon receiving the egg from the shepherd, Leda decided to guard it in a coffer, and when Helen was born, she was so lovely that Leda decided to raise her as her own daughter.

LEDA AND THE SWAN
Copy from Leonardo da Vinci
1505–1507
Gallerie degli Uffizi, Florence

☐ Before a softly fading, faraway landscape, Leda is enclosed in a sensual embrace by Jupiter in the form of a swan. At her feet, the twins Helen and Clytemnestra and Castor and Pollux (the famous Dioscuri) are born from the broken eggs.

The rape of the daughters of Leucippus

Castor and Pollux, the twin sons of Leda, are known as the Dioscuri, which means "children of Zeus," though only Pollux, a skilled wrestler, was Jupiter's real son, and therefore immortal. His brother Castor, who was the mortal son of Tyndareus, was a talented tamer of horses. In one of their many exploits, the twins kidnapped Phoebe and Ilaeira, known as the Leucippides, or daughters of Leucippus, king of Argos and Tyndareus's brother. The sisters were betrothed to Idas and Lynceus, who were nephews of Leucippus.

After the abduction, the latter chased the Dioscuri and engaged in a fierce battle with them. Castor was killed by Idas, while Pollux killed Lynceus. Even Jupiter intervened, striking Idas with a thunderbolt. Crazed by his brother's death, Pollux asked his father to send him to the same death. The king of the gods then allowed him to give up half his immortality on behalf of Castor. Thus the twins lived forever together, one day in Olympus, one day in Hades. In another version of the myth, Jupiter placed the two brothers among the stars, creating the constellation Gemini.

THE RAPE OF THE DAUGHTERS
OF LEUCIPPUS
Pieter Paul Rubens
c. 1618
Alte Pinakothek, Munich

☐ Astride a horse and protected by armor, Castor grabs one of the daughters of Leucippus. On the ground, Pollux helps his brother and snatches the other maiden. In the heat of the abduction, two little cupids try to contain the restive horses.

Jupiter and Latona

›››

THE BIRTH OF APOLLO AND DIANA

A daughter of the Titans Coeus and Phoebe, Latona (Leto in Greek) belongs to the first generation of gods. Upon learning Latona had been impregnated by Jupiter, a wrathful Juno forbade all places on Earth to shelter the maiden, in an effort to prevent her from giving birth. After wandering far and wide and being ousted from all places, Latona finally found shelter on Delos, a barren, moving island that was not anchored to the Earth, and thus had nothing to fear from Juno's wrath. There, in the shadow of a palm and an olive tree, she gave birth to Apollo and Diana. Grateful for the hospitality afforded to Latona, Neptune anchored the island to the bottom of the sea with powerful columns.

☐ This fresco depicts the birth of Diana and Apollo on the island of Delos under a palm, as ancient sources relate. Diana, on the right, embraces her mother, while Apollo gazes at the shore, where some sea divinities rise from the waves to offer him gifts.

BIRTH OF DIANA AND APOLLO
Alexandre-Denis Abel de Pujol
1822–25
Castle of Fontainebleau, Fontainebleau

Jupiter and Latona

THE PEASANTS TRANSFORMED INTO FROGS

After giving birth to Apollo and Diana, Latona and her children were again forced to hide from Juno. Finally, Latona reached Lycia. Weary from the long wandering and the heat, she saw a pond and some peasants nearby gathering wicker, rushes, and marsh algae. She approached and had just knelt to drink when they stopped her. Insensitive to her entreaties, they threatened and insulted her. Still unsatisfied, they began to jump in the pond to stir the muddy bottom and dirty the water. Angered, the Titaness raised her hands to heaven and prayed that those peasants who were mocking her should live forever in the pond, and immediately they became frogs.

LANDSCAPE WITH LATONA AND FARMERS
(detail)
Herman van Swanevelt
c. 1634
Staatliche Museen, Berlin

44

☐ This episode takes place before a quiet water course framed by richly foliaged trees. Latona stands with her children in the center of the scene and looks at the sky while the metamorphosis is happening, for behind the peasants who threaten her as they approach, others have already turned into frogs or are in the process of doing so.

Jupiter and Latona

THE DEATH OF THE CHILDREN OF NIOBE

The daughter of Tantalus, Niobe was married to Amphion, king of Thebes, with whom she had seven boys and seven girls. One day, the gods sent a soothsayer into the streets of Thebes to exhort the city's women to honor Latona and her children, Diana and Apollo. The Theban women were about to start the rituals when the haughty, splendidly attired Niobe arrived on the scene. Boasting of her divine origins, she claimed to be Latona's superior because the latter only had two children. She then ordered the women to stop the rituals and return to their homes.

The punishment for this offense came swiftly: Sent by their mother, Apollo and Diana landed in the city under cover of a cloud and mortally struck all of Niobe's children with their arrows. Mad with grief, Amphion took his own life, while a grief-stricken Niobe was turned into a stone. The wind flew her back to her native land, where the rock still drips tears drop by drop.

□ In the foreground lie her children struck by arrows, while in the center Niobe raises her arms heavenward in a gesture of despair. Apollo and Diana hide atop a cloud; the former is apparently resting, while the latter is still shooting arrows.

THE DEATH NIOBE'S CHILDREN
Abraham Bloemaert
1591
State Museum of Art, Copenhagen

Jupiter and Io

Io was a nymph, the daughter of Inachus, a river in Argolis. A smitten Jupiter seduced her by disguising himself as a cloud, but Juno, suspicious of the unusual daytime fog, went in search of her husband. Jupiter turned the girl into a lovely heifer in an effort to mislead his wife. When she learned of her husband's deceit, Juno asked him to present her with the heifer as a gift, then turned the animal over to Argus, the famed hundred-eyed watchman, to guard her.

Now Jupiter regretted this sad turn of events and asked Mercury to free Io. The divine messenger caused Argus to fall asleep with the sweet sound of his syrinx, then killed him. Enraged, Juno retaliated by driving an invisible goad into the heifer's chest. The desperate animal began to run wild all over the world. After much pleading from Jupiter, Juno's anger subsided, and Io was returned to her original body.

☐ Correggio has depicted Io being embraced by Jupiter, who is in the form of a cloud. We see only a hand and the facial features of the king of the gods.

JUPITER AND IO
Antonio Allegri, known as Correggio
c. 1531
Kunsthistorisches Museum, Vienna

Jupiter and Io

▶▶

☐ The artist narrates the part of the episode in which Juno descends to Earth on her cart drawn by peacocks and asks Jupiter to make her a gift of the heifer. In the composition are two figures not mentioned in the original tale, which allude respectively to love and deceit: Cupid, with the bow on the ground, and a masked man, who tries to hide the heifer with some drapery and Cupid's help. The tails of the peacocks pulling Juno's wagon do not have "eyes" as yet: The queen of the gods added them after Argus was slain (see p. 56).

JUNO DISCOVERING JUPITER WITH IO
Pieter Lastman
1618
National Gallery, London

Jupiter and Io

MERCURY AND ARGUS

Jupiter asked Mercury for help in freeing Io from Argus's custody. Mercury descended to Earth disguised as a shepherd leading some young she-goats to pasture, and he began to play an unusual instrument made from reeds tied together— the panpipe. Attracted by the music, Argus invited the false shepherd to sit with him. Throughout the day, they engaged in pleasant conversation and Mercury continued to play, hoping to put the many watchful eyes of Juno's faithful servant to sleep. Instead, Argus kept asking questions about the musical instrument and the details of its invention. Only after Mercury satisfied his curiosity (see p. 404) did Argus fall into a deep sleep. Then the messenger of the gods struck him a deadly blow and completed his task.

☐ This Roman fresco depicts Mercury offering the syrinx to Argus, with Io watching. The nymph is dressed like a maiden, her head veiled, and she is also depicted as the heifer into which she was transformed.

MERCURY, ARGUS, AND IO
70 CE

Jupiter and Io

MERCURY AND ARGUS
Diego Velázquez
1659
54 | Museo del Prado, Madrid

☐ In this canvas, Argus has fallen into a deep sleep and Mercury is about to kill him. In the background is Io as a heifer. Here the legendary Argus, a hundred-eyed monster, is rendered as a simple cowherd, while Mercury is identified by the winged hat.

Jupiter and Io

JUNO AND THE EYES OF ARGUS

To honor her faithful servant Argus, who had been slain by Mercury at Jupiter's command, Juno took his eyes and arranged them on the tails of the peacock, the animal consecrated to her. Deeply offended, she then turned her wrath upon the unlucky nymph–turned–heifer, thrusting into her chest an invisible goad that sent her running in a frenzy all over the world. Finally, Jupiter was able to intercede on Io's behalf and begged his wife to free her, swearing that he would never again cause her grief. Once Juno's wrath subsided, Io was returned to her human shape.

☐ In this painting, Juno mourns Argus and is about to place his eyes on the peacock's tail. Iris, the messenger of the gods and the overseer of the rainbow that connects Heaven and Earth (one is visible in the background), helps her: Here, she offers Juno the eyes she has detached from the head of the faithful watchman.

JUNO AND ARGUS
Pieter Paul Rubens
1611
Wallraf-Richartz Museum, Cologne

The rape of Europa

Europa, daughter of the Phoenician king Agenor, enjoyed going to the seashore near Tyre to play with her maids by the sea. One day, during a game, Jupiter saw her and immediately fell in love. To approach her, he took the semblance of a bull, white as snow with small, well-rounded horns and a meek look. Europa was surprised to see this friendly bull; afraid at first, she slowly approached the animal and began to stroke it and adorn it with flower garlands. Encouraged by the animal's meekness, she mounted it, and immediately the bull dove into the sea and fled with the terrorized girl on its back. The bull stopped on the island of Crete; there, Europa gave birth to Minos (who would become the island's king), Sarpedon, and Rhadamanthus. Then Jupiter gave her hand in marriage to Asterion, king of Crete.

THE RAPE OF EUROPA
Metope from the Temple at Selinunte
c. 550 BCE
58 | Museo Archeologico Nazionale, Palermo

☐ This metope is one of the earliest representations of the myth of Europa. She is rendered as a young woman riding a bull toward the island of Crete. Seen in profile, the girl clutches one of the bull's horns with her left hand, steadying herself with her right. Under the bull's legs are two fish, indicating the sea.

◄◄

The rape of Europa

▶▶

☐ Titian has narrated the most dramatic moment of the abduction, when the bull swims across the sea and the frightened girl holds onto his horns so as not to fall. To the left, we see the beach with the agitated, terrorized maids. High in the sky are two infant cupids: One holds the bow, the other the quiver. A third rides a dolphin behind the couple. The dolphin may be considered an attribute of Venus, the goddess born of the sea. Even the marine landscape seems to participate in the drama: The cliffs are buffeted by a stormy wind and almost disappear in the faraway blue, fading into the rosy clouds that turn increasingly dark and threatening as they approach Europa and the bull.

THE RAPE OF EUROPA
Tiziano Vecellio, known as Titian
1562
| Isabella Stewart Gardner Museum, Boston

The rape of Europa

☐ In one of his rare mythological works, Rembrandt's Europa holds onto a horn with her right hand, while the left digs her nails into the bull's snow-white neck, and turns terrified to look at the shore, where two handmaids watch helplessly. One of them raises her arms signifying danger, while the garland that she was making for the animal falls into her lap; the other servant, unable to react, joins her hands in dismay. In the middle ground, the wagon driver stands and looks petrified at the scene. The softly rendered city in the distance is the port of Tyre, Europa's hometown.

This painting has also been attributed an allegorical meaning: The human soul (personified by Europa) turns away from earthly passions to seek a higher, divine realm.

THE RAPE OF EUROPA
Rembrandt von Rijn
1632
The J. Paul Getty Museum, Los Angeles

Jupiter and Semele

Semele was a daughter of Cadmus, the founder of Thebes, and Harmonia. Jupiter fell in love and impregnated her. While expecting, she fell victim to Juno's wrath. The queen of the gods took on the semblance of Beroe, Semele's wet nurse, and appeared before her. During the conversation, the topic turned to Jupiter, and the fake Beroe hinted to Semele that her child's father might not, indeed, be the king of the gods. To banish all doubts, she suggested that Semele ask Jupiter to appear before her in all his splendor, as he did with Juno.

When Jupiter next visited her, the girl asked him for a gift, and he replied that he would give her anything she wished, swearing so on the Styx, the infernal river of the underworld feared even by the gods. When Semele told him her wish, Jupiter could not renege on his promise and was forced to rise to Heaven and arm himself with his thunderbolts. When he appeared before her, she could not withstand the unbearable brightness and died instantly, struck by lightning. Bacchus, the child she was carrying, was saved (see p. 356).

JUPITER AND SEMELE
Paolo Pagani
c. 1780
Moravská Galerie, Brno

☐ The artist has captured the moment when Jupiter must appear to Semele in all his splendor. The king of the gods and the eagle, his attribute, are surrounded by the clouds that he usually gathers around himself.

Jupiter and Danaë

Danaë was the daughter of Acrisius, king of Argos. An oracle had predicted that the king would die at the hand of his grandson, so he kept his daughter secluded in an underground chamber. But Jupiter took a fancy to her and was able to enter the room by taking on the semblance of a thin shower of gold. Perseus (see p. 512) would be born from this union.

When he learned what had transpired, Acrisius ordered that mother and son be thrown into a crate and hurled into the sea, but they were rescued. After many mishaps, Acrisius and Perseus were reunited and the oracle was fulfilled, for the youth, by mistake, killed the king during a javelin-throwing contest.

☐ The painter has set the myth of Danaë in a splendid semicircular colonnade with a view of stately buildings from different historical epochs in the background. The girl sits on cushions while the golden shower falls over her from above.

DANAË
Jan Gossaert, known as Mabuse
1527
66 | Alte Pinakothek, Munich

◄◄

Jupiter and Danaë

☐ Correggio has set the episode of Danaë in a room from whose window we glimpse a landscape with a monumental building. The young woman lies on a white bed, only partially covered by a sheet. Before her, Cupid tries to pull the sheet even as, somewhat reluctantly, she holds on to it. Above the bed, drops fall from a golden cloud. In the foreground on the right are two seated putti, one of them with wings; they are assaying the gold's quality on the so-called touchstone, a sort of jasper—a stone that was used to test the metal and its degree of purity.

DANAË
Antonio Allegri, known as Correggio
1531
68 | Galleria Borghese, Rome

Jupiter and Antiope

One of Jupiter's many loves was Antiope, a singularly beautiful maiden, daughter of Nycteus, king of Thebes. Disguised
as a satyr, the father of the gods lay with her while she was
asleep. Fleeing her father's wrath, Antiope found shelter in
Sicyon, where King Epopeus welcomed her and made her his
wife. Then Nycteus waged war against him in an effort to get
his daughter back, but failed; after him, Lycus, Nycteus's
brother and successor to the throne, defeated Epopeus and
enslaved Antiope.

During the journey home, she gave birth to Jupiter's
children, Amphion and Zethus; left to the elements, the twins
were found and raised by a shepherd. Once they became
adults and learned the truth, the two young men marched
against Thebes and avenged their mother, becoming lords of
the city.

JUPITER, ANTIOPE, AND EROS
Hans von Aachen
1595–98
Kunsthistorisches Museum, Vienna

☐ In this painting, Antiope embraces
Jupiter transformed into a satyr,
complete with goat's legs and horns
on his head. She doesn't seem
frightened by the unusual appearance.
Next to the couple, an impertinent
Cupid steals away after shooting
one of his famous arrows, as we can
tell from the bow lying on the rock
behind him and the quiver in the
foreground.

MINERVA

The daughter of Jupiter and Metis, goddess of prudence, Minerva is one of the most important Olympian deities, fulfilling several roles: She counsels men, both in times of war and during peace, and she is the bearer of all good things. Originally worshiped as the goddess of war, she later took on the role of guardian deity of the sciences, the arts, and all knowledge and wisdom. As a warrior goddess, she is equipped with spear, shield, helmet, and the aegis, a sort of breastplate made of goatskin. Perseus presented her with Medusa's head, which she attached to the center of the aegis to strike terror into her enemies (see p. 468).

Unlike Mars, who embodies the brutal, violent aspect of war, Minerva guarantees order and the law, strengthening and giving prosperity to the state, and as the guardian of man's intellectual endeavors, she also protects the arts of spinning and weaving. Being very clever, Minerva designed the war chariot and the quadriga; she also assisted Argus in building the *Argo*, in which Jason and the Argonauts sailed on their quests (see p. 606).

Greek name: Athena

Attributes: spear, shield, helmet, aegis. She is sometimes represented with the owl and the olive tree, both consecrated to her.

ATENA PARTHENOS
Roman copy of an original by Phidias
from 438 BCE

National Archaeological Museum, Athens

☐ Armed with a richly decorated helmet and a shield, Minerva wears the aegis with the head of Medusa in the center. In her right hand, the goddess holds a statuette of Nike (Victory).

Juno in Hades

The son of Jupiter and Semele (see p. 356), Bacchus was raised by Ino, who was his mother's sister and the wife of Athamas, king of Thebes. Ino had enthusiastically spread the cult of Bacchus, angering Juno, who had been jealous of Bacchus for some time already. Her rage and hatred were such that she even journeyed to the underworld. There, in the presence of Tityus, Tantalus, and Ixion, she beseeched the terrible Furies to help her seek revenge.

One of the Furies, Tisiphone, rose up to Earth and so unsettled the minds of Athamas and Ino that the former, in a fit of madness, killed his youngest son Learchus; Ino fled with the older son, Melicertes, but having gone mad, threw herself and the child from a cliff into the sea. But Neptune saved them and took them into his kingdom, making them immortal and changing their name to Leucothea and Palaemon, the sea deities that come to the aid of seafarers in stormy seas.

□ Brueghel depicts Juno's arrival in Hades on her peacock-drawn cart. Surrounded by monstrous, terrifying creatures, she turns for help to the Furies, who have snakes for hair.

JUNO IN HADES
Jan Brueghel the Elder
1630
Private collection

The creation of the Milky Way

This myth recounts the episode in which Mercury was ordered by Jupiter to lay the infant Hercules, born from Jupiter's union with the lovely Alcmene (see p. 540), on the breast of the sleeping Juno, for the baby would become immortal only if he tasted divine milk. But Hercules suckled so violently that some drops of milk trickled down from his lips and became a crown of stars. In another version, it was Juno who pushed baby Hercules away as soon as she understood that the breastfeeding child was not her son.

☐ In this painting, Tintoretto shows Juno waking up startled as Mercury, the divine messenger, places Hercules on her breasts. In the center of the composition, the eagle clutching the thunderbolts evokes the image of Jupiter, Hercules's father, while the two peacocks at right in the foreground are Juno's attributes. In the center, above the outstretched hand of the goddess, is the circle of stars named the Milky Way.

THE ORIGIN OF THE MILKY WAY
Jacopo Robusti, known as Tintoretto
c. 1575
National Gallery, London

84

MINERVA

☐ This Greek bas-relief offers an unusual image of Minerva leaning on her spear before a stele in a pensive pose. The unknown artist has succeeded in conveying a world of inner feelings to Minerva's face. The goddess is wearing the helmet, one of her distinctive attributes.

PENSIVE ATHENA
c. 460 BCE

Acropolis Museum, Athens

MINERVA

☐ In this seventeenth-century rendition, Minerva is a lady donning a sumptuous robe that recalls her role as guardian deity of weaving. All around the room are her attributes: the shield and helmet, with which a putto is playing; the spear leaning against a balustrade; and perched on that, a little owl, the bird sacred to Minerva.

MINERVA DRESSING
Lavinia Fontana
1613
92 | Galleria Borghese, Rome

MINERVA

☐ Minerva is rendered in her most fearful aspect of warrior goddess: Hieratic and threatening, she has a bold, fearless gaze. Her long tresses fall below the helmet to frame the aegis bearing the head of the Medusa that strikes terror in her enemies. The artist has drawn the Gorgon's image from a metope from the Temple at Selinunte that depicts Perseus slaying the monster (see p. 516).

PALLAS ATHENE
Gustav Klimt
1898
Kunsthistorisches Museum, Vienna

The birth of Minerva

Gaea and Uranus had predicted to Jupiter that the child he would sire with Metis would have his father's strength and his mother's wisdom and rule over men and gods in his stead. To ward off this danger, he swallowed Metis just as she was about to give birth and held her inside of him so that he alone could benefit from her counsel. But the child was still alive, and when her time to be delivered came, the father of the gods ordered Vulcan to open his head with an ax. From his forehead sprang a fully armed maiden: Minerva. The story says that the miraculous birth took place in Libya near Lake Tritonius.

☐ In this scene, Minerva is shown fully armed, born into this world from her father's head. On the left, Vulcan has just opened Jupiter's head with his two-edged ax. According to the myth, as a reward Vulcan received Minerva as his bride, but she disappeared from the nuptial chamber, and in fact, she is always represented as a chaste young woman.

THE BIRTH OF ATHENA
Attic red-figure *pelike*
from Vulci
c. 450 BCE
| British Museum, London

The quarrel between Minerva and Neptune

When mortals began to organize in communities, the gods decided to distribute among themselves the cities and regions that were being born, from whom they could receive their just honors and whom they would protect in exchange.

Because Minerva and Neptune were both seeking control of Attica and Athens, its capital, Jupiter decided to assign the city and the region to the god that gave the more precious gift to men. Then Neptune struck a rock with his trident, sending forth on the Acropolis either a sea or a saltwater spring, or a horse, depending on the sources, while Minerva gave the city an olive tree—and won the contest.

THE DISPUTE BETWEEN MINERVA
AND NEPTUNE
Merry-Joseph Blondel
1822
Musée du Louvre, Paris

□ Meeting in a plenary session on the clouds of Mount Olympus, the gods follow the dispute between Neptune and Minerva. The god of the sea, here shown holding a trident, generates an indomitable horse. On the left, Minerva points to an olive tree before her. Seated on his throne, Jupiter judges Minerva the winner.

Minerva and Arachne

Arachne, the daughter of a cloth dyer, was known for her weaving skills. Although everyone understood that she derived her mastery from Minerva's protection, the young woman persisted in denying the evidence and openly challenged the goddess to a weaving contest.

At first, Minerva disguised herself as an old woman and visited Arachne in hopes of dissuading her from the contest, but she failed, even provoking the girl's anger and disdain. Minerva then appeared in her true form before Arachne, who was very calm and began the contest by weaving a tapestry depicting the loves of the gods. Minerva was not pleased with the theme, and after tearing up the tapestry, she struck Arachne repeatedly with the shuttle. Thoroughly humiliated, the maiden was about to hang herself, but the goddess was moved to pity and transformed her into a spider (*aráchne* in Greek), which continues to weave its web today.

☐ This canvas narrates the final episode of the myth of Arachne. Terrified, the young woman is about to be turned into a spider, as we can see from the web hovering over her, as Minerva appears in all her might and points an accusing finger. On the floor are some unused balls of wool, and on top of one on the left is the owl, Minerva's sacred bird.

MINERVA AND ARACHNE
Luca Giordano
c. 1695
San Lorenzo Monastery, El Escorial

100

APOLLO

The son of Jupiter and Latona and the brother of Diana, Apollo is the god of the Sun—the light rising from night's darkness. He is a benign deity but can be vengeful, and as such he is often depicted with his bow and arrow. Just like the rays of the Sun, his arrows can be beneficial or bring evil, punishing men by sending plagues or causing sudden death. If suitably appeased, he can also help ward off evil.

Apollo is considered the inventor of music and an excellent kithara player; he directs the choir of the Muses, and so he is also called *Musagete*. But he is especially celebrated for his divining powers, and his oracles are crucial in solving both political and private issues. The most famous shrine dedicated to him is at Delphi; there, the Pythia (the sacred priestess) transmitted the will of the god after reaching a state of ecstasy. Described as an uncommonly handsome youth, Apollo was said to have had many liaisons with both nymphs and mortal women.

Attributes: lyre, bow, arrows, laurel tree

APOLLO
White-background *kylix*
470 BCE
102 | Archaeological Museum, Delphi

☐ The painting at the bottom of this cup depicts Apollo intent on pouring libations. Sitting on a stool, the god holds a lyre with his left hand; his hair is pulled up and held by a laurel wreath. Before him is a crow, the god's sacred animal.

APOLLO

☐ This statue represents Apollo *Sauróktonos*, "the lizard slayer." He is rendered as an adolescent, leaning against a trunk on which a lizard is climbing. In his right hand he probably held a small weapon, an arrow perhaps, with which he was about to strike the animal. Among Apollo's roles were assisting and healing the sick; in this case, the lizard probably symbolizes sickness.

APOLLO SAURÓKTONOS
Roman copy of an original by Praxiteles
from *c.* 360 BCE

| Musei Vaticani, Vatican City

APOLLO

☐ Apollo is represented as *Musagete*, the guide of the Muses. As such, he is imagined on Mount Parnassus, his head encircled by a laurel wreath, playing the kithara to accompany the dances and songs of the nine Muses, who are gathered around him.

PARNASSUS
Andrea Appiani
1811
Museo dell'Ottocento
Villa Belgiojoso Bonaparte, Milan

◄◄

APOLLO

☐ At first, Apollo and Sol (see p. 214) were distinct gods to whom primary functions were attributed. Over the centuries, probably in Roman times, the image of the two deities fused, and Apollo began to be represented on his horse-drawn chariot as he crossed the sky.

In this work by Redon, the god becomes one with the bright light that illuminates the blue sky and reflects on the backs of the white horses that pull the chariot. Below, the coils of Python rise up from darkness; the monster has been fatally struck by one of Apollo's arrows.

APOLLO'S CHARIOT
Odilon Redon
1905–14
| Musée d'Orsay, Paris

Apollo and the serpent Python

The Delphic shrine to Themis, goddess of the law, was guarded by Python, a serpent that infested the plain with all sorts of looting and foul deeds. Apollo slew the monster after striking him with more than a thousand arrows, finally freeing the countryside.

In memory of this feat, the god instituted the Pythian Games, held annually at Delphi. He also took over the shrine and dedicated it to himself. To cleanse himself of the stain caused by the monster's death, Apollo had to journey to Thessaly. From that time on, every eight years the residents of Delphi commemorated the slaying of the monster with solemn celebrations.

☐ Enveloped in a warm light that breaks through the gray, threatening sky, Apollo battles the dragon Python from his chariot, while behind him a goddess, perhaps his sister Diana, holds the quiver full of arrows. All around is a whirling mass of gods who watch the scene and assist the Sun god. To the right, a threatening Minerva and Mercury hurl themselves against a Harpy, a terrible monster that tortured men.

APOLLO SLAYS PYTHON
Eugène Delacroix
1850–51
110 | Musée du Louvre, Paris

Apollo flays Marsyas

Minerva is credited with inventing the flute, but she immediately discarded it after noticing in a stream how her face became ungraceful when she played the instrument. The satyr Marsyas happened upon it and discovered that he could create wonderful sounds with it. Proud of his discovery and convinced that the flute made the sweetest music in the world, he challenged Apollo to a contest, daring him to create a sound just as lovely on his lyre; the winner could do whatever he pleased with the loser.

The Muses made up the jury. They awarded the victory to Apollo, who could play the lyre even upside down, something that Marsyas failed to do with the flute. In fulfillment of the wager, the Sun god did whatever he pleased to Marsyas: He hung the satyr from a tree and flayed him alive. The other satyrs and the woodland deities mourned him bitterly, and their tears formed a river that took the name of the unfortunate satyr.

APOLLO AND MARSYAS
Jusepe de Ribera
1637
112 | Museo Nazionale di Capodimonte, Naples

☐ In this painting, Apollo has just tied the satyr down and is about to flay him alive, as we can see from the skin that the god is cutting. Marsyas's agony is visible on his face, torn by a tragic cry of pain. To the right, woodland divinities desperately mourn the satyr.

Apollo and Daphne

After slaying the monstrous snake Python (see p. 110), Apollo was proud of his victory. He met Cupid, who was bending his bow, trying to attach a string to it. Apollo mocked the child god, saying that such large weapons were not suited for a child, but for a valiant god such as he, who had just slain the frightful snake. Cupid's reaction was swift. The god of love took two arrows from his quiver. The first one, pointed and golden, aroused love, and he struck Apollo with it. The second arrow, blunted and with a lead point, made one insensitive to love; with this one, he struck the nymph Daphne, daughter of the river god Peneus. Apollo immediately fell in love with Daphne and tried to seduce her, but the nymph was resistant to his love and kept fleeing him. Finally, worn out and exhausted, she asked her father for help, and he turned her into a laurel tree. From that time on, the tree became sacred to Apollo.

APOLLO AND DAPHNE
Miniature
c. 1450
Bodleian Gallery, Oxford

☐ Dressed in Renaissance finery, Apollo reaches Daphne just as she turns into a laurel tree. On a rise in the center middle ground is Cupid; teased by Apollo, he has retaliated. The child god holds two arrows in his hand, perhaps alluding to his revenge, and is blindfolded, to signify that love is blind and strikes everyone, including gods.

PHEBUS

DAPHNE

FLEUVE·PE
NEE

Amour premier au cueur de pheb[us] nee
Ce fut Daphne fille au fleuue penee
Laquelle amour dauāt cas dicduictur

◄◄

Apollo and Daphne

☐ Having entreated her father, Peneus, Daphne is about to be metamorphosed into a plant, while Apollo embraces her despairingly, for he cannot stop the transformation. The tale of Daphne and Apollo was very popular throughout the ages, perhaps because the imagery of this myth was seen as an allegory of chastity mastering passionate love.

APOLLO AND DAPHNE
Antonio del Pollaiuolo
1470–80
National Gallery, London

◀◀

Apollo and Daphne

☐ The artist has focused on Apollo and dressed him in precious green drapery. He is about to play a *viola da braccio* and wears a laurel wreath to show that the metamorphosis has already occurred and the plant has become sacred to him. This is confirmed by the fleeing maiden barely visible in the background, changing into a tree. The god is probably about to intone a dirge in honor of his beloved.

APOLLO AND DAPHNE
Dosso Dossi
c. 1525

| Galleria Borghese, Rome

Apollo and Coronis

Coronis, whose name means "crow," was the lovely daughter of Phlegyas, king of the Lapiths. Apollo fell in love with her, but she betrayed him with a young mortal. The crow, which is consecrated to the god, immediately flew to his lord to give him the news. Enraged, Apollo took revenge by striking Coronis with an arrow. Before dying, the maiden revealed that she was pregnant with his child. Immediately repenting of his cruelty, the god cursed himself and the bird that had babbled the news to him. He tried everything to save her, but Coronis died; still, Apollo was able to save the child by tearing open the mother's womb as she lay on the funeral pyre. He then entrusted the boy to the centaur Chiron. Thus was born Aesculapius (Asclepius), the god of medicine who learned the art from the centaur. As to the crow, which was expecting a reward for the service rendered, Apollo changed his feathers from white to black.

APOLLO KILLS CORONIS
(detail)
Pietro Novelli
120 | Private collection

☐ Apollo has just taken revenge: He has struck Coronis, the young woman who betrayed him with a mortal, with one of his deadly arrows. In the background, a lifeless Coronis lies on the funeral pyre; Apollo will miraculously save their son from her womb.

Apollo and the cattle of Admetus

Aesculapius, the god of medicine and the son of Apollo and Coronis, had become so skillful in the medical arts that he could even revive the dead. Fearing that he might upset the world's order, Jupiter killed him with a bolt of lightning. In retaliation, Apollo slew the Cyclopes who made his father's thunderbolts in Vulcan's forge. Jupiter in turn punished Apollo by enslaving him to King Admetus of Thessaly: He would herd the king's cattle for one year.

☐ While Apollo was in Thessaly looking after the herds of King Admetus, Mercury, then still a boy, stole the cattle and hid them. Jupiter intervened and order was restored, but Apollo, who had listened to the magic sound of the lyre Mercury had invented, exchanged the cattle for the instrument. In this scene, Apollo is busy playing the lyre (actually a violin in this painting), while a satisfied Mercury leaves with the oxen.

LANDSCAPE WITH APOLLO GUARDING
THE HERD OF ADMETUS
Claude Lorrain
1645
Galleria Doria Pamphilj, Rome

Apollo and Hyacinth

Hyacinth was a young Spartan whom Apollo loved so much that he neglected his duties, preferring to spend entire days with the youth. One day they decided to have a discus-throwing contest. Apollo threw first and the discus fell on the ground, rebounded, and hit Hyacinth, who was running to catch it, in the face. The boy tuned pale and died a while later, even after the god tried to heal the deep wound. Over-come with grief, Apollo turned the blood that had spilled from Hyacinth's wound into the flower of the same name, inscribing on its petals the words "alas, alas." In another version of the myth, Zephyrus, the spring breeze, took a fancy to the boy, who did not return his love; Zephyrus turned the discus against him in revenge.

THE DEATH OF HYACINTH
Giambattista Tiepolo
1752–53
124 | Museo Thyssen-Bornemisza, Madrid

☐ Tiepolo has set the myth in his own time. In the foreground is the lifeless Hyacinth, and at his side Apollo, identified by the laurel wreath, mourns him. The presence of Cupid next to them alludes to the deep feelings that united them. On the right is the flower into which the youth has metamorphosed, while before them, on the ground, are some balls and a racquet, eighteenth-century substitutes for the discus.

The metamorphosis of Cyparissus

In the city of Ceos lived Cyparissus, an extraordinarily handsome youth loved by Apollo. The boy owned a sacred deer, his dearest playmate, with whom he spent most of his time. On a sweltering summer day, as the animal was resting in the shade of a tree, Cyparissus struck it inadvertently with a javelin, killing it. Although Apollo tried in vain to comfort him, the boy beseeched the gods to let him mourn forever. Then his limbs began to metamorphose into branches; the tree was named "cypress," the tree of sadness and mourning.

□ The beloved deer lies lifeless on the ground, while young Cyparissus lifts his arms to the gods, who are granting his wish, for cypress branches are sprouting from his head and fingers; the metamorphosis is taking place, in eternal remembrance of his grief.

THE TRANSFORMATION OF CYPARISSUS
Domenico Zampieri, known as Domenichino
1616–18
National Gallery, London

DIANA

The daughter of Jupiter and Latona and the twin sister of Apollo, Diana is known primarily as the goddess of hunting. The myth recounts that as soon as she was born, she helped her mother deliver her brother. The goddess is the feminine equivalent of Apollo; like him, she is armed with bow and arrow, and just as he is identified with the image of the Sun, so Diana is identified with the Moon, wearing a crescent Moon on her forehead. She has no companion, and thus is the chaste goddess par excellence, the guardian deity of woman's chastity until her wedding day. Like her brother, Diana can inflict plagues and sudden death with her arrows, especially on women. As a beneficial deity, she banishes illness and evil from the mortals. Finally, as the goddess of the hunt, she enjoys this activity and is often depicted hunting with her friends the nymphs, followed by her dogs, in valleys and woods.

Greek name: Artemis

Attributes: bow, arrows, crescent Moon on the forehead, dogs, stag

DIANA WITH BOWS AND ARROWS
end 1st century BCE—early 2nd century CE
Museo Archeologico Nazionale, Naples

☐ Diana is seen in profile in this fresco as she nocks the arrow into the bowstring. Her hair is gathered in a chignon, and she is wearing the chiton and a cape that covers her shoulders and bust.

DIANA

☐ Diana is identified by the crescent Moon she wears on the forehead and the bloody arrow she holds in her hand. She keeps the hunting dogs on a leash at her side. The goddess is wearing a loose shirt with one breast uncovered, reminiscent of the Amazons, the legendary women warriors who venerated Diana as their patron goddess.

DIANA THE HUNTRESS
Cavalier d'Arpino
c. 1600
Musei Capitolini, Rome

DIANA

☐ Although they were directly inspired by ancient imagery, Renaissance artists and those of later ages often interpreted Diana's hunting scenes in original ways. In this seventeenth-century work by Domenichino, the central theme is an archery contest between Diana and her nymphs, while all around other maidens return from the hunt or hold their dogs in check.

The first arrow, shot by the nymphs, hits the pole from which a dove is hanging; the second one undoes the ribbon that tied it to the pole, and the third arrow kills the dove. In the center of the composition, Diana holds high her bow and quiver, delighted at her nymph's victory.

THE HUNT OF DIANA
Domenico Zampieri, known as Domenichino
1616–17

Galleria Borghese, Rome

DIANA

☐ A frequent image of Diana is the bathing and dressing scene. Artists have frequently used this theme to draw the female nude, as in this painting by Boucher. The goddess is identified by the crescent Moon held in place on her head by a string of pearls. She is resting after the hunt, and a nymph attends to her. Totally naked, Diana sits on her dress by a stream, as indicated by the white sleeve falling to the ground. The game she has just caught lies next to her, while the quiver and arrows are on the left side of the composition. In the middle distance are two dogs, her faithful hunting mates; they are running about, perhaps attracted by a new prey.

DIANA BATHING
(detail)
François Boucher
1742
| Musée du Louvre, Paris

Diana and Actaeon

Actaeon was a very proficient hunter who had been trained in the art by Chiron, the wise centaur. One day as he walked the woods during a hunting party, Actaeon entered the valley of Gargaphia, sacred to Diana. In the deepest and most hidden part of the forest was a cave with a crystal-clear spring where Diana usually went with her nymphs to rest from hunting. The hunter came upon the goddess and unexpectedly saw her naked, bathing in the spring with her handmaids. After chasing him away by squirting water on him, she decided to punish his insolence by turning him into a stag. Actaeon ran away, surprised at his own speed, until he saw his reflection in a pool and realized what had happened. As he was looking at his image, his own dogs caught sight of him; after a lengthy chase, they reached him and mangled him to death.

DEATH OF ACTAEON
Attic red-figure krater
Pan painter
c. 470 BCE

| Museum of Fine Arts, Boston

☐ This scene depicts Actaeon attacked by his dogs. He is represented in human form, making it easier to understand the myth and to avoid mistaking this for just any hunting scene. On the left is Diana, her bow pointed at Actaeon as he vainly cries for help.

◄◄

Diana and Actaeon

☐ In this painting, Titian narrates the first part of the legend, when the young Actaeon, escorted by his dogs on the left, happens upon Diana bathing. The goddess, identified by the crescent Moon on her forehead, is depicted as her maids dry her after the bath and groom her. Actually, the artist has given a personal interpretation of the myth, for he does not depict Diana bathing as ancient sources narrate, but the scene after the bath. The young hunter's surprise is denoted by his raised hands. The deer skull on top of the arch pier, behind the nymph drying Diana's leg, seems to allude to Actaeon's imminent, tragic death.

DIANA AND ACTAEON
Tiziano Vecellio, known as Titian
1558
National Gallery of Scotland, Edinburgh

Diana and Callisto

Callisto was the daughter of Lycaon, king of Arcadia. She entered Diana's retinue after taking a vow of chastity. One day Jupiter saw her and fell in love. Disguised as Diana, the father of the gods seduced the maiden and impregnated her. After several months, at the end of a long hunt, Diana asked her retinue to stop at a spring to rest. As she was about to undress, however, Callisto hesitated, but the nymphs removed her clothes and discovered her condition. Angered, the goddess banished her from her court.

In the meantime, Juno had discovered her husband's betrayal and sought out the girl, who had by then given birth to a boy, Arcas. In a fit of jealousy, Juno transformed Callisto into a she-bear. Years later, unaware of her mother's fate, the youth tried to kill the she-bear during a hunt, but Jupiter took pity and stopped him just as he was about to slay the animal. He then raised mother and son to the heavens and gave them a home there as two constellations: Ursa Major and Ursa Minor.

JUPITER AND CALLISTO
Jacopo Amigoni
1736–37
Hermitage Museum, Saint Petersburg

140

☐ In this painting, Jupiter, transformed into Diana, seduces Callisto. The girl, whose name means "the fairest," is represented as a huntress. To the right of the king of the gods, a putto raises the red curtain to hide the eagle clutching the thunderbolts.

Diana and Callisto

☐ This painting by Ricci narrates the part of the fable when Diana discovers Callisto's secret. The nymphs around the girl undress her while she fearfully tries to cover herself. Standing on the right, Diana points an accusing finger at the girl who betrayed her, commanding her to leave.

DIANA AND CALLISTO
Sebastiano Ricci
1712–16
Gallerie dell'Accademia, Venice

MARS

A son of Jupiter and Juno, Mars is the god of war. His violent, aggressive nature makes him unwelcome to the other gods, his parents included. Homer writes that the fully armed god took pleasure even in just the wild sound of the war cry as he ran through the battlefields sowing death. Only Venus fell in love with this god, betraying Vulcan, her spouse. The ancient Greeks believed that the palace of this god was in Thrace, a wild region with a rigid climate, peopled by war-mongering tribes such as the Amazons, who were considered his daughters.

Unlike Minerva, who embodies the image of wise, prudent counsel in war, Mars incarnates its more violent, savage, and bloodthirsty currents. But the god of war does not always win; for all his brutal strength, he is often deceived and defeated by the keener, shrewder strength of Hercules or Minerva.

Greek name: Ares

Attributes: helmet, shield, spear, sword, wolf, woodpecker

COLOSSAL STATUE OF MARS
1st century CE
144 | Musei Capitolini, Rome

☐ Mars is represented standing and wearing the *lorica*—the Roman military armor with the image of Medusa in the center and two winged griffins below. On his head is a splendidly decorated helmet, and in his right hand is what remains of a spear. With his left hand he holds the shield that rests on the ground.

Mars, Venus, and Vulcan

Although married to Vulcan, Venus fell in love with Mars and became unfaithful to her husband. Apollo, the Sun god, apprised Vulcan of the affair, and he decided to punish his wife and her lover. In his forge, he built a strong, extremely thin net, invisible even to divine eyes. After fastening it to the bed, he feigned a trip to the island of Lemnos, his native land. Mars immediately took advantage of Vulcan's absence to lie with his lover, but they were trapped in the net. Vulcan then summoned all the gods to be witnesses, and they laughed until Neptune freed the lovers.

☐ Elegantly attired in a Renaissance gown, Venus watches Mars resting. The god is in a deep sleep; not even the sound of the conch a little satyr is playing in his ear awakens him. Other child satyrs mock him by playing with his weapons. This mythological theme conveys the message that love conquers all violence and all wars.

VENUS AND MARS
Sandro Botticelli
c. 1485

◄◄

Mars, Venus, and Vulcan

 In a richly festooned nuptial chamber, Vulcan, seen from the back, holds the invisible net he had built specifically to trap the two lovers. Mars seems surprised, while Venus lowers her eyes in shame. Above them, the gods amusedly look at the unfolding scene. Mercury, identified by the caduceus, hovers above the couple; next to him, Jupiter sits on a cloud, thunderbolts in hand; and Minerva is at his side, armed with a spear. To the far left, above Vulcan, we glimpse Diana with the crescent Moon on her head and Saturn with the reaping hook.

VENUS AND MARS SURPRISED BY VULCAN
(detail)
Joachim Wtewael
1601

VULCAN

Another son of Jupiter and Juno, Vulcan is the god of fire and the blacksmith of heroes and gods, many of whom wear the lovely armor he forges for them. This god is lame, and different versions of the myth explain the disability. In the most popular one, after quarreling with Juno, in a fit of rage Jupiter took little Vulcan and hurled him from Mount Olympus. The unlucky child fell on the island of Lemnos, where he was found and healed by the Sinties, the local people. In another version, the god was born lame and his mother, ashamed of his disability, hid him from the other gods by throwing him down from Olympus; the child fell into the ocean and was raised by Thetis.

Vulcan learned the art of forging metal as a child. In his forge, located either on Mount Etna or in another volcano, the Cyclopes work as his assistants. Jupiter gave him Venus in marriage, but she fell in love with Mars and soon betrayed him.

Greek name: Hephaestus

Attributes: anvil, hammer

☐ This vase painting narrates Vulcan's return to Olympus, the abode of the gods. To persuade him to return, Bacchus caused him to become drunk. Now the inebriated and wobbly god of fire is led to the mountaintop by Bacchus and his maenads.

HEPHAESTUS RETURNS TO OLYMPUS
(detail)
Attic red-figure amphora
550–500 BCE

Kunsthistorisches Museum, Vienna

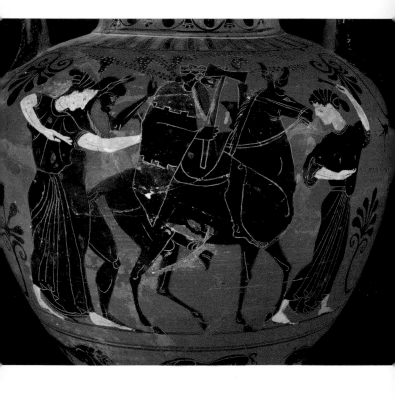

VULCAN

□ The artist has transposed the representation of Vulcan's forge to his own time. The forge of the god of fire is in an open space, with a broad country landscape visible in the background. On the left, Vulcan is forging a piece of metal on his anvil; next to him, Cupid, quiver in his lap, plays with a dog. All around are copper and pewter objects and armor pieces scattered casually. To the extreme left of the painting a woman, probably Venus, leans from a door.

VULCAN'S FORGE
Jacopo Bassano
1580
| Galleria Sabauda, Turin

◄◄

VULCAN

□ Velázquez has chosen to illustrate the episode in which Apollo tells Vulcan that Venus and Mars are lovers. Standing before the anvil, the god of fire turns abruptly from his task and looks surprised and disbelieving at Apollo. Around him are the Cyclopes, depicted as simple laborers, who listen, surprised. The artist has depicted Apollo with the laurel wreath to identify him; he has also added a sort of luminous halo around his head to stress his role as the Sun god. In fact, in the Homeric poems, it is Sol (see p. 214) who discloses the dalliance to Vulcan; here the artist has synthesized the images of the two distinct gods into that of Apollo.

APOLLO AT THE FORGE OF VULCAN
Diego Velázquez
1630
Museo del Prado, Madrid

MERCURY

The son of Jupiter and Maia, a nymph, Mercury was born in a cave near Mount Cyllene in Arcadia. Soon after his birth, the child displayed precocious gifts (see p. 160). Realizing his uncommon energy, Jupiter decided to appoint him messenger of the gods.

It is said that the fast-running god—he wears winged sandals—would fly over mountains and seas to bring news of the gods' intentions. Mercury usually carries the caduceus, a stick with two coiling snakes, and wears the petasus, a wide-brimmed traveler's hat. Among his many tasks is that of Psychopomp, or escorter to the netherworld of the souls of the dead. A clever, shrewd god who is something of a trickster, the divine messenger is also worshiped as the guardian god of thieves, of commerce in general, and of wayfarers. Country crossroads and city thoroughfares were frequently punctuated by statues representing him (herms) to point the way to travelers.

Greek name: Hermes

Attributes: winged sandals, petasus, caduceus

HERMES WITH CADUCEUS AND PURSE
4th century BCE
Musée du Louvre, Paris

☐ As the protector of wayfarers, Mercury is here portrayed with mantle and petasus, typical travel wear. The money purse he clutches in his right hand recalls that he is also the god of commerce. In the other hand is the caduceus.

◄◄

MERCURY

☐ Mercury is shown here in his role
of *Psychopomp*, the guide of the
dead. He is holding Myrrhine, a
young woman who has just died, by
the hand, to escort her across the
Acheron—the underground river that
all souls must cross to reach the
kingdom of the dead. To the left of
this relief, we see the girl's distraught parents taking leave of her.
Mercury is recognizable by the
winged sandals, a hint of his
legendary speed. The girl's name
is immortalized above her figure.

HERMES PSYCHOPOMP
Relief from a Greek vase
c. 420 BCE

National Archaeological Museum, Athens

Mercury and the herd of Apollo

Soon after birth, Mercury gave signs of uncommon liveliness and energy. He was born in the morning, and at noon he had already wriggled out of his swaddling clothes and invented the lyre, using a turtle shell to which he had attached some suitable strings. That same day, in the evening, he went to Thessaly, where his brother Apollo had been sent to work for King Admetus, watching his cattle (see p. 122). Taking advantage of the Sun god's momentary inattention, Mercury stole the cattle. Only an old peasant, Battus, saw him but promised to keep the secret. Still, the clever child god decided to test him and, appearing in disguise, tried to corrupt the old man, who finally gave in to his cajoling. Because Battus had promised to be as mute as a stone, the god turned him into one.

In the end, Jupiter ruled that the cattle should be returned to Apollo, who made peace with his little brother. The myth also recounts that Apollo was so charmed by the sound of the lyre invented by Mercury that he gave the child the cattle in exchange.

MERCURY STEALING THE CATTLE OF THE GODS
Edward John Poynter
1860
160 | Walker Art Gallery, Liverpool

☐ Mercury is here depicted as a child. Already wearing the winged petasus, somewhat cheekily he asks Battus not to reveal that he stole the god's cattle. The shepherd looks amusedly at the child god; the stolen oxen are visible in the back.

Mercury and Herse

One day Mercury saw the daughters of the Athenian king Cecrops walking back from a ritual to Minerva and fell in love with Herse, the loveliest of them. The god offered to pay one of her sisters, Aglauros, to let him into the room of his beloved. While Mercury left to get the promised gold, Aglauros was bitten by Envy and began to deeply hate her sister's happiness. Therefore she broke the agreement and decided not to satisfy the god's request. Mercury tried in vain to soothe her and persuade her to let him in; after the hundredth refusal, he turned the girl into a dark stone, as dark as her thoughts.

☐ In this canvas, the daughters of Cecrops are walking back from the ceremony honoring Minerva, bearing flower garlands and carrying baskets on their heads. Mercury flies overhead, pointing his caduceus, and gazes at the women below.

MERCURY WATCHES HERSE
AND AGLAUROS
Hendrik van Balen
Musée des Beaux-Arts, Valenciennes

Mercury and Herse

☐ The tragedy of Aglauros, all the way to the right in the painting, unfolds in a richly decorated chamber. Mercury is about to turn her into stone; in the center of the composition, Herse looks speechless at the scene, while the other frightened sisters rush to her aid.

MERCURY, HERSE, AND AGLAUROS
Jean-Baptiste Marie Pierre
1763
Musée du Louvre, Paris

VENUS

Many legends surround the birth of Venus, the goddess of
beauty and love. Homer narrates that she was born from the
liaison between Jupiter and Dione, a daughter of Uranus and
Gaea, but the poets preferred the version of Venus born from
the foam of the sea, where Saturn had thrown his father's
genital organs after castrating him (see p. 22). As soon as she
rose from the waves, the winds took her first to Cythera,
then to Cyprus. In yet another version of the myth, the
goddess was born from a seashell and brought in the seashell
to the island of Cythera.

Venus married Vulcan, the god of fire, but soon betrayed
him with Mars, the god of war (see p. 146). She had many
other lovers, including young Adonis and Anchises, with
whom she begot the Trojan hero Aeneas.

Greek name: Aphrodite

Attributes: doves, myrtle, rose, apple

APHRODITE OF CNIDUS
Roman copy of an original by Praxiteles
from *c.* 360 BCE
166 | Musei Vaticani, Vatican City

☐ The Cnidian Aphrodite is a celebrated statue from ancient Greece.
The goddess of beauty is caught as
she drops her clothes on an urn, just
before taking a bath. The statue
takes its name from the residents of
the city of Cnidus, who purchased
the statue and venerated it in a
small temple.

VENUS

☐ Venus is here depicted as *Sosandra*, in Greek, "the savior of men." The goddess stands, enveloped in a full, heavy mantle that barely reveals her form; hidden by the drapery, the left knee is barely discernible. The veil frames the oval of her face. It is a rather unusual, original image compared to the traditional iconography that depicts this goddess primping at the mirror, often surrounded by cupids.

APHRODITE SOSANDRA
mid-1st century CE
168 | Museo Archeologico Nazionale, Naples

◄◄

VENUS

☐ Elegantly dressed, a serene
Venus rides a white goose in the sky.
Her right arm is stretched and the
hand holds a plant, a sort of curly
vine, while with her left hand she
holds onto the docile bird.

APHRODITE RIDING A GOOSE
(detail)
Attic white-background cup
c. 460 BCE
170 | British Museum, London

VENUS

☐ Venus is often represented lying on a bed or primping at her daily toilet, irrespective of what mythological episodes are being narrated. She personifies feminine beauty, and as such, her figure becomes a pretext for studying the female body. Here the goddess is gracefully stretched on a couch while the faithful Cupid holds a mirror, in which she admires herself. The child god, identified by the wings, has his hands crossed and a ribbon on his wrists, an allusion to the deep bond that joins them.

THE TOILET OF VENUS
(THE ROKEBY VENUS)
Diego Velázquez
1647–51
National Gallery, London

172

VENUS

☐ Boucher has given us a soft, gentle image of a Venus whose femininity, though still unripe, is already seductive. The goddess of love is surrounded by her identifying attributes: doves, roses, pearls, and a silver seashell lying at the foot of the bed, which recalls the legend of her birth from the foam of the sea.

THE TOILET OF VENUS
François Boucher
1751

The Metropolitan Museum of Art, New York

VENUS

☐ Botticelli narrates the version of the birth of Venus in which the goddess of love rises from a sea-shell and is carried in it to the island of Cythera. The figures on the left personify the springtime winds: Zephyrus, wearing a blue mantle, carries Aura, the breeze, in his arms. On the opposite side of the scene, a handmaid of the goddess—possibly one of the Graces or the Hours—welcomes the goddess by covering her with a precious mantle.

THE BIRTH OF VENUS
Sandro Botticelli
1484–86
Gallerie degli Uffizi, Florence

VENUS

☐ Stretched out on a finely carved bed, Venus is stroking some doves, one of her attributes. Cupid, identified by the quiver on his shoulder, is nearby. This winged boy, whose arrows cause all who are within his reach to fall in love, is generally considered the child of Mars and Venus. The god of war is in the background, fully armed; he stealthily approaches his beloved, almost fearful of being discovered.

VENUS AND CUPID
Lambert Sustris
c. 1540
Musée du Louvre, Paris

VENUS

VENUS, MARS, AND CUPID
Piero di Cosimo
c. 1505

Gemäldegalerie, Berlin

☐ The goddess of love is depicted as she watches Mars, her lover, who is asleep. In her arms, she holds Cupid, who is believed to be the fruit of their illegitimate love. Many objects in this painting are her attributes, such as the myrtle bush in the background, a symbol of everlasting love because it is an evergreen, and the two cooing doves, an allusion to the embracing lovers and Venus's favorite birds.

VENUS

☐ Leaning on the bed, Mars takes Venus by the hand and invites her to lie down, when Cupid bursts into the scene, leading the war god's horse by the bridle. The two lovers turn amused toward the animal, which seems to look curiously inside the room.

VENUS AND MARS WITH CUPID
Paolo Veronese
1575–80
182 | Galleria Sabauda, Turin

Venus and Adonis

THE BIRTH OF ADONIS

Adonis was the son of Cinyras, king of Cyprus, and his daughter Myrrha. Having reached the marriageable age, the myth recounts, the maiden kept refusing all her suitors because she bore a secret passion for her father. Despairing because she saw no solution to her plight, she resolved to hang herself but was saved by her wet nurse, who learned the terrible truth and decided to help. One evening, the nurse told the king about a lovely maiden who was desperately in love with him; under cover of darkness, she led Myrrha to her father's nuptial thalamus and the girl lay with him for nine nights. One night the king, curious about his lover, lit her face and discovered the terrifying truth. He immediately tried to kill Myrrha, but she escaped and begged the gods to transform her into another living being, that she might no longer offend either the living or the dead. The gods heard her, and metamorphosed her into the myrrh tree. The child she carried in her womb continued to grow inside the tree until, with the help of Lucina, the goddess of childbirth, the bark broke and the child was born. He was called Adonis.

THE BIRTH OF ADONIS
(detail)
Tiziano Vecellio, known as Titian
1507
Museo d'Arte Medioevale e Moderna,
Padua

184

☐ Adonis is born from Myrrha just as she is transformed into a tree. Lucina, the goddess of childbirth, assisted in the delivery, pulling the baby from the tree trunk. Around her, some naiads witness the miraculous event.

Venus and Adonis

DEATH OF ADONIS

Struck in error by one of Cupid's arrows, Venus fell madly in love with Adonis and would spend entire days hunting with him, neglecting her divine duties. The goddess knew the young man's destiny, and often counseled Adonis to avoid hunting fierce prey and concentrate instead on tamer ones. One day, while Adonis was hunting alone, his dogs smelled a wild boar and began to follow the tracks. Heedless of Venus's advice, he followed the dogs, found the prey, and struck it— but could not kill it. The fierce animal attacked and mortally wounded him. In vain Venus ran to him. In memory of the youth, she transformed his blood into anemones, the flowers whose life is as short as that of Adonis.

□ Adonis is depicted leaving for the hunt with his dogs. To the left is Venus, who gazes raptly at him while Cupid sports an impertinent, amused air as he points to the goddess. Pleased about his mischief, he still holds an arrow in his hands, an allusion to the arrow that he shot at his mother, whose breast appears punctured.

VENUS, ADONIS, AND CUPID
Annibale Carracci
1590–95
186 | Museo del Prado, Madrid

◄◄

Venus and Adonis

☐ Venus and Adonis are hunting. The goddess of love is dressed like Diana, goddess of the hunt, her gown pulled up above the knee, an arrow in her hand. At her side, Adonis has just killed a stag. Venus, who knew the fate of her beloved, always counseled him to hunt tamer animals. Cupid, Venus's faithful escort, surveys the scene from the air; a little putto next to him blows on the hunting horn.

VENUS AND ADONIS HUNTING
(detail)
Marcantonio Franceschini
1629–1709
188 | Liechtenstein Museum, Vienna

◀◀

Venus and Adonis

▶▶

☐ In this painting, Titian has freely interpreted the fable. Venus tries to hold back her beloved, who is going hunting with his dogs and seems determined to leave, despite the goddess's entreaties. In the middle ground, Cupid sleeps under a tree, no longer watching over their love. In the sky, we glimpse Aurora's chariot—in another version of the story, it is that of Venus—and the rays radiating from it point to the path that Adonis will take to his imminent, tragic fate.

VENUS AND ADONIS
Tiziano Vecellio, known as Titian
1553–54

| Museo del Prado, Madrid

◄◄

Venus and Adonis

☐ Despite Venus's warnings, Adonis lies lifeless on the ground, killed by a wild boar. To the right, behind a tree, the animal flees. A grief-stricken Venus has rushed to the scene on her swan-drawn cart, but it is too late for her beloved. Next to Adonis are some red anemones that have sprouted from his blood. They are short-lived flowers whose leaves the wind scatters just after they have flowered, their name being derived from the Greek *ánemos*, which means "wind."

THE DEATH OF ADONIS
Domenico Zampieri, known as Domenichino
c. 1629–31

| Palazzo Durazzo Pallavicini, Genoa

Atalanta and Hippomenes

The daughter of Schoeneus, king of Scyros, Atalanta was a strikingly beautiful maiden and an excellent huntress. She eschewed men because an oracle had predicted that, once married, she would be forever changed. To discourage her suitors, she usually challenged them to a race, promising her hand to the winner and death to the loser. For many years Atalanta went unconquered, until Hippomenes challenged her. To win, he resorted to a ruse that Venus suggested: The goddess gave him three golden apples from the Garden of the Hesperides and advised him to throw them one by one on the ground, to slow down the girl's race. Inevitably attracted by the golden fruits, Atalanta stopped three times to pick them up and lost.

But Hippomenes forgot to give thanks to Venus for the help he had received, and so she punished them. One day, while the couple was in a forest near the temple of Cybele, Hippomenes and Atalanta were seized by a sudden passion caused by the goddess of love. Guilty of desecrating the sacred shrine, the lovers were transformed into lions.

ATALANTA AND HIPPOMENES
Guido Reni
c. 1612

| Museo Nazionale di Capodimonte, Naples

☐ The artist has captured the salient point of the myth, when Atalanta stoops to retrieve the golden apples, which the goddess of love made heavier to handicap the young girl. Hippomenes seizes the opportunity and overtakes her, winning the race.

VESTA AND THE VESTALS

A daughter of Saturn and Rhea, and therefore a sister of Jupiter and Juno, Vesta is one of the twelve major gods. She is the goddess of the hearth and family life in general. In Rome, Vesta was also worshiped as the guardian goddess of that extended family, the state, so that consuls, praetors, and dictators made sacrifices to her when inaugurating their mandates.

The shrine dedicated to her had no statues, only a sacred fire that burned perennially and was guarded by the Vestals, for should the fire go out, it would be considered an unlucky omen. The Vestals were virgin priestesses who reported to the highest religious authority, the pontifex maximus. They had many privileges, but many duties as well, including keeping themselves chaste for the length of their service; those who broke the vow were buried alive.

Greek name: Hestia

☐ The goddess of the hearth is shown fully dressed, a rich mantle covering her head, standing at an altar. In one hand she holds the sacrificial cup, in the other a sort of scepter topped by a torch, an allusion to the sacred fire that must always be kept burning.

LUNETTE WITH VESTA
Antonio Allegri, known as Correggio
1519
Abbess Room
196 | Convent of San Paolo, Parma

Tuccia

There are very few tales about the goddess Vesta, but many about the priestesses who guarded her fire. Among them was Tuccia, a Vestal virgin accused of breaking her vow of virginity. After asking protection from the goddess, to prove her innocence Tuccia carried a sieve full of water from the Tiber River to the temple of the goddess without spilling even one drop.

☐ This work by Mantegna depicts young Tuccia with a sieve in her hands. Simply attired, the young woman looks bewildered and somewhat frightened as she undergoes the trial that will prove her innocence.

THE VESTAL VIRGIN TUCCIA WITH SIEVE
(detail)
Andrea Mantegna
1495–1506

| National Gallery, London

Claudia Quinta

Like all Vestal priestesses, Claudia Quinta had taken the vow of chastity. Accused of having broken the vow, she was able to prove her innocence by performing a prodigy. A ship originating from Asia had run aground at the mouth of the Tiber while carrying a heavy stone statue of the goddess Cybele. Claudia was able to pull the ship upstream inside Rome using only her slender belt. When she reached the city, the priests delivered the statue to Scipio Africanus.

□ The artist has given us a contemporary version of the Claudia Quinta episode, setting it in his own time. In the foreground, the young woman pulls the boat, while on the opposite shore of the river, against the background of a medieval city, the admiring public follows the prodigious event.

CLAUDIA QUINTA CARRIES
THE STATUE OF CYBELE
Miniature
c. 1450
Public Library, New York

quute claudic

JANUS

Among the Olympian gods is Janus, one of the earliest deities in the Roman pantheon, with no corresponding god in Greek mythology. Although he occupied a prominent position in Roman religion, his role was never clearly defined. The ancients held him in great consideration; Macrobius, a fifth-century Roman author, even claimed that he was superior to the other gods and referred to him as *deus deorum*, the "god of gods." Still, although only scant information about him has survived, it is possible that his role, at least in the early period of the Roman civilization, was held in higher consideration than that of Jupiter.

This god had many functions: He was the god of beginnings and ends; he presided over every entrance or departure. Janus began the new year, inaugurated the seasons, and was considered a sort of "doorman." For these reasons, he was given the attributes of Patuleius, "he who opens," and Clusius, "he who closes."

HEAD OF TWO-FACED JANUS
from Vulci
2nd century BCE
Museo Nazionale Etrusco di Villa Giulia, Rome

☐ On Earth, Janus was the patron god of passages and doorways; for this reason, archways were called *iani*. Because each passageway looks on two opposite directions, front and back, the god was personified with two faces back to back, and was called two-faced Janus.

JANUS

☐ Janus had several other functions. Because beginnings were sacred to him, he protected the start of all activities or undertakings and was invoked before every deed. During the Renaissance, the image of Janus with his two-faced head representing the past and the future became part of the allegory of Prudence. This fresco depicts the personifications of Strength, Prudence, and Temperance—the virtues, according to Plato, that marked a just man. The central double-faced figure holding a mirror is Prudence. The mirror suggests the wise man's ability to see himself as he is, while the two faces evoke the knowledge of time past and time future, as well as a related concept—circumspection. To the left sits Strength with her attributes: an oak branch and lion. To the right, Temperance holds a horse bit in her hands, symbolizing moderation.

THE CARDINAL VIRTUES
(detail)
Raffaello Sanzio, known as Raphael
1511
Segnature Room
Palazzi Vaticani, Vatican City

SIBYLS

The Sibyls were renowned female prophets of antiquity. Generally speaking, their image is that of the priestess who guards the cult of Apollo and interprets his oracles. The Sibyls have very ancient origins, and many lands claim to have been their birthplace. The name is apparently derived from Sibyl, the daughter of the Trojans Dardanus and Neso. A maiden endowed with the gift of prophecy, her reputation soon expanded to all the known world. After her, all female prophets were attributed her name. The number of Sibyls varies according to the sources. The most important ones were the Eritrean, Persian, Libyan, Delphic, Samian, Cumaean, Cimmerian, Hellespontine, Tiburtine, and Phrygian Sibyls. These priestesses also guarded the famous Sibylline books, a collection of oracles and prophecies kept in the temple of Capitoline Jupiter in Rome and consulted in times of disasters or extraordinary events.

Attributes: book

SIBYL READING
Angelica Kauffmann
1780–85
206 | Galleria Sabauda, Turin

☐ The artist has portrayed the Eritrean Sibyl. The myth narrates that immediately after her birth she began to prophesy in verse. She suggested that Tarquinius purchase the nine Sibylline books. Each time the king, who thought the price exorbitant, refused, the Sibyl burned three of the books. After the second refusal, he bought the last three and deposited them in Jupiter's temple.

SIBYLS

☐ Initially thought to be an allegory of music on account of the *viola da gamba* and the musical score, this painting actually represents the Cumaean Sibyl, who escorted Aeneas to the netherworld to speak with the dead. Behind the Sibyl are visible a laurel tree, sacred to Apollo, and a vine, an allusion to Bacchus but also to Christ, for in the Middle Ages the Sibyls were assimilated to the prophets and considered the very first messengers of the coming of Christ.

A SIBYL
Domenico Zampieri, known as Domenichino
1617

Galleria Borghese, Rome

Apollo and the Cumaean Sibyl

When she was young, the Cumaean Sibyl had been loved by Apollo. To seduce her, the god promised her that he would grant her any wish. The young girl took a fistful of dust from the ground and asked to live as many years as the grains of dust she held in her fist, but she forgot to also ask for eternal youth. For this reason, she had a very long life as an old woman.

☐ The Cumaean Sibyl, whose oracle site was at Cumae near Naples, where Apollo was worshiped in very ancient times, is depicted as an old woman intent on reading a volume, a probable allusion to the Sibylline books.

THE CUMAEAN SIBYL
Michelangelo Buonarroti
1508–12
Sistine Chapel

Palazzi Vaticani, Vatican City

CVMAEA

Augustus and the Tiburtine Sibyl

One legend narrates that the Roman Senate had suggested that Augustus be made a god. Undecided, the emperor turned to the Tiburtine Sibyl for advice on the matter. The young prophetess announced the coming of a child who would be greater than all the gods combined. When these words were spoken, the sky was rent, revealing an apparition of the Virgin Mary with the infant Jesus in her arms.

❑ Before an architectural background, a fantasy Rome, the Sibyl points out to the kneeling Emperor Augustus the apparition of the Virgin and Child whom the Roman people would soon worship. She holds a volume in her hands, a reminder of the Sibylline books.

AUGUSTUS AND THE TIBURTINE SIBYL
Antoine Caron
1575–80
Musée du Louvre, Paris

SOL (SUN)

Sol, the god of the star bearing the same name, belongs to the first generation of gods, the Titans. He is the son of Hyperion and Theia, as well as the brother of Aurora (Dawn) and Luna (Moon). The ancients represented this god as a young, bright-eyed man with resplendent curls and a golden helmet on his head.

Sol's main role was to bring light to the gods and to men: In the morning, he rose from the ocean in the East, crossed the vault of the sky, and plunged again into the sea in the West at sunset. The Sun god crossed the sky on a fiery chariot pulled by very fast horses. The ancients believed that the god had a golden palace in the West where he and his horses went to rest. As a deity who hears and sees everything and whose light penetrates each minute corner, he was invoked in oaths and protestations. Later, his image became fused with that of Apollo, although originally the two gods were distinct.

Greek name: Helios

THE RACE OF THE SUN CHARIOT
(detail)
Giambattista Tiepolo
c. 1740
Palazzo Clerici, Milan

□ Starting in late Roman times, the image of Sol, the Sun god, began to coincide with that of Apollo, and artists assimilated the two identities. In this fresco by Tiepolo, the chariot of the Sun is ready to bring the light of a new day. The chariot is pulled by four splendid horses: Pyrois, Eos, Aethon, and Phlegon.

Phaeton

Phaeton was believed to be the son of Sol and the ocean nymph Clymene. He was raised by his mother, who had shielded him from his father's identity until he came of age. Wanting proof that the god was really his father, Phaeton visited Sol; eager to dispel all doubts, the god promised to grant him any wish. When the boy asked to drive his chariot, the father consented, albeit unwillingly. Sol's powerful steeds did not recognize their master's bit and suddenly veered from the usual course and began to race high in the sky. Frightened by the height, Phaeton tried to turn the horses first down toward Earth, setting it on fire, then up in the sky, burning the stars. To avoid a universal conflagration, Jupiter was forced to kill him with a thunderbolt.

☐ A kneeling Phaeton asks Sol permission to drive his chariot. The horses, groomed by the Hours, are visible in the background on the left, where he is pointing. With his golden mantle, the lyre, and a laurel wreath as crown, the Sun is here identified with Apollo. Seated around him are the four Seasons, and in the center, in the guise of the god of time, stands Saturn.

HELIOS AND PHAETON WITH SATURN
AND THE FOUR SEASONS
Nicolas Poussin
c. 1635
Staatliche Museen, Berlin

Phaeton

☐ Seized by panic, Phaeton has lost control of the chariot and crashes down to Earth, struck by Jupiter's bolts of lightning. The king of the gods, after calling all the divinities as witnesses, sat on the peaks from which he was wont to rain clouds, thunder, and lightning down to Earth and acted immediately to avoid a worldwide fire.

THE FALL OF PHAETON
Sebastiano Ricci
1703–1704
218 | Museo Civico, Belluno

Phaeton

☐ Struck by Jupiter's thunderbolts, Phaeton crashes to Earth, and his lifeless body falls to the bottom of the Eridanus River. The Heliades, daughters of the Sun and the sea nymph Clymene and Phaeton's sisters, recovered his body and lowered him into a tomb. They mourned him four days and four nights until, gradually, their inconsolable grief turned them into poplar trees. This tapestry depicts their metamorphosis along the river banks, while the surrounding animals ignore the event.

THE FALL OF PHAETON
Tapestry
Battista Dossi
1545

Musée du Louvre, Paris

The blinding of Orion

The son of Neptune and Euryale, Orion was a giant renowned for his good looks and prodigious strength. Eonopion, king of the island of Chios, asked for his help in freeing the island from a plague of wild beasts. The giant accepted the assignment; while on the island, he fell in love with Merope, the king's daughter, but she did not return his love. One day, a drunken Orion raped the girl, who blinded him in revenge while he lay sleeping. An oracle told the giant that he could regain his sight only by exposing his eyes to the Sun's rays.

He then traveled to Vulcan's forge, where he took a boy, Cedalion, sat him on his shoulders and asked him to guide him in the direction of the rising Sun. Thus, by exposing his eyes to the beneficial rays, he was healed. Once he regained his sight, the giant began to hunt with Diana. One day, he tried to rape Diana, who punished him by sending a scorpion that stung him to death. After he died, Orion was metamorphosed into the constellation that bears his name.

BLIND ORION SEARCHING FOR
THE RISING SUN
Nicolas Poussin
1658

☐ Blinded by Merope, Orion wanders with young Cedalion perched on his shoulders. From Earth, Vulcan guides the steps of the giant toward the East, for the ancients believed that if one looked constantly at the Sun, he could be cured of blindness. High on a cloud, Diana follows the scene.

Clytia and Leucothea

Because he had revealed her secret affair with Mars (see p. 154) to her husband Vulcan, Venus retaliated by causing Sol to fall in love with Leucothea, a mortal girl who was the daughter of King Orcamus. To win her love, Sol disguised himself as the girl's mother. Once in her room, he dispatched the hand-maids with an excuse. Finally alone, the god revealed his identity, and Leucothea allowed herself to be seduced.

But Clytia, an ocean nymph whom Sol had loved in the past, became jealous and revealed what had happened to Leucothea's father, who buried his daughter alive. In vain Sol tried to revive her with his warm rays; unable to do so, he sprinkled her burial mound with scented nectar; thus, incense was born. Repudiated by Sol, Clytia spent her days watching her former lover cross the sky; she stopped eating and drinking until her limbs were transformed into a flower— the sunflower, which always turns its face toward the Sun.

CLYTIA TURNED INTO A SUNFLOWER
Charles de La Fosse
1675
Musée National du Château et Trianon,
224 | Versailles

□ A despairing, grief-stricken Clytia sits by the sea. After completing his journey across the sky, Sol now plunges into the sea heedless of her tears. Some maidens, perhaps sea nymphs, try in vain to console her. Behind the maiden is the sunflower into which she will be transmuted.

LUNA (MOON)

A sister of Sol and Aurora, Luna is described as a lovely maiden with snow-white arms, her head decorated with a diadem of rays. She is also called "the night eye"; each evening she rises from the sea and crosses the dark vault of the sky on her chariot pulled by two white horses. Sometimes she appears on an ox-drawn cart, a survival of a very early legend in which Selene, the Moon deity, had taken the form of a heifer in order to lie with the Sun god, who had been turned into a bull. Later, as was the case for Sol and Apollo, the image of Luna was superimposed on Diana's, who also wears a crescent Moon on her head.

Greek name: Selene

Attributes: the crescent Moon

☐ The Moon goddess is portrayed in this vase painting as she drives her chariot pulled by two white horses across the night sky. Elegantly attired, she wears the Moon disk on her head over a richly embroidered cap.

SELENE
(detail)
Red-figure painting on vase
500–450 BCE
Antikensammlung, Berlin

Luna and Endymion

Several love affairs have been attributed to Diana–Luna, including her love for Endymion, a young, handsome shepherd who was the son of Calyce and Aethlius, the king who founded Elis. According to the more popular version of this myth, the goddess fell madly in love with the youth and each night visited him on Mount Latmos, in Asia Minor. She asked Jupiter to grant one of her beloved's wishes, whereupon he immediately asked to sleep the eternal sleep, thus becoming immortal and preserving his youth. From the love between Luna and Endymion, fifty daughters were born.

☐ Endymion sleeps under a tree, watched by Diana–Luna. Behind the goddess is the Moon disk, her attribute. Just behind Endymion, a little Cupid, armed with bow and arrows, his finger on his lips, invites us to silence. Next to the youth, his dog also sleeps. Sleeping animals are often part of the iconography of Luna and Endymion.

DIANA AND ENDYMION
Pier Francesco Mola
c. 1660
Musei Capitolini, Rome

AURORA (DAWN)

Aurora is another daughter of Hyperion and Theia. She personifies the very first daylight and daily drives her chariot pulled by winged horses, scattering rose petals along the way to announce the arrival of the Sun. Several loves have been attributed to her, including Orynoe, Cephalus, and Tithonus, whom she married. One legend tells of her as Mars's lover; Venus punished her by causing her to be always in love, but never happily.

Greek name: Eos

☐ Before a blanket of clouds, the chariot of the Sun appears surrounded by the Hours holding each other by the hand. The image of the Dawn, she of the "rosy fingers," appears laden with flowers. A putto with a lit torch hovers above the horses: Phosphor, the morning star whose name means "he who brings light."

AURORA
Guido Reni
1614
Casino Rospigliosi, Palazzo Pallavicini, Rome

Aurora and Tithonus

Tithonus, the son of Laomedon and a brother of Priamus, king of Troy, was loved by Aurora and had a child with her, Memnon, prince of the Ethiopians, who was slain by Achilles before the walls of Troy. Because of the great love she felt for her husband, the goddess persuaded Jupiter to grant him immortality, the most coveted prize, but forgot to also ask for eternal youth. Therefore, Tithonus became eternally old and his body shrunk so much that she had to carry him in a child's wicker basket, until she was moved to pity and transmuted him into a cicada.

☐ Aurora appears with her spouse, Tithonus, by now old and sleeping soundly on a blanket of clouds. She is about to leave for her daily round, for she holds a rose that she will soon scatter across the sky. On her head is a star, possibly an allusion to the morning star.

AURORA AND TITHONUS
Giovanni da San Giovanni,
known as Lo Scheggia
c. 1620
Gallerie degli Uffizi, Florence

WINDS

The Winds (*Venti* in Latin) were worshiped as gods and offered propitiatory sacrifices, especially by anyone setting out on a sea journey. The sons of Aurora and the Titan Astraeus, the four principal Winds are Boreas, Zephyrus, Eurus, and Notus. The most feared one was Boreas, the cold north wind that made the earth shiver and shook the sea. Just as dangerous was Notus, the warm, humid south wind that brought rain and storms. The best-loved wind was Zephyrus, the sweet, beneficial west wind that heralded spring and ripened the fields. Finally, Eurus, the southeastern wind, usually blew during the winter solstice. According to the myth, the Winds resided on Aeolia in Thrace, locked up in a cave and guarded by Aeolus, who, depending on need, opened a passage so they could blow all over Earth.

BOREAS ABDUCTING OREITHYIA
Francesco Solimena
1729
234 | Kunsthistorisches Museum, Vienna

☐ The most popular representation of the Winds is in the iconography of the rape of Oreithyia, the daughter of King Erechtheus, by Boreas. The latter seized her while she was on the banks of the river Ilissus and took her to Thrace, where he sired two children, Calais and Zetes, with her. In this canvas Boreas, the winged god, has grasped Oreithyia; while some women try in vain to free the maiden, others flee, panic-stricken.

THE MUSES

The daughters of Jupiter and Mnemosyne (Memory), the Muses were nine sisters born from nine nights of love. With their sweet voices, they entertained the gods, making them forget their worries—in fact, these graceful deities presided over the art of singing as well as all kinds of poetry, the arts, and intellectual activity in general. The poets always invoked them for inspiration, and all those who challenged them met a sad end. As the deities of song, the Muses are linked to Apollo, the god of art and music, who directs their choir. According to the prevailing tradition, each Muse oversees a specific art: for Calliope it is epic poetry; Clio, history; Polyhymnia, heroic hymns; Euterpe, lyrical music; Terpsichore, dance; Erato, love poetry; Melpomene, tragedy; Thalia, comedy and idyllic poetry; and finally, Urania presides over astronomy.

SARCOPHAGUS OF THE MUSES
280–90 CE
Palazzo Massimo, Rome

☐ On this side of the sarcophagus are sculpted five of the nine Muses. The first one on the left is Terpsichore, with a lyre at her feet; Thalia, with a comic mask, follows; then Euterpe with an aulos, a wind instrument similar to the oboe. Next to her is Melpomene, holding a tragic mask, and, finally, at the extreme right, Erato with the kithara.

THE MUSES

☐ In this fresco by Raphael, Apollo is seated and plays a string instrument. He is surrounded by the Muses, who are identifiable by their attributes. To the right of the god is Polyhymnia holding a book, Terpsichore is pointing, Calliope holds a kithara, Erato a mask, and Urania is seen from the back. To the left of the god, Melpomene leans pensively on Thalia's shoulder, and next to the Sun god is Clio seated, holding the tuba, while Euterpe stands behind her.

THE PARNASSUS
(detail)
Raffaello Sanzio, known as Raphael
1510–11
Segnatura Room
Palazzi Vaticani, Vatican City

THE MUSES

☐ The Muses meet in a grove permeated by a magical, suspended atmosphere. The young women wear contemporary clothes and are divided into four groups. Three are seated in the foreground, while the others stroll about in groups of two. Their attributes almost fade in this composition, and the figures are defined by a sinuous, linear silhouette.

THE MUSES
Maurice Denis
1893
240 | Musée d'Orsay, Paris

THE MUSES

☐ This statue portrays Urania, "the Celestial," seated. The Muse wears a chiton; a mantle rests on her knees. With her right hand she holds a stylus, a small stick usually made of bone or metal with a pointed end, used in antiquity to write on wax tablets. In her left hand she holds a globe.

THE MUSES

☐ Calliope or Calliopea, "she of the fair voice," is the muse of epic poetry. Sitting on a rock, she wears a short-sleeved chiton, and her full mantle rests on her legs. In her hands she holds her attributes: a stylus and a wax tablet.

CALLIOPE
early 2nd century CE
Palazzo Altemps, Rome

THE MUSES

□ Polyhymnia, "she of the many hymns," is the Muse of sublime music. Sometimes, as in this case, she is represented without attributes, but with a pensive, dreamy expression. Draped in a mantle that envelops her entire body, she leans against a rocky column; her right elbow rests on the rock, while the hand, covered by the mantle, holds up her chin. With her rapt face, the eyes fixed on a faraway point, this maiden is the personification of absorbed solitude that projects a deep sense of melancholy. This pensive posture, so different from the other iconographic types, has led experts to identify in this statue the figure of Polyhymnia.

POLYHYMNIA
late 2nd century CE
Centrale Montemartini, Rome

THE MUSES

□ Totally unlike the preceding image (see p. 247), the young woman in this painting is also Polyhymnia, though here she is represented as the deity who presides over the harvest. Such iconography is due to the peculiar exegesis of ancient texts by some humanists. Actually, the iconography of the Muses that has come to us through archaeological finds was often unknown to the Renaissance scholars; hence, based on their interpretations of a Byzantine text of the Greek poet Hesiod's *Works and Days*, this Muse had become "she who invented farming; with her gathered gown she arranges hoes and seed vases, and holds spikes of wheat and grapes in her hands," and this is how she has been depicted here.

POLYHYMNIA
Ferrarese artist
1455–60
| Gemäldegalerie, Berlin

THE MUSES

□ Art critics have interpreted this young woman, a work of Cosmè Tura, as an iconographic revival of the image of Calliope, the Muse of epic poetry. She sits on a rich throne of polychrome marble, crowned by a seashell held up by the two marine creatures that also decorate the throne's arms. With one hand she holds a cherry branch, while the other hand rests on her knee.

A MUSE (CALLIOPE?)
Cosimo Tura
1455–60

THE MUSES

☐ Thalia sits on a gem-encrusted, elaborately decorated gilded throne and holds a branch with golden grapes in her right hand. At each side of the throne, finely wrought vases hold lilies, an emblem linked directly to the client who commissioned the work. Thalia, whose name means "the blooming one," is the Muse of comedy and idyllic poetry, though in this painting she takes on the guise of a vegetation goddess. Once more (see p. 248), the artist has drawn from humanistic texts of the time that spoke of the Muse as a contributor to agriculture and the inventor of farming.

THE MUSE THALIA
Michele Pannonio
c. 1456–59

Szépmûvészeti Múzeum, Budapest

THE GRACES

The Graces are daughters of Jupiter and Eurynome, a Titaness and the daughter of Oceanus. They are the deities of beauty and personify the element of harmony in the world, spreading joy and gracefulness in nature and in the hearts of men and gods. They are said to live on Mount Olympus with the Muses, with whom they sometimes sing. They are part of the retinues of Apollo or Venus, some of whose attributes they share. According to the most common version of the legend, the three Graces are Euphrosyne (Joy), Aglaia (Ornament), and Thalia (Abundance).

Greek name: Charites

Attributes: rose, myrtle, apple, dice

□ The three Graces are depicted naked, holding each other by the shoulder to form a circle. Two look at the viewer, and the third, in the center, is seen from the back. This ancient image was revived by Renaissance artists, who used the same compositional design.

THE THREE GRACES
1st century CE

Museo Archeologico Nazionale, Naples

◀◀

THE GRACES

☐ This artist has reinterpreted
the image of the three Graces.
The objects they hold in their hands,
and those scattered on the ground,
allude to the intellectual activities
which the Graces influence benefi-
cially. The book could be interpreted
as an allusion to the seven liberal
arts, and the lute is an image of
music. Below, on the left, a putto
holds a swan, a probable allusion
to love poetry.

HARMONY, OR THE THREE GRACES
Hans Baldung Grien
c. 1544

Museo del Prado, Madrid

VICTORY (VICTORIA)

The goddess Victory personifies victorious, irresistible power, especially Jupiter's. The daughter of the Titan Pallas and Styx, she belongs to the first generation of gods, before the Olympian divinities. She fought alongside Jupiter in the Battle of the Titans (see p. 22), but is also Minerva's companion. Initially worshiped only in the context of the cults of Jupiter and Minerva, she gradually became the symbol of all victories and favorable events, whether human or divine. Thus she was invoked not only in times of war, but also during the frequent sports and music contests.

Greek name: Nike

Attributes: represented as a winged deity

☐ The goddess Roma sits on a throne. The legend recounts that she came to Italy with Aeneas, who had a key role in resettling the Trojans in Italy. The goddess holds in her hand an effigy of winged Victory, who in turn holds the globe and a vexillum, the Roman military standard. This image of Victory follows a traditional iconography in which she is always shown next to important divinities that bestow success.

THE BARBERINI GODDESS
early 4th century CE
Palazzo Massimo, Rome

VIRTVS · HONOR · IMPERIVM

VICTORY

☐ The winged goddess leans forward, as if her rapid motion were dictated by the fluttering wings rather than her feet. Victory (Nike) faces the wind that ruffles her chiton, making it fit tightly against her breasts, while the mantle that has fallen from her shoulders twists and swells, adding realism to the image.

NIKE OF SAMOTHRACE
c. 190 BCE
Musée du Louvre, Paris

HEBE

Hebe is the personification of youth. The daughter of Jupiter and Juno, she is introduced in the *Iliad* as the cupbearer of the gods, pouring wine at their banquets. She is represented as a servant or "household daughter" on Mount Olympus, for she helps Juno ready her cart; she is also described dancing with the Hours or the Muses at the sound of Apollo's lyre. After Ganymede took over the role of divine cupbearer (see p. 264), Hebe was given in marriage to Hercules when he was raised to Olympus, and had two children by him. Later traditions attribute to Hebe the power of restoring youth.

□ Hebe, the goddess of youth, is portrayed as a lovely maiden, a cup in her left hand and a finely wrought pitcher in her right, from which she is about to pour the sacred drink of the gods, her first occupation being that of cupbearer to the gods.

HEBE
Antonio Canova
1816–17
Pinacoteca Civica, Forlì

GANYMEDE

After Hebe (see p. 262), Ganymede took on the role of cupbearer to the gods on Mount Olympus. Traditionally, he is believed to be the son of the Trojan king Tros and Callirhoe, and he is described as an extraordinarily beautiful youth, the loveliest of all mortals.

He was looking after his father's cattle on the mountains of Troy, when he was suddenly kidnapped by Jupiter, who had fallen hopelessly in love with him, and carried to Olympus. Several versions of the abduction exist. According to one, it was Jupiter who abducted the boy; in others, the king of the gods asked the eagle, the animal sacred to him, to seize the youth with its sharp talons and carry him to Olympus. To compensate the father for having abducted the boy, Jupiter gave him either some divine horses or a vine of finely decorated gold that Vulcan had made, and the eagle was transmuted into a constellation.

□ Having taken on a human form, Jupiter runs holding young Ganymede tightly to his chest. He carries a knotty club in his right hand, and the boy holds a cock, a conventional courting gift that adult Greek men gave to their beloved boys.

ZEUS AND GANYMEDE
470 BCE
Archaeological Museum, Olympia

GANYMEDE

☐ In this canvas, the abduction of Ganymede is set against a mountainous landscape dotted with ancient buildings. It shows a different version of the myth in which Jupiter turns into an eagle to kidnap the youth to whom he had taken a liking, and carry him to Mount Olympus.

THE RAPE OF GANYMEDE
Anonymous artist
c. 1550

Stiftung Preussische Castle, Potsdam

CUPID (EROS)

Cupid, also known as Eros, is described in early literary sources as having been created at the same time as Earth from aboriginal Chaos. He symbolizes the natural force of attraction that drives all things to unite. Next to this image of a cosmogonic deity there is another, better-known one, that of the child of Mars and Venus and the god of love. In this later version, he is a winged, naughty, somewhat cheeky boy. Several anecdotes and tales describe his cunning and the sometimes cruel tricks he plays on both gods and mortals, for not even Jupiter, the father of the gods, can escape Cupid's power.

Armed with bow and arrows, and sometimes also a torch, the god strikes anyone who comes within range of his bow. He has two types of arrows: The gold-tipped ones raise a feeling of love in those who are hit; the leaden, blunt ones cause aversion in the heart of the lover.

Greek name: Eros

Attributes: quiver, bow, arrows, torch

☐ This is a statue of Eros in a classical pose. The young, handsome winged god is portrayed as he stretches the bowstring. Behind him, the quiver hangs from a branch stump.

EROS STRINGING THE BOW
c. 1st century BCE

| Musei Capitolini, Rome

MUNIFICENTIA · SS · D · N · BENEDICTI
PP · XIV · A · D · MDCCLIII

CUPID

☐ Looking at the viewer with eyes at once innocent and provocative, Cupid builds his bow. The weapon stands on top of some books, possibly an allusion to the intellect spurned by the power of passion. Below, in the middle ground, are two young putti: The one with the annoyed look is Liseros, personification of the initiating power to love or lust. He is hugged by Anteros, personification of requited love.

CUPID CARVING HIS BOW
Francesco Mazzola, known as Parmigianino
1533–34

Kunsthistorisches Museum, Vienna

CUPID

☐ The central theme of this painting is inspired by a verse from the poet Virgil's *Bucolics*, "amor vincit omnia" (love conquers all). Cupid is represented as a god who mocks and scorns the emptiness of earthly ambitions symbolized by the musical instruments. To the right in the painting is a suit of armor on which rests a laurel wreath, both symbols of the longing for fame earned on the battlefield, a further reference to earthly ambitions, contrasted with divine love, which rises above everything.

AMOR VINCIT OMNIA
Michelangelo Merisi da Caravaggio
1602–1603
Gemäldegalerie, Berlin

CUPID

◄◄

►►

☐ The inclusion of Cupid in this painting shows that love is the subject, for it was probably created for a wedding. The god of love appears with Venus, who is wearing a bridal veil and earrings. The rose and the myrtle, both attributes of Venus, are also in this painting. Other details also allude to love and faithfulness, such as the red curtain in the background, the ivy climbing the trunk behind Venus, and the thurible that the goddess holds in her hand. Finally, Cupid's gesture—urinating through the myrtle wreath—was considered a good omen and a wish for happiness and fertility.

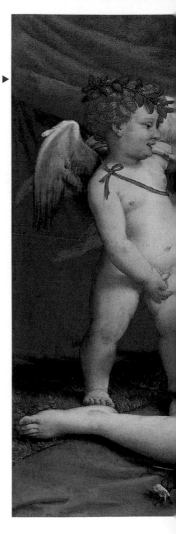

VENUS AND CUPID
Lorenzo Lotto
1520–30
274 | The Metropolitan Museum of Art, New York

CUPID

☐ In this painting, Cupid suggests the clearly amorous theme, for this was possibly a wedding painting. The bride and groom, or the betrothed couple, are portrayed as Mars and Venus and are crowned by winged Victory with myrtle wreaths—the myrtle tree was sacred to Venus and a symbol of eternal love. Little Cupid has dropped his bow and quiver under a quince tree and hastens to offer the couple a basket of roses.

VENUS AND MARS,
VICTORY AND CUPID
Paris Bordone
c. 1560

Kunsthistorisches Museum, Vienna

CUPID

☐ The image of the triumphal cart with a mythological or allegorical figure and their attendant train developed in the fifteenth century as the illustrations of the *Trionfi* (Triumphs), an allegorical poem by Petrarch, became widespread. This image shows the Triumph of Love. A boy Cupid hovers over the richly appointed cart and is about to shoot one of his arrows. Below him, sitting around a brazier, are Mars, Jupiter, and Venus. The cart is pulled by four white horses and is escorted by a train of elegantly attired gentlefolk. Instead of the usual traits of impudent, witty boy, Cupid is here rendered as a nimble, slim youth.

THE TRIUMPH OF LOVE
Jacopo del Sellaio
15th century
| Museo Bandini, Fiesole

CUPID

☐ Sometimes Venus and Cupid are portrayed independently of the mythological episodes in which they appear. In this unusually graceful, gentle painting, mother and child are caught in an intimate domestic vignette. The child god, rendered with small sparrow wings, has laid down bow and quiver and leans on his mother's lap. Venus is combing his hair and is almost unrecognizable in the full red skirt that enhances her pale skin.

VENUS COMBING CUPID'S HAIR
Giovanni da San Giovanni,
known as Lo Scheggia
1627

Palazzo Pitti, Florence

CUPID

☐ Often Cupid is represented in the company of his mother, who punishes his mischief. In this fresco, against a vague landscape, we see Cupid from the back, his hands to his eyes, as if about to cry for one of his pranks; Venus holds the child god, who looks like an innocent, defenseless little boy, and for a second we forget his divine powers that cause cruel injury to both gods and mortals.

EROS IS PUNISHED
c. 79 CE

Museo Archeologico Nazionale, Naples

CUPID

☐ In vain, little Cupid tries to reach his mother's arm to recover his bow. He must have done some mischief, for Venus has just grabbed his weapons—the bow in her raised hand, and one of the arrows in the other—to prevent more pranks. The artist has interpreted Cupid's punishment as an innocent skirmish between mother and child.

CUPID DISARMED BY VENUS
Jean-Antoine Watteau
1710
284 | Musée Condé, Chantilly

Cupid blinded

The blind Cupid motif is not part of ancient Greek and Roman iconography; it first appeared in the Middle Ages and results from a free interpretation of classical literary sources. The blindfolded Cupid took on different features depending on the historical context. In Renaissance Italy, the image of love is that of the classical winged boy, and the blindfold underscores his blindness, since he can strike anyone anywhere, but also points to the darkness that is associated with sin. With time, as this particular image became very common, its original significance was lost.

☐ This image of Cupid is directly inspired by classical models. The god of love appears as a naked, winged child armed with bow and arrow and blindfolded. This last touch belongs to medieval iconography, probably underscoring love's irrational quality.

BLIND CUPID
Piero della Francesca
c. 1464–65
Church of San Francesco, Arezzo

◄◄

Cupid blinded

☐ Like the painting on page 279,
this table is an illustration inspired
by a somewhat literal reading of
Petrarch's *Trionfi*. Four white horses
pull the fiery cart, above which
Cupid stands ready to strike, with
the bow and a quiver full of arrows
slung from his shoulder. Immortalized as he is about to shoot one of
his feared arrows, the child god is
blindfolded, perhaps an allusion to
love's blunting effects.

THE TRIUMPH OF LOVE
Giovanni da San Giovanni,
known as Lo Scheggia
c. 1450

Museo di Palazzo Davanzati, Florence

Cupid and the Honeycomb

Once, Cupid was trying to steal honey from a honeycomb, and a cruel bee stung all his fingers. The child god felt a sharp pain, and kicking and jumping nervously about, showed Venus the stings, asking how such a small insect could cause so much harm. Then his mother laughed, pointing out how similar he was to the bee, so little and so dangerous as well, and so capable of inflicting great wounds.

☐ Wearing a trendy, wide-brimmed hat, Venus looks pleased, while Cupid, still holding the honeycomb, complains to her. The anecdote is narrated in the *Idyls* of Theocritus, but the artist also seems to warn the viewer about the dangers of lust; during the sixteenth century, so-called venereal diseases were quite common.

VENUS WITH CUPID STEALING HONEY
Lucas Cranach the Elder
c. 1531
Galleria Borghese, Rome

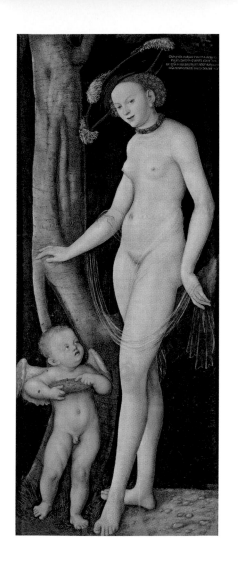

Cupid and Psyche

Psyche was the youngest and prettiest of three sisters. Her beauty was almost supernatural, such that it provoked Venus's wrath. Angered, the goddess turned to Cupid, asking him to make the girl fall in love with a man from a low station in life. But as soon as he saw her, Cupid fell madly in love and decided to take her to his palace, which he visited only at nightfall. He also prevailed upon the girl not to try to discover his identity, or he would leave her. But one night the curious Psyche, prodded by her envious sisters, lit an oil lamp to see the face of her beloved; unfortunately, a drop of oil fell on his shoulder, and he awakened. Disappointed, he left. The desperate girl roamed the entire Earth in search of her beloved, until she came to Venus's palace, where the goddess subjected her to a number of trials that Psyche was able to overcome only with the help of divine intervention. In the meantime, Cupid had come to regret his action and longed for Psyche. He searched for her, and when he found her, he asked Jupiter permission to marry her and take her to Mount Olympus. His wish was granted.

☐ This Roman fresco depicts Cupid and Psyche in a tender embrace. The god of love is identified by the angel wings sprouting from his shoulders, while Psyche is often represented with butterfly wings.

CUPID AND PSYCHE
early 1st century CE
Museo Archeologico Nazionale, Naples

◄◄

Cupid and Psyche

PSYCHE IS LED TO CUPID'S PALACE

Psyche's sisters were married, but Psyche was not; her supernatural beauty instilled fear in her suitors. The worried father decided to consult an oracle, which suggested that he dress the young woman in her bridal finest and take her to a mountain, where a monster would abduct her. The desperate parents did as the oracle advised and left her on top of the mountain. Suddenly, Psyche was lifted and carried by the wind into a deep valley, and lowered into a soft meadow, where she promptly fell asleep. When she awakened, she was in the garden of a splendid, wondrous palace. At the end of the day, having retired to sleep, Psyche felt the presence of the monster the oracle had described, who lay with her, but did not seem as terrible as the oracle had prophesied. Before he left at daybreak, the lover warned not to try to discover his identity, or he would desert her forever.

THE ABDUCTION OF PSYCHE
Pierre-Paul Prud'hon
1805
Musée du Louvre, Paris

☐ Psyche has fallen into a deep sleep and Zephyrus, the gentle spring breeze here personified as a winged youth, carries her to Cupid's palace. He is aided by *amorini*.

◄◄

Cupid and Psyche

PSYCHE AND HER SISTERS

For weeks, Psyche's life unfolded quietly in Cupid's palace. During the day she was alone, but at night her lover visited her. After a while, the young woman began to feel lonely and homesick, and asked her beloved for permission to invite the sisters. He granted her wish, and Zephyrus carried them to Cupid's palace. Psyche had prepared precious gifts for them, but realizing her happiness, they felt jealous and decided to take revenge by insinuating doubts about her lover's identity, and they tried to convince her to discover his true face.

THE LEGEND OF CUPID AND PSYCHE
Angelica Kauffmann
c. 1800

| Museo Revoltella, Trieste

☐ In keeping with her traditional image, Psyche is depicted with butterfly wings. Seated at a table, she shows her sisters the precious gifts she has prepared for them, but the latter—one looks pensive, the other holds her by the shoulder—already seem to be plotting. In the middle ground, almost in the shadow, Cupid watches without speaking.

Cupid and Psyche

PSYCHE DISCOVERS CUPID ASLEEP

Psyche's sisters finally convinced her that she had to find out her groom's true identity, saying that perhaps he was a wild beast who sooner or later would kill her. One night, a fearful Psyche took a knife and lit the face of her beloved as he lay sleeping. She was shocked to discover that it was Cupid, the handsomest of men. Enraptured, she stood in contemplation until a drop of hot oil dripped from the lamp she was holding in her hand; the god of love woke up, and flew away without uttering a word.

☐ The artist has captured the moment when Psyche, fearful that her beloved groom might be a monster, approaches him with an oil lamp and a knife, and is struck by his beauty. Cupid's bow and arrows are lying on the floor next to the god, who is still in a deep sleep.

CUPID ASLEEP
Andrea Appiani
1810–12
Villa Reale, Monza

◄◄

Cupid and Psyche

►►

THE TRIAL OF THE SEEDS

After Cupid deserted her, a wretched Psyche went in search of her beloved, roaming the world, until she came to Venus's palace. After striking her and tormenting her, the goddess subjected the maiden to several challenging trials. The first consisted of separating chick peas, lentils, fava beans, kernels of wheat, barley, millet, and poppy seeds that were all mixed together. The young woman stood petrified before the mound of grains and legumes, despairing over the challenge; luckily, a country ant took pity on her and called all the ants in the area, who came to help and completed the great task.

☐ A despairing Psyche sits on the floor surrounded by mounds of seeds, while before her a veritable army of ants completes the task that a jealous, pitiless Venus had assigned to her.

THE TRIAL OF THE SEEDS
Giulio Romano and assistants
1526–28
Palazzo Del Te, Mantua

CONSTRVI

Cupid and Psyche

THE TRIAL OF THE STYGIAN WATER

Still angry even after Psyche won the first challenge, Venus ordered her to go at dawn to gather wool from some fierce wild rams. Psyche successfully completed this task, but the goddess of beauty was still dissatisfied and subjected Psyche to an even harder challenge: Handing her a small urn, she ordered her to bring it back full of water from the Styx. This was the infernal river feared even by the gods; it was began at a spring hidden deep inside rocks on top of a steep, rugged mountain, then crashed below ground down to Hades. This time, Jupiter was moved to pity and asked his sacred animal, the eagle, to help the maiden. Seeing Psyche return with the urn full of water, Venus was shocked and even angrier and decided to subject her to yet another terrible trial.

☐ Identifiable by the wings visible on her back, Psyche is about to receive from Venus the pitcher in which to collect water from the river Styx. Enraged, the goddess points her finger in a threatening gesture, while the young woman, her head bent, submits resignedly to yet another trial from her cruel mother-in-law. Venus is also identifiable by the two billing doves in the foreground on the right.

VENUS DELIVERS THE PITCHER TO PSYCHE
Felice Giani
1790
Palazzo Altieri, Rome

Cupid and Psyche

☐ Psyche sits on a rock in a wooded, forbidding landscape, and delivers the urn to Jupiter's eagle. To the right, water from the Styx crashes down from the top of a high, unreachable crag into the river below, sending forth great clouds of steam.

LANDSCAPE WITH PSYCHE AND JUPITER
Paul Brill and Pieter Paul Rubens
1610
304 | Museo del Prado, Madrid

◄◄───

Cupid and Psyche

───►

PSYCHE IN THE NETHERWORLD

For the last trial, Venus ordered Psyche to descend to the
infernal regions and deliver to Proserpina an urn into which
the goddess of the netherworld should put a little of her
beauty. Psyche climbed a tall tower and threw herself into the
void, intending to end her life and thus reach the kingdom
of the dead as quickly as possible. But the tower suddenly
began to speak, offering sound advice on how to reach the
netherworld, how to behave once there, and especially what
to do in order to return to Earth and how to avoid the traps
that Venus had prepared. The tower also advised Psyche to
take two coins for Charon, the ferryman of the dead souls,
and two barley cakes to throw to Cerberus, the terrible
three-headed monster that guarded Proserpina's palace.

□ In the netherworld, Psyche is
about to step off Charon's boat. The
soul of a dead man clings to the
boat, begging to be picked up, but
mindful of the warnings the tower
has given her, Psyche does not
answer his entreaties. Behind her
are three women bent on weaving a
piece of cloth; although they also
ask for help, Psyche knows that she
must not, for divine law forbids it.

PSYCHE IN THE UNDERWORLD
Ernest Hillemacher
1865
| National Gallery of Victoria, Melbourne

Cupid and Psyche

PSYCHE ASLEEP

After finally climbing back from the netherworld, Psyche was walking with the urn toward Venus's palace. Curious about its contents, she stopped and, heedless of the advice she had received, she raised the small cover. Immediately, an infernal sleeping vapor spread into the air and surrounded the girl, who promptly fell into a deathlike sleep. In the meantime, Cupid had forgiven Psyche and longed to see her again. He went in search of the maiden and found her asleep. After imprisoning the death-inducing vapor back into the urn, he awakened Psyche by striking her with one of his arrows. Then he flew to Olympus, and after long entreaties, Jupiter granted him Psyche in marriage and ordered Mercury to carry her atop the sacred mountain, where the wedding finally took place.

☐ Van Dyck has illustrated the scene when Cupid runs to Psyche and finds her in a deep sleep. Next to her is the upturned coffer that sent off Stygian vapors, causing her to fall into a mortal slumber.

CUPID AND PSYCHE
Anton van Dyck
1638
The Royal Collection
Kensington Palace, London

◄◄

Cupid and Psyche

☐ Boucher has depicted the wedding of Cupid and Psyche before all the divinities, including Venus, whose rage has finally subsided; she holds a lit torch, symbolizing love. From the union of Cupid and Psyche, Voluptas (Pleasure) was born.

THE MARRIAGE OF CUPID AND PSYCHE
François Boucher
1744
| Musée du Louvre, Paris

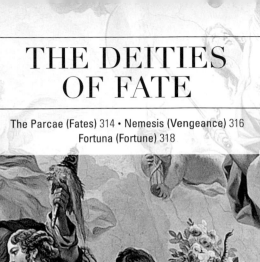

THE DEITIES OF FATE

The Parcae (Fates) 314 • Nemesis (Vengeance) 316
Fortuna (Fortune) 318

THE PARCAE (THE FATES)

The Parcae are the deities who oversee the destiny of mortals and gods. The daughters of the Night (or, alternatively, of Jupiter and Themis), their Greek name, Moerae, means "share," for each human being is assigned from birth his or her "share" of life, happiness, and sorrows—in a word, his or her fate. In any case, the ancients were convinced that human existence was ruled by fate and that everyone's life events were established a priori. Although they believed that human life was guided by the gods, they also believed that fate was more powerful than Jupiter, a power to which even the king of the gods had to submit.

For example, the Parcae stepped into events to prevent a god from helping a hero who was in danger, if in fact the hero's fate was to die. There are three Parcae: Nona (Clotho in Greek), "the spinner"; Decima (Lachesis), "the measurer"; and Morta (Atropos), "the inflexible." The first spins each human being's life course; the second, representing the randomness of life, winds up the thread and measures it; while the third, representing death, cuts it.

Greek name: Moerae

Attributes: distaff, thread, shears

THE CAVE OF ETERNITY
(detail)
Luca Giordano
1682–86
314 Palazzo Medici Riccardi, Florence

☐ In the cave of eternity, the Parcae are on the right, intent at their work. Nona holds the distaff in her hand while Decima, at her side, measures the thread of human life, and Morta is about to cut it.

NEMESIS (VENGEANCE)

Nemesis is the personification of divine vengeance and generally represents the gods' indignation and wrath at hubris, the human flaw of insolence or arrogance. This deity has the power of crushing "excess," thereby maintaining a sort of balance between man's good and bad luck.

Nemesis would send all sorts of punishments to those who were too fortunate, seemed too happy, or felt too proud, the last being a typical prerogative of kings. She struck anything that was meant to inject disharmony and lack of order into society's normal equilibrium and was dissatisfied until order was reestablished. Later, the image of Nemesis as the bearer of bad luck was assimilated with that of the Furies.

☐ Nemesis appears as a winged woman, holding in her left hand some leather strips, a symbol of the fate that rules human life. In her right hand, she balances a cup on her fingers, an allusion to the instability of the gifts that luck offers humankind.

NEMESIS
Albrecht Dürer
1501–1502
| Whitworth Art Gallery, Manchester

FORTUNA (FORTUNE)

Among the deities who are directly associated with the vicissitudes of human life is Fortuna, the goddess of good or bad luck, traditionally considered a daughter of Oceanus and Tethys. She rules the world's events and personifies the uncertainty and the sudden turn of events in human life.

Greek name: Tyche

Attributes: rudder, blindfold, globe

☐ Fortuna flies over the globe of the world, dispensing riches at random. Her wind-blown tresses underscore her fickleness, while the presence of Cupid, who holds her by the veils distracting her, alludes to her preference for love.

LA FORTUNA
Guido Reni
1637
Musei Vaticani, Vatican City

THE SEA AND WATER DEITIES

Neptune 322 • Tritons and Nereids 328

NEPTUNE

The god of the sea, Neptune is a son of Saturn and Rhea and a brother of Jupiter. After battling the Titans (see p. 22), the gods divided the lordship of the universe among themselves: Neptune was given the kingdom of the seas, Jupiter the sky, and Pluto the netherworld. The ancients believed that Neptune's wondrous palace was located in the abysses; the god moved about on a splendid chariot pulled by wild horses with bronze hooves that allowed them to race nimbly upon the waves.

Neptune has the power to raise storms; with a simple stroke of his trident, he causes earthquakes and tidal waves, raises new islands from the depths of the sea, and makes water spring from rocks. At the same time, a wave of his hand calms the threatening sea breakers and smoothes out the waters. Neptune has many loves, but while Jupiter's offspring are for the most part benign deities, Neptune's are often violent and evil creatures, such as Polyphemus (see p. 714) and Antaeus. Neptune's favorite animal is the horse.

Greek name: Poseidon

Attributes: trident

POSEIDON ENTHRONED WITH HIS SON
THESEUS AND A NEREID
Attic red-figure krater (from Agrigento)
Syriskos painter
480–70 BCE
Cabinet des Médailles, Paris

□ Neptune is portrayed sitting on a throne holding his attribute, the trident. Before him is his son Theseus, slayer of the Minotaur, born of his relationship with Aethra. Behind Neptune is a Nereid.

NEPTUNE

☐ Here Neptune is depicted on his horse-drawn chariot with his bride Amphitrite, a Nereid. It is said that having seen her dance near the island of Naxos, the god of the sea fell madly in love and kidnapped her. In another version, Amphitrite successfully flees Neptune by hiding in the depths of the sea, but one of the god's dolphins finds her and delivers her to him. In this mosaic, two putti hold a fluttering cloth over their heads, an image that appears often in the iconography of marine deities and is usually interpreted as an attribute of Aura, one of the spirits of the air.

TRIUMPH OF NEPTUNE AND AMPHITRITE
Mosaic
3rd century CE

Musée du Louvre, Paris

NEPTUNE

☐ In the center of an architectural setting is a young Neptune, almost unrecognizable but for the trident he holds in his hand, sweetly embracing a maiden identified as his bride, Amphitrite. In the Homeric poems, she is the personification of the swell of the sea, a deity who takes pleasure in surrounding herself with dolphins and other sea creatures; it was only in the late Greek culture that Amphitrite became linked to Neptune and was worshiped as his bride.

NEPTUNE AND AMPHITRITE
Jan Gossaert, known as Mabuse
1516
Gemäldegalerie, Berlin

TRITONS AND NEREIDS

The only son of Neptune and Amphitrite, Triton lives with his parents in the abysses. This deity is half-man and half-fish and carries the *bucina*, a sort of spiral conch; when he blows into it, the waves swell and the sky darkens, raising a storm. At other times, a sweeter sound calms the stormy waters. Later, classical authors began to use the name "Triton" in the plural to indicate other beings whose role in the seas is analogous to that of the satyrs and centaurs on Earth. The Tritons live in the sea and spend their days frolicking with marine monsters and Nereids. The latter are also benign marine creatures, the daughters of Nereus, an ancient sea god who preceded Neptune, and Doris, as well as the grand-daughters of Oceanus. Perhaps the personification of the sea waves, their number varies from fifty to one hundred. They lived in the palace of their father, Nereus, at the bottom of the sea and sat on golden thrones. Some celebrated Nereids are Galatea, who was loved by Polyphemus; Thetis, who was Achilles's mother; and Amphitrite, who married Neptune (see p. 324).

☐ In this ancient Greek sculpture, a Nereid rides a sea monster, the pistrix, here rendered as a half-horse, half-fish creature with an elongated snout.

NEREID RIDING THE PISTRIX
4th–3rd century BCE

Museo Archeologico Nazionale, Naples

TRITONS AND NEREIDS

☐ This painting narrates the kidnapping of Europa (see p. 58): The bull crosses the sea with the maiden on its back, while Tritons and Nereids festively play in the waves around them and watch, now amused, now surprised. In the background at right is Neptune's chariot, pulled by dolphins and carrying Amphitrite and the god of the sea with the trident in his left hand.

THE RAPE OF EUROPA
Noël Nicolas Coypel
1727

Philadelphia Museum of Art, Philadelphia

THE EARTH DEITIES

Ceres 334 • Cybele 344 • Bacchus 346 • Nymphs 380
Satyrs 390 • Silenus 398

WOODLAND AND MOUNTAIN CREATURES
Pan 402 • Centaurs 410 • Chiron 422

ITALIC RURAL DEITIES
Vertumnus and Pomona 424 • Flora 428

CERES

An early divinity associated with vegetation and the earth, Ceres is a daughter of Saturn and Rhea, and thus one of Jupiter's sisters. Compared to Gaea, who represents the cosmogonic aspect of Earth, Ceres is the goddess of farmed fields and wheat cultivation in particular, although she is believed to generally oversee everything that pertains to agriculture, which she herself taught to men.

Among the many legends about Ceres is the abduction of her daughter Proserpina by Pluto, the god of the underworld, and Ceres's desperate search for her. After learning the truth from the Sun god, especially that Jupiter had condoned the abduction, a wrathful Ceres began to wander alone, giving vent to her grief and neglecting her duties. As a result, Earth became a wasteland and a universal famine threatened humankind. Jupiter had to intervene, ruling that Proserpina could live with her mother for two-thirds of the year and spend the remaining third in the kingdom of the dead.

Greek name: Demeter

Attributes: spikes of wheat, serpent- or dragon-pulled cart.

CERES
Mosaic
250 CE
Museo del Bardo, Tunis

□ Ceres appears in her classical guise of harvest divinity. Spikes of wheat crown her head, and she holds a horn of plenty overflowing with the fruits of the land.

CERES

☐ In this painting, Ceres is represented in search of Proserpina. The goddess is driving a dragon-pulled cart. Originally, the dragon was a large serpent—a symbol of fertility. For this reason, sometimes she also appears with two snakes in her hands, since *draco* in Latin means both "dragon" and "serpent."

CERES IN SEARCH OF PROSERPINA
Giorgio Vasari and Cristoforo Gherardi
c. 1563

Palazzo Vecchio, Florence

Ceres and Stellion

During her search for her daughter, an exhausted, thirsty Ceres saw a hut. She was welcomed by an old woman, who immediately offered her food and a sweet drink. While the goddess was avidly restoring herself, a cheeky boy named Stellion appeared and began to mock her, laughing loudly at her hunger and thirst. Offended by the ill manners, she threw the drink at him, causing the boy's face to fill with stains and his body to slowly turn into a reptile smaller than a lizard.

☐ According to ancient sources, this episode takes place at night. Ceres stands and drinks before the old woman, who holds a candle to light up the scene. With the other hand, she tries to hold back Stellion, who mocks the thirsty goddess. The lit torch behind Ceres alludes to her desperate search for her daughter.

CERES AND STELLION
Adam Elsheimer
1608
Museo del Prado, Madrid

Ceres and Triptolemus

Still in search of Proserpina, Ceres stopped at Eleusis, where Celeus gave her hospitality. Grateful for the king's kindness, she presented his son Triptolemus with a cart pulled by winged dragons and a supply of seeds, exhorting him to travel all over the Earth sowing wheat kernels and teaching agriculture to men. The boy was not welcomed everywhere; after covering Europe and Asia, he stopped in Scythia, where he was a guest of King Lyncus. After listening to his story, the king became envious and tried to kill the youth and take his place. He was about to plunge a sword into his heart when Ceres turned the king into a lynx, urging Triptolemus to continue on his journey.

☐ Triptolemus sits on a cart pulled by winged serpents, a gift of Ceres. The goddess of farming is portrayed as she presents the youth with the seeds that he is to sow throughout the world. Triptolemus was worshiped as the founder of agriculture and of the civilization that developed from it.

TRIPTOLEMUS ON THE CART
WITH DEMETER
(detail)
Vase painting
460 BCE

"Sine Cerere et Baccho friget Venus"

This saying, "without Ceres and Bacchus, Venus is cold," is taken from a comedy by the Roman poet Terentius and means that love suffers without good food and wine. The quote began to be illustrated in the seventeenth century, especially by Flemish artists.

☐ Holding a bunch of grapes, Bacchus offers his hand to Ceres, who is crowned with spikes of wheat. They seem to walk out of the painting. Behind them, in a chiaroscuro background, a chilly Cupid and Venus warm themselves by a fire.

SINE CERERE ET BACCHO FRIGET VENUS
Bartholomaeus Spranger
c. 1595
Kunsthistorisches Museum, Vienna

CYBELE

The cult of Cybele originated in Asia Minor and from there spread to Greece and then Rome. She is a Phrygian deity, part of the group of early female deities known as "Great Mother." This goddess oversees all of nature and personifies the power of vegetation, its life force. She moves about on a lion-drawn cart with a retinue of priests, the Corybants, and lives on mountains and deep in the woods. Because of a dearth of legends specific to her, this goddess was assimilated to Rhea, the mother of Jupiter and the other children of Saturn, including Ceres.

In one famous legend, Attis, her Phrygian lover, pre-ferred a mortal woman to her. On the day of the wedding banquet, the goddess took revenge by striking fear into the hearts of the guests. Attis fled to the mountains, went mad, and took his own life. Then the grieving goddess instituted a funeral ceremony in his honor, to be celebrated during the spring equinox. This rite gave rise to an orgiastic cult that continued until the fourth century CE.

Attributes: lions, a turreted crown

□ In this statue, Cybele is enthroned and flanked by two lions, animals sacred to her. She holds a tambourine, a clear allusion to the orgiastic rites dedicated to her, and wears a tower-shaped crown that marks her role as founder and custodian of cities.

CYBELE ENTHRONED
3rd century CE
Museo Archeologico Nazionale, Naples

BACCHUS

The god of wine, viticulture, and mystic frenzy, Bacchus is a son of Jupiter and Semele. He is a beneficial god who generally personifies nature's productive energy that causes the fruits of the earth to ripen. He was already a young man when Juno, who had always hated him because he was the offspring of one of Jupiter's liaisons, caused him to go mad. Rendered distraught, Bacchus began a long period of roaming, teaching men wherever he went how to cultivate the vine and till the soil, and presiding over the foundation of new cities. He first wandered into Egypt, then Syria and Phrygia, where the goddess Cybele welcomed him and purified him, initiating him into her own cult. Finally cured of madness, Bacchus continued his roaming and even reached India. In his honor, the bacchanals were instituted. At these feasts the worshipers—mostly women— were taken with divine frenzy and roamed the countryside, dancing and uttering ritual cries.

Greek name: Dionysus

Attributes: vine, thyrsus (a staff tipped with a pine cone and entwined with ivy and vine leaves and shoots), a cart pulled by panthers, tigers, leopards, she-goats

☐ In this fresco, Bacchus is totally covered by a bunch of grapes. In one hand he holds the thyrsus and in the other a pitcher, from which he is pouring wine for a panther, an animal consecrated to him. In the background is Mount Vesuvius, planted with vineyards.

BACCHUS AND VESUVIUS
1st century CE
Museo Archeologico Nazionale, Naples

BACCHUS

☐ In his wanderings, Bacchus took on the guise of a boy and sailed on a pirate ship directed to the island of Naxos. But the sailors changed route and turned toward Asia, hoping to sell the boy into slavery. When Bacchus realized this, he conjured up the music of invisible flutes that filled the boat with vines and changed the oars into snakes, driving the sailors so mad that they jumped into the sea, where they turned into dolphins.

In this painting, Bacchus is shown reclining comfortably in the boat, crowned with vine leaves. Vine shoots have sprung up around him, and the pirates-turned-dolphins surround the boat. After performing this wonder, Bacchus's powers were universally recognized, and he joined the rest of the gods on Olympus.

DIONYSUS WITH DOLPHINS
Cup
Exekias (from Vulci)
540–30 BCE
Staatliche Antikensammlung
und Glyptothek, Munich

BACCHUS

☐ Michelangelo has sculpted a young, seemingly inebriated Bacchus: A cup of wine in his hand, a wreath of grapes and vine leaves crowning his forehead, he can barely stand. The body leans slightly backward as if about to lose his balance. With the other hand, he clutches the skin of a tiger—an animal consecrated to him—and a bunch of grapes. Behind him, a sprightly young satyr mocks him by stealing the grapes.

BACCHUS
Michelangelo Buonarroti
1496–97
Museo Nazionale del Bargello, Florence

BACCHUS

☐ In this painting, Titian narrates an episode from the life of Bacchus. The god is recognizable by the garland of vine leaves that crowns his forehead. He is arrested by Pentheus, king of Thebes, who was taking strong measures to prevent the cult of the god from taking hold in his lands. The king paid dearly for challenging the god; not only did Bacchus free himself, but he led Agave, the king's mother, into a divine frenzy, such that she mistook her son for a panther and killed him. She then hung the head of the animal from a thyrsus. In ancient thought, Pentheus represents the evildoer whose sin of hubris brings on divine retribution.

THE BRAVO
Tiziano Vecellio, known as Titian
16th century
Kunsthistorisches Museum, Vienna

BACCHUS

☐ This pale boy with livid lips, dressed in a plain white tunic, is a self-portrait of Caravaggio as Bacchus. His head is wreathed with vine leaves, his hands hold a bunch of white grapes, and he leans against a low wall where more fruits—a bunch of black grapes and two peaches—are on display. Inevitably, all these elements hint at Bacchus, the god of wine. This melancholy hymn to life is more than a simple self-portrait, and art critics still debate the painting's many symbols and meanings.

YOUNG SICK BACCHUS
Michelangelo Merisi da Caravaggio
1593–94

Galleria Borghese, Rome

The birth of Bacchus

The son of Jupiter and Semele, the latter died when Jupiter accidentally struck her with a bolt of lightning (see p. 64). Still, Jupiter was able to save the baby that Semele carried in her womb by extracting it and sewing it into his thigh until he gave birth to the child by loosening the strings that tied his leg. For this reason, Bacchus was surnamed "the twice-born."

The child was entrusted to Mercury, who in turn took him to Athamas, the king of Orchomenus, and his wife, Ino, asking them to raise him in secret, dressed in girl's clothes, to thwart Juno's murderous designs in retaliation for her husband's infidelity. But the shrewd queen of the gods learned the truth and caused Ino and Athamas to become deranged (see p. 86). Then Jupiter took the child and transmuted him into a young goat, asking the nymphs of Mount Nisa to care for him. Later, Bacchus was reverted to his human form and educated by the old satyr Silenus.

□ Jupiter is reclining in the center of the composition, delivering little Bacchus from his thigh. Before him, Juno, who had caused the death of Semele, the child's mother, witnesses the birth. The queen of the gods forever persecuted Bacchus, even punishing those who dared help him.

THE BIRTH OF BACCHUS
(detail)
Red-figure krater
400–380 BCE
Museo Archeologico Nazionale, Taranto

◄◄

The birth of Bacchus

☐ Dressed in a short red cape, Mercury takes little Bacchus, who already wears an ivy wreath, to the Nisan nymphs. He points his hand heavenward toward Jupiter, the father of the gods, who is resting after his labors while Hebe serves him a cup of ambrosia. At the foot of the bed, an eagle clutches the god's thunderbolts. To the left of the composition, five nymphs look on with interest, while from the top of a hillock Pan welcomes the baby god by playing on his syrinx. On the extreme right is the episode of Echo and Narcissus.

THE BIRTH OF BACCHUS
Nicolas Poussin
1657
Fogg Art Museum,
Cambridge (Massachusetts)

Bacchus and his court

☐ Instructed by Jupiter, Mercury carries the child Bacchus, wrapped in a sort of mantle, to Silenus and the nymphs. The divine messenger is identifiable by the winged sandals and the petasus he wears on his head. Silenus appears as an old, white-haired deity carrying a thyrsus, the traditional staff entwined with ivy and vine leaves and tipped with a pine cone. On each side of the composition are two nymphs. One supports Silenus; the other, sitting on a rock, holds a flower in her hand.

MERCURY LEADS BACCHUS TO SILENUS
White-background *kalyx* krater
(from Vulci)
Boston *phiale* painter
c. 440–35 BCE

Museo Gregoriano Etrusco, Vatican City

Bacchus and his court

The myth narrates that in his protracted wandering Bacchus even reached India. It was at this time, according to one version of the myth, that the god's triumphal retinue was created, in which he advanced on a cart pulled by panthers and decorated with ivy and vine leaves, followed by his acolytes, sileni, maenads, satyrs, and other woodland deities, who danced and sang, uttering joyful cries at the sound of flutes and tambourines.

☐ The Bacchae or maenads (the name is derived from the Greek *mainomai*, "to be mad") were part of Bacchus's court. They personified nature's orgiastic spirits. This semi-naked maenad is caught in a frenzied dance; she vigorously twists her torso and throws her head backward in an obsessive, Dionysian dance inspired by a sort of mystic madness.

DANCING MAENAD
350 BCE

◄◄

Bacchus and his court

□ This raving maenad, her head thrust backward, has a snake in her hair instead of the usual wreath of vine leaves, probably a reminder that among the rituals dedicated to Bacchus was the handling of snakes. Her shoulders are covered with fur, and in her left hand she holds a live feline by the leg, for there was a belief that the maenads could tame wild beasts, which were sacred to Bacchus. In her right hand, she carries the traditional thyrsus.

MAENAD
Attic white-background cup
Brigo painter
490–85 BCE
Staatliche Antikensammlung
und Glyptothek, Munich

◄◄

Bacchus and his court

☐ Some intoxicated maenads offer libations to a Bacchus idol. At his left, one of them pours a drink—probably wine—while another priestess raises the thyrsus, an ancient symbol of fertility. To the right of the idol, a third priestess plays the tambourine, a musical instrument used in bacchanals, while the last one holds a torch at his side.

MAENADS DANCING AROUND
THE IDOL OF DIONYSUS
Stamnos
Dinos painter
420–10 BCE

Museo Archeologico Nazionale, Naples

◄◄

Bacchus and his court

☐ The god is depicted riding a richly
decorated triumphal cart pulled by
leopards, which were consecrated
to him and allude to the spreading
of the cult to Asia. All of the god's
symbols are present: the thyrsus he
holds in his hands, the ivy wreath,
and the leopard skin thrown over his
shoulders. Next to him, Ariadne, his
bride (see p. 370), is driven in a cart
pulled by billy goats, evoking an
ancient legend in which the god, to
flee Juno's wrath, was transformed
into a goat by his father, Jupiter.
All around, the swirling maenads
and satyrs that make up the lively
train dance and play different instruments. At the head of the train is
Silenus, Bacchus's teacher; thoroughly intoxicated, he advances,
swaying on his donkey.

TRIUMPH OF BACCHUS AND ARIADNE
Annibale Carracci
1595–1605
Palazzo Farnese, Rome

Bacchus and Ariadne

The daughter of Minos, king of Crete, Ariadne had helped Theseus, with whom she had fallen in love, slay the Minotaur and exit the labyrinth by giving him a magic thread (see p. 536). Once out of the labyrinth, the Athenian hero had begun his journey home with Ariadne, but he abandoned her on a beach. The grieving Ariadne moved Bacchus to pity; he fell in love and married her. Furthermore, the god took the crown she was wearing and threw it into the sky, turning it into a constellation.

☐ The artist illustrates the wedding of Bacchus and Ariadne. Kneeling slightly, the god of wine is about to slip a ring on the maiden's finger, while a child Cupid crowns her with a diadem of stars, a memento of the crown that the god had thrown up into the sky, transforming it into a constellation.

BACCHUS AND ARIADNE
Sebastiano Ricci
c. 1713
370 | Chiswick House, London

Bacchus and Ariadne

☐ There are several versions of the myth of the encounter between Bacchus and Ariadne in Naxos. In one version, Ariadne, deserted by Theseus, suddenly comes upon Bacchus, who is returning with his retinue from India. The god of wine and his followers appear all of a sudden from behind the trees and catch Ariadne by surprise, frightening her. Maenads and satyrs make up the retinue; semiferal creatures, they make merry with percussion instruments, typical of Dionysian music (just as string instruments evoke Apollo's music). Bacchus almost jumps down from his cart as he throws the maiden's crown in the sky, transforming it into a constellation. To the left of the composition, we glimpse the *Argo* with Theseus on board, disappearing in the distance.

TRIUMPH OF BACCHUS
Tiziano Vecellio, known as Titian
1520–23

| National Gallery, London

Midas's wish

While traveling through Phrygia with Bacchus and his retinue of satyrs and maenads, Silenus, who was the god's teacher, lost his way. He was found by some peasants as he wandered drunk about the fields, and led before Midas, the local king, who recognized him and gave him hospitality. After some time, the king returned him to Bacchus, who thanked him for the generous hospitality and offered to grant him a wish. Midas asked that everything he touched be transformed into gold. Bacchus unwillingly complied, and immediately everything the king touched became gold, including the soil on which he walked, stones, and wheat plants. When time for dinner came, Midas sat at the table but realized that even the food he took in his hands turned to gold.

Realizing his tragic mistake prompted by greed, the king asked Bacchus forgiveness, imploring him to take back such a destructive gift. Then the god of wine instructed him to go to the river Pactolus, walk upstream until he came to the spring, stand under the spot where the water came out from the rocks, and wash his body, thereby washing away his guilt.

MIDAS AND BACCHUS
Nicolas Poussin
c. 1630

Alte Pinakothek, Munich

☐ Bacchus is standing, and next to him a drunk Silenus sleeps in an unseemly pose. Kneeling before the god, Midas thanks him for releasing him from the power of turning everything he touched into gold.

Coresus and Callirhoe

A Bacchic priest, Coresus had fallen in love with a young woman named Callirhoe, who had rejected him. The priest complained about it to the god, who sent an epidemic of madness to Callirhoe's land. Not understanding the reason for such punishment, the residents questioned the Dodona oracle, who revealed that the god's wrath would subside only when the maiden, or anyone who wished to die in her stead, was sacrificed at the altar where Coresus performed his rituals. There being no one willing to die in her place, Callirhoe was led to the sacrificial altar where Coresus himself was to perform the sacrifice. When the time for the ritual came, the priest, who was still in love with the maiden, turned the dagger on himself and plunged it in his chest. At that sight Callirhoe, shaken by such great proof of love and repenting of her own cruelty, took her own life near the spring, which from that time on has been called by her name.

CORESUS SACRIFICING HIMSELF
TO SAVE CALLIRHOE
Jean-Honoré Fragonard
c. 1765
Musée du Louvre, Paris

☐ This painting narrating the sacrifice of Coresus is laid out like a theater scene. The priest is portrayed as he plunges the sacrificial dagger into his heart. Next to him, supported by a female figure, Callirhoe has fainted. Above the central scene, the allegorical figures of Despair and Love fly about. To the left, desperate bystanders witness the event.

The bacchanal of the Andrians

The island of Andros in the Aegean Sea was famous in antiquity for its excellent wine, being therefore an important center of the cult of Bacchus. According to the myth, the god of wine visited the island every year, and upon his arrival wine would begin to flow from a spring. There the Andrians, wearing ivy wreaths, celebrated a bacchanal near the wine stream, indulging in the pleasures of wine by singing and dancing.

☐ This painting by Titian depicts the bacchanal. In the background is the ship that carried Bacchus to the island. The residents are partying near the wine stream. Some are dancing, others drink greedily, still others have fallen into a wine-induced stupor. On the right, a woman lies alone, like the old man on the hill on the far right middle ground. In the foreground center, two women musicians play the flute; on a scroll, we read: "He who drinks without drinking again, knows not how to drink."

THE BACCHANAL OF THE ANDRIANS
Tiziano Vecellio, known as Titian
1523–25
378 | Museo del Prado, Madrid

NYMPHS

Among the lesser divinities of the earth are the nymphs, usually beneficial spirits of nature personified as lovely, sweet maidens who inhabit groves, springs, streams, shady forests, or deserted islands where nature is bountiful and friendly. They spend their time spinning or weaving, or singing and dancing. The nymphs are often in the court of major deities such as Bacchus and, in particular, the huntress Diana and Venus. The naiads, water nymphs, live in rivers or freshwater springs. The Nereids are the sea nymphs, especially of the calm sea. The oreads are the mountain nymphs that inhabit mountains, crags, and valleys, while the dryads or hamadryads are tree nymphs. These deities were quite popular in folk imagination, and appear in mythological tales almost like modern fairies.

□ This spring nymph lies languidly on a red cloth, in front of a broad landscape, and seems asleep. All around the rim of the fountain is carved a Latin saying that reads: "I am the nymph of the sacred fountain. Do not disturb my sleep, for here I rest."

THE WATER NYMPH
Lucas Cranach the Elder
1518
Museum der Bildenden Künste, Leipzig

Acis and Galatea

Lovely Galatea was a Nereid, or sea nymph. Polyphemus, the infamous Cyclops, fell madly in love with her, but she preferred Acis, the son of Pan and a Simetus River nymph. The nymph tried to escape the giant's heavy compliments; for his part, the giant was pining away and neglecting his duties. One day, while Acis and Galatea were resting in the shadow of a rock, they heard the songs that Polyphemus liked to sing to her. After looking for the nymph in valleys and woods, the one-eyed giant discovered her in the company of Acis. At the sight of the angry Cyclops, Galatea dove deep into the sea while Acis fled, pursued by Polyphemus, who wrested a large rock from a mountain and threw it at him, killing him. Galatea transmuted the blood from the wounds of her beloved into the river by the same name.

☐ In this painting, the artist has set the lovers in the midst of sea divinities. They are insensitive to the imploring songs that the giant offers Galatea, and hide from him behind blue drapery. Before the giant is a volcano—Mount Etna, probably, for the myth of Acis and Galatea is set in eastern Sicily.

ACIS, GALATEA, AND POLYPHEMUS
François Perrier
c. 1645–50
382 | Musée du Louvre, Paris

Glaucus and Scylla

One day, young Glaucus had spread his nets out to dry on a meadow, along an unknown shore. While he was counting the many fish he had caught, he noticed that as soon as they touched the grass they dove again into the sea. The fisherman realized that the grass was miraculous, and ate some of it, becoming an immortal sea deity. In the depths of the sea, the goddesses purified him of everything mortal and gave him a new form, half-fish and half-man. Now Glaucus fell in love with Scylla, who listened to his tale, but in the end rejected him. Angered by the nymph's refusal, Glaucus turned for help to the sorceress Circe, who fell in love with him, but he refused her. Angered, the sorceress took her revenge on Scylla, transforming her into the terrible monster that attacks the sailors near the Strait of Messina (see p. 724).

☐ Glaucus has just been metamorphosed into a half-man, half-fish sea divinity; he casts a loving glance at the young Scylla, who draws back, almost frightened.

GLAUCUS AND SCYLLA
Bartholomaeus Spranger
1580–82
Kunsthistorisches Museum, Vienna

Echo and Narcissus

The nymph Echo was keeping Juno busy with long conversations to prevent her from discovering Jupiter's betrayals; for this reason, the queen of the gods sentenced her to repeat only the last words of what was being said. Now the nymph fell madly in love with Narcissus, an exceedingly handsome young man loved by women and nymphs alike, but who was insensitive to love. Echo also was refused, and she hid in the woods and was wasting away until only her voice remained, her bones having been turned into stones.

One day, another rejected lover turned to Nemesis for vengeance, and she promised to help. On a very hot day after a long hunt, Narcissus stopped at a spring to refresh himself, saw his image reflected in the water, and fell in love with it. Longing for that reflection, the young man wasted away. In the place where his lifeless body lay, a flower appeared—the narcissus.

ECHO AND NARCISSUS
Nicolas Poussin
1627–28
| Musée du Louvre, Paris

☐ Narcissus lies lifeless near the spring; next to his head, the flowers into which he has been transformed are blooming. Behind him, a putto with a lit torch alludes to his death, for it was with torches that the funeral pyre was lit. Leaning on a rock is the disappearing figure of Echo.

Picus and Canens

Picus, the king of Latium and a son of Saturn, fell in love with Canens, a nymph daughter of the god Janus, and married her. In addition to her beauty, Canens had such a sweet voice that it was said she could even move trees and stones and tame wild beasts. One day, while Picus was hunting for wild boars in the countryside, the sorceress Circe saw him and was smitten. To capture him, she caused a wild boar to appear, leading the young king to pursue it and stray from his party. At that point, the sorceress materialized and tried to seduce him, but he rejected her. Deeply offended, Circe retaliated by transforming Picus into a woodpecker. In the meantime, Canens, worried because her husband had not come home, wandered in the countryside for days on end until, exhausted, she reached the Tiber River and, after one last song, dissolved into air.

☐ This painting narrates three episodes of the myth of Picus. In the foreground, the group of hunters that follows the king has captured the boar; to the right, vengeful Circe pours a magical potion over the unfortunate king, who is turning into a woodpecker; in the background, a dejected Canens searches for her husband.

PICUS TRANSFORMED INTO
A WOODPECKER
Benvenuto Tisi, known as Il Garofalo
early 16th century
Galleria Nazionale d'Arte Antica, Rome

SATYRS

The satyrs are the male equivalents of the nymphs. They are lascivious nature demons associated with fertility. Considered the sons of Mercury and the naiads, the freshwater nymphs, they are described as half-human, half-animal beings with billy goat legs, pointed ears, and two small horns on the forehead. Satyrs live in mountains and forests, where they usually hunt. Together with nymphs and maenads, they form Bacchus's retinue (see p. 362) and are often described in the god's company, dressed in animal skins and crowned with wreaths of vine leaves, drinking, making music and singing, or pursuing the nymphs and bacchants who sometimes fall prey to their lust. The satyrs were considered hostile deities, since, according to the most common lore, they attacked animals, killed cattle, harassed women, and frightened people.

□ With feral eyes and ears and windswept hair, this rapturous, inebriated satyr dances and swirls. Here he is about to jump: The torso is turned, the arms are stretched, and the head is thrown backward. He probably had a wild animal skin on his left arm and the thyrsus and a cup of wine in his hands.

DANCING SATYR
c. 360 BCE
Museo del Satiro, Mazara del Vallo

SATYRS

☐ This satyr is represented as he pours wine—symbolized by the bunch of grapes he holds in his right hand—into a horn. His head bends slightly forward and is adorned with a garland of vine leaves. Next to him, on a tree stump, are a sheep-skin, a flute, and a curved stick that resembles a shepherd's staff.

SATYR POURING WINE
late 2nd century CE
Palazzo Altemps, Rome

SATYRS

☐ In the Middle Ages and the Renaissance, the image of the satyr came to embody evil, vice, and often lust. This painting by Lotto presents the viewer with a moral choice between virtue and vice. In the foreground are two different scenes, separated by the tree that stands at the center. On the left, a putto with a compass in his hand is about to draw a circle. In front of him are books and geometric and musical instruments that symbolize the cultural and intellectual pursuits of the man who commissioned the work. On the right, an inebriated satyr is hugging a sort of amphora full of wine. Other amphorae lie upturned around him, creating an image of vice.

The two separate scenes in the background illustrate the effects of the two ways of life. On the right, a ship is sinking in the stormy sea of vice; on the left, another putto climbs the steep path that leads to spiritual enlightenment.

ALLEGORY OF VIRTUE AND VICE
Lorenzo Lotto
1505
National Gallery of Art, Washington, D.C.

The satyr and the peasant

One legend narrates that once upon a time a satyr and a peasant became friends. When winter and the icy winds came, the man used to blow into his hands. When the satyr asked him to explain, the peasant replied that he blew on his hands to warm them and get some relief from the cold. Later, at supper time, while everyone was at the table, the man blew on the piping-hot soup before eating it. When the satyr looked at him perplexed, he replied that he was cooling the soup because it was too hot. Then the satyr became angry and left, claiming that he did not want to be friends with a being as ambiguous as man, from whose mouth issues both cold and heat.

☐ The tale of the satyr and the peasant became a popular subject of seventeenth-century Flemish painting. Here a man dressed in red is blowing on a bowl of soup to cool it, while earlier he had been blowing on his hands to warm them. On the opposite side of the table, the satyr, rendered with goat legs and two small horns on the forehead, is skeptical and scolds the peasant for his duplicity.

THE SATYR AND THE FARMER'S FAMILY
Jacob Jordaens
c. 1625
Szépművészeti Múzeum, Budapest

SILENUS

The name Silenus usually identifies the old satyr who raised the child Bacchus and became his faithful companion. In later times, Silenus was imagined as a round, plump middle-aged man with slightly flattened nose, usually staggering drunkenly about and following Bacchus on a donkey, assisted by other satyrs. There are many versions of his origins; according to some, he is the son of Pan or Mercury and a nymph. Silenus was said to be a very wise man with the gift of divination. He could predict the future when he lay sleeping off the wine, as long as men surrounded him or tied him with flower garlands.

In classical mythology, unlike satyrs, which are woodland and mountain spirits, the sileni are considered the spirits of the fertile running waters. Finally, they were believed to have the gift of prophecy and to have invented musical instruments. These differences notwithstanding, over time sileni and satyrs became assimilated.

SILENUS INEBRIATED RIDES AN ASS
Mosaic
2nd century BCE–79 CE
398 | Museo Archeologico Nazionale, Naples

☐ This mosaic portrait of Silenus follows the traditional iconography: He is a bald, potbellied, tottering old man trying to climb on his ass; the animal is held steady by two assistants. Silenus carries the thyrsus, which is Bacchus's attribute.

◄◄

SILENUS

☐ Crowned with an ivy wreath, Silenus reclines languidly on the ground, already drunk, though he still asks that his cup be filled from a wineskin. On the left side of the scene, a boy keeps the ass tied, the animal being a distinctive attribute and companion of this deity. Below left in the foreground is a scroll bearing the artist's signature, held by a snake, suggesting the Bacchic rites that included handling these reptiles. Behind Silenus is Pan—his father, according to the myth.

DRUNKEN SILENUS
Jusepe de Ribera
1626
Museo Nazionale di Capodimonte, Naples

The Earth Deities

PAN

An ancient woodland deity, Pan was believed to be the son of Mercury and a nymph. He is imagined as half-man and half-animal, with a jutting chin and a keen, sharp expression on his bearded face. Pan has two small horns on his forehead and a hairy body with billy goat legs and hoofs. The myth recounts that his mother was frightened by the infant's appearance at his birth; but Mercury led him to Mount Olympus to show him to the other gods, who were favorably impressed. Because everyone liked the child, he was called Pan, which means "all" in Greek. Bacchus was charmed by him and accepted him in his court; it is not unusual to see Pan among the maenads and satyrs in traditional Bacchic iconography.

This god spends his days in the Arcadian valleys hunting and making music in the company of nymphs. He is feared by travelers because he purposely makes strange sounds and unexpected noises to frighten them, and his image was associated with sudden fear; in fact, the word "panic" derives from Pan.

Attributes: syrinx, shepherd's staff

PAN PLAYS THE DOUBLE FLUTE
WITH A DANCING MAENAD
(detail)
Krater
Maron painter (attr.)
late 4th century BCE
Museo Archaeologico Eoliano, Lipari

402

☐ Pan intently plays the flute while a maenad holding a thyrsus presents him with a container, probably filled with wine.

Pan and Syrinx

Syrinx was a naiad, a water nymph. A follower of Diana and therefore bound to chastity, she fled from the lecherous satyrs and gods who lived in the woods and the countryside. Pan fell in love with her and tried to conquer her, but the naiad refused, as she had done with previous suitors, and began to run, pursued by the god. When she reached the Ladon River, she had to stop. She then desperately asked her sisters to transmute her; Pan, convinced he had seized her, was only grabbing marsh reeds. Full of sorrow, the god began to sigh, and the air from his sighs, vibrating inside the reeds he still held in his hands, created a sweet, light music. Enchanted by the music, Pan cut some reeds of different lengths and glued them together with wax, creating a new instrument to which he gave the name of the beloved nymph he had lost: Syrinx.

☐ This painting captures the instant just before the nymph is transformed. Having reached the river Ladon, Syrinx raises her arms to the heavens, begging her naiad sisters for help. Behind her, Pan, identifiable by his part-human, part-feral face and the goat's hooves, is about to grab her.

THE NYMPH SYRINX PURSUED BY PAN
Jan Brueghel the Elder
1623
404 | Pinacoteca di Brera, Milan

The judgment of Midas

One day, Pan, finding himself near Mount Tmolus, dared to
belittle Apollo's songs and challenged him to a contest. The
Sun god accepted, and the old mountain spirit was chosen
as the judge. After Pan played, it was Apollo's turn; gently
stroking the strings of his lyre, he sang so sweetly that the
judge had to declare him the winner. King Midas was present
at the contest and took Pan's side, claiming that the decision
was unfair. Hearing these words, an angry Apollo caused two
long ass's ears to sprout on his head. Unable to hide the
shameful ears, Midas began to wear a crimson miter on his
head, but the servant who cut his hair found out his secret.
He did not dare to reveal what he had seen, but since he also
could not stay quiet, he decided to dig a hole and to speak
into it what he had seen; then he buried his secret by filling
the hole with dirt. After a year, however, a thicket of reeds
had sprouted on that spot, and whenever the wind moved
them, they revealed the secret to the passersby.

☐ This artist has set the myth in
his own times. Pan is rendered as a
shepherd intent on playing the flute,
while Apollo, lyre in hand, is dressed
like the god of the Sun. Below on the
right is Midas with the long ass's ears
that Apollo has caused him to grow.

THE JUDGMENT OF MIDAS
Miniature
1410–11
British Library, London

◄◄

The judgment of Midas

☐ On the left, Tmolus, the old mountain spirit, is crowning Apollo (holding the lyre) with the victory wreath. Next to the judge, Pan plays the syrinx. The woodland divinity is portrayed with his traditional beard and feral ears, but without the goat's hooves that are also part of the classical iconography. To his right is King Midas, with the ass's ears that Apollo gave him for preferring Pan's music to his own.

APOLLO DEFEATING PAN
Jacob Jordaens
1637

408 | Museo del Prado, Madrid

The Earth Deities

CENTAURS

Sired by Ixion, king of the Lapiths, and a cloud, the centaurs are half-man and half-horse, violent and boorish beings. Their human torso has two arms, and the lower equine half has four hoofed legs. They lived in Thessaly near Mount Pelion and led the life of wild beasts. Over time, the centaurs grew less wild in the folk imagination and were treated as spirits linked to Bacchus, like the satyrs and the sileni. Two centaurs stand out for their unusual character: Chiron and Folus, both kind, benign deities who were nonviolent friends of man.

☐ This young centaur, a creature half-man and half-horse, advances happily with fresh prey on his left arm.

YOUNG CENTAUR
117–38 CE
Musei Capitolini, Rome

CENTAURS

□ Cupid, the god of love usually rendered as a winged boy, is riding an old, afflicted-looking centaur. His suffering and fatigue are probably due to the pains of love, as symbolized by Cupid and the fact that the centaur has his hands tied behind his back, as if the child god had bound him.

CUPID RIDES A CENTAUR
1st–2nd century CE
| Musée du Louvre, Paris

The birth of the centaurs

Ixion, king of the Lapiths, a strong, wild tribe that made its home in Thessaly, fell in love with Dia, daughter of Deioneus, and was able to marry her by promising large gifts to the future father-in-law. After the wedding, Deioneus claimed the gifts that had been pledged to him, but Ixion killed him by treachery, causing him to fall into a pit full of burning coals. Guilty of the worst offenses—oath-breaking and the shedding of family blood—Ixion was sentenced to madness. Only Jupiter was moved to pity and purified him, freeing him from his madness, but once again Ixion was ungrateful, for not only did he fall in love with Juno, but also tried to take her by force. The king of the gods (or Juno, in other versions) then shaped a cloud that replicated Juno's features, and Ixion made love to the apparition. From this sacrilegious union the centaurs were born. Ixion's action did not go unpunished; he was thrown into Tartarus (see p. 444).

IXION, KING OF THE LAPITHS,
DECEIVED BY JUNO
Pieter Paul Rubens
c. 1615
414 | Musée du Louvre, Paris

□ To the left, the Lapith king Ixion seduces a cloud that has the semblance of the queen of the gods, while the true Juno, on the right, walks away. From the high heavens, the king of the gods looks on. A torch held aloft, an *amorino* takes Juno by the arm and turns to Jupiter, as if confirming his wife's faithfulness.

The battle of the Lapiths and the centaurs

One of the best-known legends is the fierce battle of the Lapiths and the centaurs. Both violent, boorish races, they lived in Thessaly, the former near the southern slopes of Mount Olympus, the latter in the woods that covered Mount Pelion. When Pirithous, king of the Lapiths and Ixion's son, married Hippodamia, he also invited the centaurs, who were his relatives, sons of the same father (see p. 414). During the wedding banquet, the centaurs, who were not accustomed to drinking wine, became inebriated. One of them, Euritos, became very drunk and tried to rape Hippodamia, causing a general brawl that degenerated into a bloody fight that ended with the victory of the Lapiths, while the defeated centaurs were forced to leave Thessaly.

CENTAUR AND LAPITH
Metope from the Parthenon
447–32 BCE
416 | British Museum, London

□ This sculpture from the Parthenon depicts the battle between a centaur—a creature half-man and half-horse—and a Lapith. The battle of the centaurs was a frequent subject in Greek art, having been interpreted since earliest times as the victory of Greek civilization over the primitive Pelasgian civilization, which was considered barbarian.

◄◄

The battle of the Lapiths and the centaurs

☐ In the center of the scene in this vase painting, a Lapith throws a powerful punch to a centaur about to hit him with an amphora. The legend tells that in the fight all kinds of objects, such as cups and goblets, were used as weapons. To the left, another centaur is stopped by a Lapith just as he is about to throw a table, and on the ground is a frightened female figure, probably Hippodamia.

BATTLE OF THE CENTAURS
Column krater
Florence painter
c. 460 BCE

Museo Archeologico Nazionale, Florence

◄◄

The battle of the Lapiths and the centaurs

☐ Identifying the various characters in the violent melee of this relief by Michelangelo is not easy. The Lapiths seem to be grouped on the left, the centaurs in the center and at right in the front and middle ground. In the center of the relief, a female figure seen from the back, probably Hippodamia, is being pulled by the hair by a Lapith and held back by a centaur. At the bottom in the foreground, two centaurs lie lifeless on the ground. Michelangelo has freely interpreted the literary sources, since the Lapiths are shown using rocks as weapons, while the centaurs are using clubs.

BATTLE OF THE CENTAURS
Michelangelo Buonarroti
1504–1505
Casa Buonarroti, Florence

CHIRON

Chiron, the best-known and wisest of the centaurs, was the son of Philyra, daughter of Oceanus, and Saturn; the latter lay with her disguised as a horse to escape his wife's anger. For this reason, Chiron is half-man and half-horse.

Born with the gift of immortality, Chiron lived in a cave near Mount Pelion, in Thessaly. Friendly with men, meek and wise, he was skilled in the arts of music, hunting, war, and medicine, and in fact was the teacher of heroes such as Hercules, Achilles, Jason, and Aesculapius; he even educated Apollo. Chiron was struck accidentally by one of Hercules's arrows and tried to treat the deep wound with medicinal ointments, but in vain: The wound was untreatable because the hero's arrows were soaked in a powerful, deadly poison. Racked with pain, the good Chiron took shelter in a cave and invoked death, even though he was immortal. Prometheus answered his prayers and lent him his own right to die, finally giving him peace (see p. 492).

APOLLO, CHIRON, AND HIPPOCRATES
1st century CE

| Museo Archeologico Nazionale, Naples

☐ In this Roman fresco, Chiron is portrayed with Apollo on his left and Hippocrates sitting on the right—the latter is the celebrated Greek physician hailed as the founder of medicine.

VERTUMNUS AND POMONA

Vertumnus and Pomona are primitive divinities associated with the fruits of the Earth. Vertumnus (or Vortumnus), whose name derives from the Latin *vertere annus* ("the turning of the year"), can adopt different forms, promotes the changing of flowers into fruits, and oversees the changing of the seasons. Pomona, whose name is derived from the word *pomum*, "fruit," is a deity of fruits and orchards.

According to the myth, Pomona was roaming the countryside fleeing the love of any man or mortal; Vertumnus had fallen in love with her and in vain had tried to seduce her. Far from losing heart, he took on different guises, now as a harvesting peasant, now as a soldier or fisherman; with the pretext of helping her in the various farming chores, he could be near her and court her. One day, he approached the goddess disguised as an old woman. After praising her work, she began to sweetly scold Pomona for her excessive pride and advised her to give her heart to someone, recommending the young Vertumnus. After a long, futile talk, Vertumnus decided to reveal himself and take her by force, but when she saw the god in all his splendor, the goddess was seduced.

□ Vertumnus is an early Etruscan deity, the god of seasonal change, especially of autumn and its fruits.

VERTUMNUS
Museo Archeologico Nazionale, Florence

VERTUMNUS AND POMONA

☐ Young Pomona sits near a still life of fruits that identifies her and holds the reaping hook she uses to work in the orchards. The crone at her side is actually Vertumnus, who has disguised himself to approach the girl and plead his cause. To the extreme right stands Cupid with his bow and arrows, suggesting the amorous nature of this scene.

VERTUMNUS AND POMONA
Anton van Dyck
1625
Galleria di Palazzo Bianco, Genoa

FLORA

Another early deity, worshiped by the Sabines, Flora is the goddess of spring, of flowers, and of flowering, the all-important natural and fascinating process that ensures a bountiful harvest.

The poet Ovid identified Flora with the Greek nymph Chloris. He narrates that on a fine spring day, Zephyrus, the god of the springtime wind, saw her wandering the fields and fell in love with her. He abducted her and decided to properly marry her. As a reward and a proof of his love, he granted Flora the power to rule over the flowers of farmed fields and orchards. As the goddess of flowers, she is believed to have given honey to men. The goddess also oversees the flourishing of youth, the happiest age of man.

☐ In this Roman fresco, a young woman seen from the back walks barefoot in a meadow, leisurely picking white flowers from a shrub and arranging them in a cornucopia. Her yellow chiton leaves a shoulder bare, and she wears an armlet and a crown. Although her identity is uncertain, this image is generally considered a representation of Flora.

FLORA
early 1st century CE
Museo Archeologico Nazionale, Naples

◄◄

FLORA

☐ A peculiarly dressed young girl wears a white tunic that leaves one breast uncovered and a headdress of the same color, on which rests a myrtle wreath. Her blond curls fall gently on her shoulders, and she wears precious jewels on her forehead and around her neck. Her enigmatic, perhaps inviting gaze is turned to the viewer, and she holds a nosegay in which an anemone and three daisies are recognizable. This painting has been subjected to several interpretations, though it is considered an allegory linked to the image of Flora.

PORTRAIT OF A LADY AS FLORA
Bartolomeo Veneto
c. 1507–1508

Städelsches Kunstinstitut, Frankfurt

FLORA

☐ The image of Flora is used frequently in female portraits. In this case, Rembrandt has given his wife, Saskia, the semblance of the flower goddess. The figure rises from the dark background, enveloped in a golden light. She wears a luxuriant garland of flowers and holds a staff in her right hand entwined with ivy and more flowers on top. In all probability, Rembrandt wanted to paint an allegory of expectant motherhood, since at the time of the painting his wife was with child. Flora is also linked to the image of flowering, thus of youth and of the joys of life and motherhood.

SASKIA AS FLORA
Rembrandt von Rijn
1463
| Hermitage Museum, Saint Petersburg

◄◄

FLORA

☐ In this large canvas by Poussin, Flora is the image of spring perennially renewing herself. She is surrounded by men and women who were metamorphosed into flowers upon dying. To her left is Ajax, who committed suicide by falling on his sword because he had not been awarded the arms of Achilles; from his blood a carnation was born. Next to him is Narcissus, for whom the flower is named; behind him, Clytia, who was turned into a sunflower. On the right are Crocus and Smilax, whose tragic love story transformed them respectively into saffron and sarsaparilla. Behind them is Adonis, from whose blood sprouted anemones, and next to him Hyacinth, who was turned into the flower that took his name. A herm of Pan, the god of fertility, rises in the left middle ground, while Apollo in the sky drives the Sun chariot that brings life to plants and flowers.

THE EMPIRE OF FLORA
Nicolas Poussin
1631

Gemäldegalerie, Dresden

THE INFERNAL DEITIES

The Infernals 438 • Pluto 448 • Proserpina 450
The Furaie (The Furies) 456 • Hecate 458

THE INFERNALS

The infernals are a dark region in the bowels of Earth with several entrances, such as caves or deep fissures in the ground. The rivers Coccyx, Pyriphlegethon, Acheron, and Styx cross it. The ancients believed that the Styx meandered several times around Hades and that one could cross it only by being ferried on Charon's boat. One had to pay for the crossing, so the ancients placed a coin in the mouth of the deceased.

Beyond the rivers was the mouth of Hades, guarded by the terrifying, many-headed dog Cerberus, who allowed all to enter but prevented anyone from leaving to return above ground. Once in Hades, Pluto's reign, souls were judged by Minos, Rhadamanthus, and Aeacus; these judges ruled on whether the souls would join the evil or the just. The former were hurled into Tartarus, where they suffered untold torments; the latter were sent on to the Elysian Fields, where they experienced eternal happiness.

☐ Brueghel has created an image of the netherworld filtered through Christianity, for he has given us a kingdom of the dead that is a terrifying place on fire. The ancients believed it was a dark, barren wasteland where the souls of the dead roamed, almost like shadows in a dream.

PLUTO'S PALACE
Jan Brueghel the Elder
438 | Pinacoteca di Brera, Milan

The torment of Tantalus

An Asian king and a forebear of Agamemnon and Menelaus, Tantalus was believed to be a son of Jupiter, and as such was allowed to sit at the gods' table and partake in their banquets. But Tantalus was conceited and proud and dared to steal nectar and ambrosia from one of the banquets to give to his mortal friends. Furthermore, seeking to test divine knowledge, he killed and dismembered his son Pelops and offered him as a dinner course to the gods. But the gods realized the terrible deed and no one dared to eat of it; on the contrary, moved to pity, they reassembled the boy's body and resuscitated him, then punished Tantalus by exiling him to Tartarus, the infernal region that imprisons the mortals guilty of the most heinous crimes, sentencing him to eternal hunger and thirst.

☐ Homer sang of a Tantalus who was plunged to his neck in water but was unable to quench his thirst, because every time he tried to drink, the water disappeared. Neither could the crafty king eat, because the luxuriant tree branches that hung full of all kinds of fruits above his head were moved aside by the wind every time he tried to grab them.

TANTALUS
Giambattista Langetti
1650–76
440 | Ca' Rezzonico, Venice

The labors of Sisyphus

Sisyphus was a hero and the founder of Corinth. Many legends celebrate his cunning. When Jupiter abducted Aegina, daughter of the river god Asopus, he was discovered by Sisyphus, who revealed everything to the girl's father; in exchange, he received the Pirene Spring near the citadel of Corinth. To punish him for the betrayal, the father of the gods sent him Death, but Sisyphus surprised her and chained her, so that no one could die any more. Then Jupiter had to intervene and personally release Death. Of course, her first victim was Sisyphus, but before dying he begged his wife not to celebrate the customary funeral rites. As soon as he was before Pluto, the hero complained about his wife's lack of piety and wrested permission to return to Earth to punish her. But once he saw the light of the Sun, Sisyphus did not return to Hades; therefore he died a natural death in his old age. Back in the netherworld, he was punished for all his deceptions: His sentence was to push a heavy rock up to the top of a steep hill, but once on top, the rock fell back to the bottom of the hill, and he was forced to start again the enormous labor.

SISYPHUS
Tiziano Vecellio, known as Titian
c. 1549
442 | Museo del Prado, Madrid

☐ In the infernal darkness, Sisyphus is forced to carry a large rock up a mountain. His body is strained by the effort, highlighting the enormous toil involved in lifting the rock.

The punishment of Ixion

Ixion, the king of the Lapiths, was struck by madness as punishment for his heinous crimes (see p. 414). Among the gods, only Jupiter was moved to compassion and decided to heal him, but the king was ungrateful to the father of the gods and dared to take a fancy to Juno and try to possess her against her will. Then Jupiter created a cloud with Juno's form and Ixion lay with her, siring the centaurs. Faced with such a sacrilegious offense, Jupiter decided to punish Ixion. He tied him to a fiery wheel that rotated continuously, and threw him into dark Tartarus. Because Ixion had been initially protected by Jupiter, he had drunk ambrosia, which makes men immortal; therefore he was forced to suffer this punishment for all eternity.

☐ In this Roman fresco, on the left, we see Ixion bound to the wheel; next to him are Vulcan and Mars. The latter, identified by the caduceus in his left hand, turns to Juno, who is witnessing the punishment. The woman shrouded in a wide mantle and seated in the foreground has been variously identified as a Fury, an infernal spirit, or the mother of Ixion.

THE PUNISHMENT OF IXION
1st century BCE –1st century CE

The punishment of Tityus

Tityus was a giant, son of Jupiter and Elara. Fearful of Juno's jealous nature, the father of the gods hid his pregnant lover deep beneath the earth, and in fact Tityus was said to be born from the earth. Later, after Latona gave birth to Diana and Apollo (see p. 42), Juno, blinded by jealousy, caused the giant to lust after Latona and sent him to her. But the mother of the divine twins was saved by Jupiter, who killed the giant with a thunderbolt and hurled him into Tartarus, where he was tied to the ground and punished by two eagles, who fed on his liver that kept regrowing.

☐ This splendid rock crystal carving depicts the punishment of Tityus. The giant lies on his back with bound hands and feet, while an eagle pounces on his liver, considered by the ancients to be the organ where emotions reside. For this reason, Renaissance artists interpreted this episode as an allegory of the body's subjection to sensual pleasure.

THE PUNISHMENT OF TITYUS
Cut rock crystal
Giovanni Bernardi
c. 1530
| British Museum, London

PLUTO

After conquering the Titans, Jupiter and his brothers Pluto and Neptune divided up the world. Jupiter became lord of the sky, Neptune king of the seas, while Pluto was assigned the world of the dead. This god rules the netherworld with a firm hand: No one who enters his kingdom can hope to leave it, save for rare exceptions that the gods themselves instituted. His wife is Proserpina, whom he kidnapped when she was gathering flowers with her maids (see p. 450). The Greek name of this god is Hades, which means "the invisible," for the ancients named him very rarely, believing that the god flew into a rage by simply hearing his name. Therefore, epithets were used, the most common one being Pluto (from the Greek pluton, "the rich one," alluding both to the wealth of the farmlands and the treasures of the underground mines).

Greek name: Hades

Attributes: scepter, pitchfork, the dog Cerberus

□ Riding his chariot with a pitchfork in his hand, Pluto enters the netherworld. To his left is Venus, who, according to Ovid, had spurred Cupid (in the center near a ruined colonnade) to shoot one of his arrows at the king of Hell, causing him to fall in love with Proserpina.

PLUTO ARRIVES IN TARTARUS
Joseph Heintz the Younger
c. 1640
Městské Muzeum, Mariánské Lázně

448

PROSERPINA

Proserpina is the goddess of the netherworld and the daughter of Jupiter and Ceres. Pluto (see p. 448) was smitten when he saw her gathering flowers in the Sicilian countryside. When she had wandered away from her friends, he took her down to the infernal world to make her his bride.

Proserpina's mother, who is the goddess of the harvest (see p. 334), roamed Earth in a futile search for her daughter until Apollo revealed to her Proserpina's whereabouts. Filled with anger, Ceres neglected her duties and a famine and drought ensued. As a result, Jupiter sent Mercury to the netherworld to retrieve Proserpina. But the young woman had eaten a pomegranate seed; this sufficed to keep her forever in the world of the dead, for the ancients believed that anyone who ate anything there could no longer return to the living. Jupiter ruled that Proserpina could spend two-thirds of the year with her mother and one-third in the underworld with her groom.

Greek name: Persephone

Attributes: spikes of wheat, torches, crown, pomegranate, fruits

THE RAPE OF PERSEPHONE
Jan Soens
c. 1580
450 | Musée des Beaux-Arts, Valenciennes

☐ Pluto has already seized Proserpina, who raises her hands in a cry for help. Cyane, a nymph who tried to stop Pluto, is in the river on the left.

PROSERPINA

☐ Bernini has immortalized this myth by sculpting Pluto as he firmly seizes the maiden, who in vain tries to escape his clutches. Next to the god is Cerberus, the three-headed dog that guards the gates of Hades and is often depicted with him. On the ground lies the pitchfork, one of the god's attributes.

THE RAPE OF PROSERPINA
Gian Lorenzo Bernini
1621–22
Galleria Borghese, Rome

PROSERPINA

☐ In this ancient bas-relief, Pluto
and Proserpina enthroned are shown
with some of their distinctive attributes: for the goddess, a spike of
wheat and a cock; for the god,
a poppy. The wheat alludes to
Proserpina's original role of rural
deity overseer of the germination
of the fields; the cock is sacred to
her, for the ancient Greeks believed
it was an animal of the underworld that was in contact with the
chthonic forces from the depths of
the earth. The poppy Pluto holds
is probably an allusion to the sleep
of death.

PLUTO AND PROSERPINA ENTHRONED
Votive tablet
late 6th–early 5th century BCE
Museo Nazionale, Reggio Calabria

THE FURIAE (THE FURIES)

Among the infernal divinities are the frightening Furies, the deities of vengeance who torment anyone who has broken the moral law, punishing especially the offenses to the family order. Issued from the blood of Uranus when he fell to Earth upon being mutilated by his son Saturn (see p. 22), these are primitive deities, who refuse to recognize the authority of the Olympian gods. As with the Parcae, the gods are subjected to their will. At first indeterminate in number, they were later restricted to three: Alecto ("the troubled one"), Tisiphone ("the murder avenger"), and Megaera ("the hateful one"). The Furies are winged deities with snakes for hair who carry torches or whips; when they seize a victim, he has no hope of escaping; fleeing is impossible, and his torments will end only with madness or death.

Greek name: Erinyes or Eumenides

Alternative Latin name: Dirae

□ The Furies are remembered especially in the myth of Orestes, who avenged his father, Agamemnon, by slaying his mother, Clytemnestra, and her lover, Aegisthus. In this work, Orestes appears with his sister Electra. The young hero is clutched by pangs of remorse for the horrible double murder he committed, while behind him the merciless Furies materialize.

ORESTES PURSUED BY THE FURIES
Philippe Auguste Hennequin
1800
456 | Musée du Louvre, Paris

HECATE

According to Hesiod, Hecate is the daughter of the Titan Perseus and Asteria. Originally, she personified an aspect of the Moon, for which reason she is linked to Diana. She probably represented the new, invisible Moon, and because she was not visible in the sky, the ancients believed that she hid in the bowels of Earth; this would explain her presence among the infernal gods. Under this aspect, Hecate was soon considered the goddess of spirits and night apparitions. She wanders at night among the souls of the dead, crossing the places where three roads meet, which are magical by definition, and walking near tombs.

Hecate was also believed to oversee the magical arts, protecting the witches who nightly look for herbs for their spells. It was believed that Circe and Medea had learned witchcraft from her and were her assistants. As a sorceress, crossroads and triple crossroads are sacred to her, and she is even nicknamed Trivia or Three-formed. This epithet also reflects her image as a deity with one body but three heads, a possible allusion to the three different phases of the Moon: new, half, and full.

☐ The goddess Hecate is represented in her traditional form of three-headed divinity on a single body.

STATUE OF HECATE
3rd century CE
458 Museo Archeologico Nazionale, Venice

HECATE

☐ Blake has imagined Hecate as
three separate deities arranged at
the points of a triangle: The two
personifications in the middle ground
hide their gaze from the viewer,
while the deity in the foreground is
turned to her right, her hand on a
book she seems to leaf through.
Depicted in her gloomiest aspect,
the goddess sits on the ground,
surrounded by darkness and by
creatures of the night, such as the
snake and the owl.

HECATE
William Blake
c. 1795
460 Tate Gallery, London

MONSTERS

Sirens 464 • Harpies 466 • Medusa 468 • Cerberus 470 • Hydra 472
Chimera 474 • Minotaur 476

SIRENS

Sea divinities, the Sirens are believed to be the daughters of the river god Asopus and a Muse, either Terpsichore, Calliope, or Melpomene. In the earliest versions of the myth, they live on a Mediterranean island, where they attract sailors with their bewitching choruses; spellbound by the sweet, tempting melodies, the seafarers recklessly approach the rocky coastline and end up smashed against the rocks. Then the terrible creatures feed on the bodies of the unwary sailors.

They appear for the first time in Homer's *Odyssey* (see p. 722), which mentions two of them; in later legends, the Sirens are three or four, with different names. Ovid writes that they were Proserpina's companions; after she was abducted by Pluto (see p. 450), they roamed Earth in search of their friend, then asked the gods for wings so that they could also look for her in the sea. According to yet another version of the myth, their metamorphosis was a punishment inflicted by Ceres because they failed to prevent Proserpina's abduction.

SIREN
Vase painting
560–50 BCE
Musée du Louvre, Paris

☐ Ancient classical iconography imagined Sirens as half-woman and half-bird creatures, sometimes with talons. Starting in the Middle Ages, these creatures began to be depicted with the lower body in the shape of a fish.

HARPIES

The Harpies, whose name in Greek means "snatchers," are winged deities daughters of Thaumas and the ocean nymph Electra. Initially, there were only two (Aello and Ocypete), to whom a third (Celaeno) was added. Their names clearly describe their nature, since they mean, respectively, "sea storm," "swift-flying," and "the dark one." They are imagined sometimes as winged women, sometimes as monsters with a woman's head, a bird's body, and sharp talons. According to the myth, they lived in the Strophades Islands in the Aegean Sea. Described as snatchers of people and souls, sometimes their image appears on tombs. The Harpies are remembered in the tale of Phineus, king of Thrace, who had been cursed. Anything he placed before him, food in particular, was snatched away by the Harpies or soiled with their excrements. The king was freed by two Argonauts.

□ The image of the Harpy, a predatory creature, has been associated with greed, but in this work she stands for Fortune. Blindfolded to underscore her randomness in dispensing favors or calamities, she stands on two globes to symbolize the fickleness of one's luck. The creature holds in her hands two pitchers with pleasures and griefs that she randomly pours on humankind.

ALLEGORY OF WINGED FORTUNE
Andrea Previtali (attr.)
early 16th century
Gallerie dell'Accademia, Venice

MEDUSA

Medusa is the best-known of the three Gorgons, daughters of the sea deities Phorcys and Ceto. The other two Gorgons, Stheno and Euryale, were immortal; not so Medusa. They are described as monsters with snakes for hair, boarlike tusks, golden wings, and brazen claws. With their fiery eyes and piercing looks, they turn anyone who looks at them to stone. The mortal Medusa was slain by Perseus (see p. 514), who presented her head to the goddess Minerva, who attached it to her aegis. Apparently, the winged horse Pegasus and the giant Chrysaor were born from the drops of blood of her chopped-off head.

The legend of Medusa is from the Hellenic Age. While initially she was considered a monster from the generation that preceded the Olympian pantheon, she later was believed to be the victim of a metamorphosis; a mortal maiden had dared to compare her beauty to Minerva's and was punished by the goddess, who turned her tresses into snakes.

MEDUSA
Michelangelo Merisi da Caravaggio
1597
Gallerie degli Uffizi, Florence

☐ Caravaggio has imagined Medusa beheaded, blood spilling from the neck. The monster's terrifying expression is heightened by the open, shrieking mouth and the deranged look. Her hair, made of entwined snakes, gives this Gorgon a superhuman, surreal aspect.

CERBERUS

The issue of the monsters Echidna and Typhon, Cerberus is the dog of the infernals. He was placed at the gate of the kingdom of the dead, the most remote area of the Styx, at the site where Charon docks his ferry that carries the souls of the dead; the dog allows anyone to enter, but prevents anyone from leaving. Generally, the dog is an identifying attribute of Pluto, the god of the infernals, but it also appears in scenes that describe Olympus or the gods' banquets. Cerberus has three heads and a tail made of snakes.

Few mortals succeeded in stepping behind the gloomy threshold guarded by Cerberus and returning among the living. Hercules caught the dog and took it to Eurystheus, and Orpheus with his sweet melody was able to appease it and remove Euridyce from the netherworld. Other heroes who traveled down to Hades were confronted with the ferocious watchdog and were able to tame it only by feeding it a poisonous loaf of bread. Among these were Psyche, whom Venus had ordered to pay a visit to Proserpina, and the Sibyl who escorted Aeneas.

CERBERUS
William Blake
1824–27
Tate Gallery, London

□ The image of Cerberus also appears in illustrations of the Christian Hell, such as this plate by Blake illustrating Dante's *Divine Comedy*. The monster stands guard at the circle of the gluttons; he holds in his claws the souls of the dead, just as Dante imagined him.

HYDRA

The legendary Hydra of Lerna is, like Cerberus, an offspring of Typhon and Echidna. The Hydra is a many-headed monstrous snake; the number of heads varies from five up to one hundred, though in the most common version of the myth she has seven, sometimes with human features, that are immediately regrown every time they are chopped off. The monster was raised by Juno, Hercules's sworn enemy, for a future battle against the famous Greek hero, who defeated the monster in one of his celebrated labors (see p. 548).

☐ In medieval iconography, the terrifying seven-headed monster sometimes took on the features of a winged dragon and evoked Satan's image. Later, it became the allegorical representation of vice. In this vision by Guercino, vice is a repelling, deformed dwarf embracing the Hydra. The monster has seven heads, like the seven deadly sins, which are so rooted in evil people that they always regrow no matter how many times they are cut off.

STUDY OF HERCULES KILLING HYDRA
Giovanni Francesco Barbieri,
known as Guercino
1618
472 | Private collection

1722   N° 62   Sebao Benedetti

CHIMERA

Born from the union of Typhon and Echidna, the Chimera is a monster with a three-part body: lion in the front, goat in the center, and either lion or snake in the back. Traditionally, she is also depicted with three heads: lion, goat, and snake, all breathing fire and flames.

According to Homer, the Chimera had been raised by Amisodarus, king of Caria. Iobates, king of Lycia, asked Bellerophon, a hero born in the city of Corinth, to kill the monster that was ravaging the countryside. Thanks to his winged horse, Pegasus, the hero won the battle and slew the terrible monster (see p. 526).

☐ This representation of the Chimera is faithful to the ancient sources: a lion with a snake's tail and a second goat's head. The monster is arched backward as it prepares to leap. The lion's head, threateningly turned towards the enemy, roars, and the muscles throb as it prepares to jump.

CHIMERA
mid-5th century BCE
Museo Archeologico Nazionale, Florence

MINOTAUR

The offspring of Jupiter and Europa (see p. 58), Minos was king of Crete. To prove his right to the throne, he asked Neptune to send him a bull from the sea, which he would then sacrifice to the god. The god of the sea answered his prayers and sent him a magnificent white bull. After being ensconced on the throne, however, Minos decided to keep the animal for himself and sacrificed another one to the god, but his action did not go unnoticed. To punish him for the offense, Neptune caused in Pasiphaë, Minos's wife, a violent passion for the bull. Hidden inside a cow decoy that Daedalus had built at her insistence, the queen lay with the bull. From the union was born the celebrated Minotaur, a monster half-man and half-bull. For his part, a frightened and ashamed Minos had Daedalus build a labyrinth, in which he imprisoned the monster. He then dictated that seven youths and seven maidens from Athens be sacrificed every year to be devoured by it. Theseus, son of the Athenian king Aegeus, sailed to Crete with the intention of killing the Minotaur (see p. 536) and succeeded thanks to the help of Ariadne, Minos's daughter.

MINOTAUR
(detail)
Vase painting
515 BCE
476 Private collection

☐ The Minotaur, "the bull of Minos," is represented in this vase painting as half-bull and half-man. In the myth survives the memory of the ancient Minoan civilization and its vast palaces, with the famous labyrinth, which were uncovered at Cnossos.

Daedalus and Icarus

A celebrated Athenian artist, Daedalus was forced to leave the city and found refuge in Crete, where he became architect and sculptor to Minos. After the Minotaur's birth, he designed the labyrinth, a highly intricate maze in which the horrible creature was imprisoned. When Theseus reached Crete to kill the monster, Ariadne, Minos's daughter, asked Daedalus for advice on how to help the youth, and he gave her a magic ball of thread. Minos was angered by Daedalus's action and shut him and his son Icarus in a tower. To escape, Daedalus built wings made of feathers and held together by wax for himself and his son. He then instructed his son on how to use them, cautioning him to fly low, far from the Sun. After the first few shaky seconds, Icarus began to maneuver the wings and, heedless of his father's advice, flew too high in the sky. The heat from the Sun melted the wax that glued the feathers together, and the wretched youth fell into the sea and drowned.

DAEDALUS AND ICARUS
Andrea Sacchi
1640–48
478 | Galleria Doria Pamphilj, Rome

☐ In this painting, the artist portrays Daedalus affectionately arranging the wings he has just invented on the shoulders of his son, Icarus. The boy raises an arm and looks skyward with a faraway expression; his tense look seems to portend his imminent death.

◄◄─────────────────────────────────────

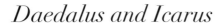

Daedalus and Icarus

───

☐ Side by side with his son Icarus, Daedalus watches helplessly the unfolding tragedy. A terrified Icarus is about to plunge into the sea, for the wax that held his wings together has melted. In some moralizing Renaissance versions of the myth, the boy's tragic fate is brought as an example of the dangers of ambition, and an exaltation of modesty.

THE FALL OF ICARUS
Jacob Pieter Gowy
17th century
Museo del Prado, Madrid

THE DAWN
OF HUMANKIND

The Golden Age 484 • The Silver Age 486 • The Iron Age 488
Astraea 490 • Prometheus 492 • Pandora 502 • Deucalion and Pyrrha 506

THE GOLDEN AGE

According to the ancients, after the creation of the world, the history of humankind was broken into four major ages: the Golden, Silver, Bronze, and Iron Ages. During the Golden Age, men lived in a state of innocence, happy and free from toil, misfortune, or illness. There were no laws to maintain order because they knew neither violence nor war. In this state of grace, of everlasting springtime, men and women lived together peacefully and serenely, eating the fruits of the fertile Earth. They did not age or grow feeble, and when their time did come, Death took them as if in a sleep. After death, they became spirits, benign demons, the custodians of mortal men and women, and wandered about Earth dispensing wealth.

THE GOLDEN AGE
Jean-Auguste-Dominique Ingres
1862
Fogg Art Museum,
Cambridge (Massachusetts)

☐ This painting depicts the state of grace in which humankind lived during the Golden Age. Men and women carry flowers and fruits, while others scatter them from above, an allusion to the bounty of nature that produces them. From the top of a hill the figure of Saturn, guardian god of the Golden Age (also known as the Age of Saturn), towers over everything.

THE SILVER AGE

The beginning of the Silver Age corresponds to the reign of Jupiter, after Saturn was confined to dark Tartarus (see p. 20). The father of the gods reduced the duration of spring (it was eternal in the previous age), and divided the year into four seasons: autumn, winter, a short spring, and summer. From that time on, the air was now hot, now icy cold, depending on the seasons, and men were forced to find shelter, farm the land, and domesticate animals. Hesiod recounts that this generation neither worshipped the gods, nor made sacrifices in their honor; for this reason, Jupiter ended the Silver Age. The Bronze Age was characterizes by crude, fearless, and cruel mortals who spent their time in violent pursuits instead of farming.

☐ This fresco imagines the Silver Age, when men developed agriculture. To the left, a youth is pressing bunches of grapes with his hands, a reference to winemaking, while behind him a man holds an ox and a third carries an animal. On the right side of the scene, women work in the fields; one of them carries a sheaf of wheat.

THE SILVER AGE
Pietro da Cortona
1637
Palazzo Pitti, Florence

THE IRON AGE

The Iron Age was the last and the worst of all; it was characterized by all sorts of ungodliness. Instead of restraint and honesty, deceit and trickery ruled. Whereas the land was previously held in common, now it was divided and fenced off; it was farmed and its bowels were mined in search for the treasures hidden near the frightful river Styx, which instigated evil, for the gold and iron that were extracted and brought to the surface stirred up war and violence. During this age, people lived by robbing each other, and trust vanished. Even Astraea, the goddess of justice, resolved to desert the bloodied Earth. After calling a council of the gods, Jupiter decided, albeit unwillingly, to destroy humankind.

☐ This painting does portrays not the effects of the Iron Age, but the divine council that was called to resolve the situation. Jupiter has convened all the gods to tell them of his decision to send a deluge that will destroy a human race that has become hopelessly violent and corrupt. All the gods of the Greek pantheon are represented, each one with his or her identifying attributes; above them, the king of the gods and his wife are seated on the throne.

THE AGE OF IRON
Jacopo Zucchi
c. 1575
Gallerie degli Uffizi, Florence

ASTRAEA

The daughter of Jupiter and Themis (the Law), and sister of Modesty, Astraea spreads feelings of virtue and justice among the people. She was active particularly during the Golden Age, but when evil and violence plagued the world in the Iron Age, she fled to the heavens and became a constellation.

☐ Astraea materializes in the clouds to a group of shocked peasants. She appears with a lion and with the sword and the scales, her attributes. The artist took inspiration from the second eclogue of Virgil's *Bucolics*, in which the poet recounts the birth of a new Golden Age ushered in by the return to Earth of Astraea, the goddess of justice. The painting seems to hint at other meanings, for it has been interpreted either as a glorification of the House of Medici or a celebration of peace after the end of the devastating Thirty Years' War.

THE RETURN OF ASTRAEA
Salvator Rosa
c. 1640
Kunsthistorisches Museum, Vienna

PROMETHEUS

The son of the Titan Iapetus and the Oceanid Clymene, Prometheus created the first men in the image of the gods by making a paste of rainwater and clay. Later, violating Jupiter's interdiction, he stole a spark of fire from the chariot of the Sun and gave it to man as a gift. A different version of the myth recounts that Prometheus stole the fire from Vulcan's forge. The Titan was held in great consideration by the mortals because, thanks to his gifts, he had enabled the development of the arts and of industry; together with Vulcan and Minerva, he was hailed as a promoter of progress. But Jupiter, angered by the theft, punished both him and men: He ordered Vulcan to chain Prometheus to a rock near Caucasus, where each day an eagle would devour his liver, which would grow back every night. As for men, he sent them Pandora (see p. 502). According to the myth, Prometheus was saved by Hercules, who struck the eagle with one of his powerful arrows and unchained him. Later, Prometheus offered his life to the centaur Chiron, who had been fatally wounded and wanted to die in his place, thus giving his immortality to the Titan (see p. 422).

THE MYTH OF PROMETHEUS
Piero di Cosimo
1515
Alte Pinakothek, Munich

492

□ Prometheus is portrayed in the act of shaping man. His brother Epimetheus kneels on the left. On the right, his task accomplished, Minerva leads him to Olympus.

PROMETHEUS

☐ Holding a lit torch, Prometheus stealthily leaves Olympus. Since the dawn of Greek civilization, several attributes have been attached to his image. At the time of Aeschylus, the great fifth-century BCE playwright, the theft of fire was hailed as a manifestation of that divine wisdom that differentiated man from other living beings, allowing him to achieve extensive knowledge in the arts and the sciences. Hence, Prometheus had made it possible for man to shed his primitive state of ignorance.

PROMETHEUS CARRYING FIRE
Jan Cossiers
c. 1637
Museo del Prado, Madrid

PROMETHEUS

☐ In this canvas, we see Vulcan in his forge, about to chain Prometheus for stealing the fire, an unforgivable offense according to Jupiter. Next to him is Mercury, the divine messenger. The Titan is on the ground in a foreshortened position, his face contorted with pain. Behind Vulcan, we barely glimpse in the chiaroscuro background the sharp-beaked, predatory eagle that will devour his liver each day.

PROMETHEUS BEING CHAINED BY VULCAN
Dirck van Baburen
1623

Rijksmuseum, Amsterdam

PROMETHEUS

☐ In the myth, the cunning Prometheus is bound to a column to prevent him from breaking free. Perched on his knees, the eagle is eating his liver—blood flows from his chest and trickles to the ground. On the opposite side of the scene is the torment of Atlas, the Titan sentenced to support the sky for having dared to rise up against Jupiter during the War of the Titans.

PUNISHMENT OF ATLAS AND PROMETHEUS
Vase painting
550 BCE
Museo Gregoriano Etrusco, Vatican City

PROMETHEUS

☐ His hands on his eyes to signify despair, Prometheus lies on his back as the voracious eagle attacks him. On the opposite side of the composition, Hercules is about to shoot an arrow at the terrifying animal. Jupiter had sworn upon the Styx, the infernal river, that he would never release Prometheus, but when Hercules freed him, he was proud of this feat that gave fame and glory to his son, and did not object. However, so as not to invalidate his oath, he forced Prometheus to wear a ring made from the iron of his chains and a fragment of the rock to which he had been bound.

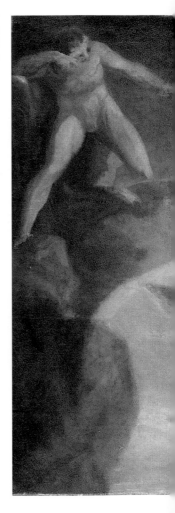

HERCULES FREES PROMETHEUS
Henry Fuseli
1781–85

| Private collection

PANDORA

Prometheus's theft of fire (see p. 492) had repercussions on humankind, in that Jupiter punished them as well. The king of the gods instructed Vulcan to take water and clay and fashion a beautiful maiden in the image of the immortal goddesses, then ordered the other divinities to each present her with a virtue or a quality. The woman was called Pandora, or "she who receives gifts from all the gods." Dressed in a resplendent gown, with a veil held fast on her head by a precious crown, Pandora was escorted to Earth by Mercury, who led her to Epimetheus, brother of Prometheus. Forgetting his brother's advice not to accept gifts from the gods, Epimetheus was charmed by the girl and decided to take her as his bride. Pandora carried with her a jar containing all sorts of misfortunes and disasters from which men had been immune until then. Once the cover was raised, the contents spread to all corners of the world, with the exception of hope, which stayed inside the jar because Pandora closed it before it could escape.

VULCAN INTRODUCES PANDORA
TO THE GODS
Johann Heiss
c. 1660–1704
| Private collection

❑ In the center of the composition, Vulcan shows Pandora to the assembled gods and each one of them presents her with a virtue: Minerva teaches her the womanly arts; Venus gives her grace and a consuming longing for love; and Mercury instills deceit and cunning in her heart.

PANDORA

☐ The lovely maiden is represented with the flower garland that the Hours have given her. In her hands is the famous vase, here rendered as a precious jewelry box. Later versions of the myth relate that the vase, which had been presented as a wedding gift to Epimetheus, contained not evils, but all sorts of good things. Curious about the contents, Pandora opened the vase and all the good things spilled out and flew back to Olympus. For this reason, all sorts of evils befell mankind, leaving hope as man's only comfort.

PANDORA
Alexandre Cabanel
1873
Walters Art Museum, Baltimore

DEUCALION AND PYRRHA

During the Iron Age, violence and ungodliness ruled Earth. Witnessing all sorts of crimes from above, Jupiter called a council of the gods, where he announced his decision to destroy humankind by sending rain from the sky instead of thunderbolts. He expressed his will, then imprisoned Boreas, the north wind, and all the other winds that dispelled the clouds, inside the caves of Aeolus, the god of the winds (see p. 234), and freed Notus, the rain-bearing south wind. He asked his brother Neptune, the god of the seas, for help, and the latter shook the earth with his trident, making the waters spread in all directions; the rivers overflowed their banks, flooding the countryside and drowning everything in their path. Most mortals were swept away by the waves, and those who ran to safety would later starve to death. Only one man and one woman survived: Deucalion, the son of Prometheus, and his wife, Pyrrha—the only just and uncorrupted mortals. Then Jupiter freed the winds and the skies were clear once more, and Neptune ordered the sea to withdraw.

□ The deluge is drowning humankind. A gloomy, dismal atmosphere pervades this painting, in which we see prostrate men and women exhausted by cold and fatigue. The dark, threatening sky is crossed by a winged figure, Notus, the south wind, its wings soaking wet.

DELUGE
Giulio Carpioni
c. 1665
| Private collection

The stones of Deucalion and Pyrrha

When Jupiter decided to let loose a deluge upon the corrupt, violent human race, he also decided to save two just individuals: Deucalion, son of Prometheus, and his wife, Pyrrha, daughter of Epimetheus. Following the advice of Prometheus, the couple built a boat—a sort of large house—where they found shelter for many days, sailing during the deluge. Once the great storm was spent and the waters receded, Deucalion and Pyrrha realized that they were the only surviving human beings. Unsure about what to do, they decided to consult an oracle near the temple of Themis, who suggested that they cover their heads, loosen their clothes, and throw the bones of the Great Mother behind their shoulders. Initially shocked and confused, Deucalion then understood that the bones of the great mother were the stones of the earth. Therefore they began to throw stones behind them: Pyrrha's became women, and Deucalion's men.

☐ In this medieval miniature, Deucalion and Pyrrha are dressed in contemporary wear. They are interpreting the words of the oracle by throwing stones at their back; the stones metamorphosed into men and women and repeopled Earth.

THE STONES OF DEUCALION AND PYRRHA
Miniature
Master of the *Bruges Book of Prayer*
c. 1500
British Library, London

HEROES

Perseus 512 • Bellerophon 526 • Cadmus 528 • Oedipus 530
Theseus 534 • Hercules 540 • Orpheus 586

PERSEUS

Perseus is the son of Jupiter and Danaë (see p. 66) and a grandson of Acrisius, king of Argos. Because an oracle had prophesied that the king would be slain by his daughter's son, he locked his daughter in an underground chamber, but Jupiter entered the girl's prison disguised as a shower of gold; their union begot Perseus. When Acrisius realized what had happened, he put daughter and child in a wooden chest and cast it into the sea. The chest drifted over the waves until it washed ashore on the island of Seriphos, where a fisherman, Dictys, brother of the island's tyrant Polydectes, found them.

Over time, the tyrant fell in love with Danaë and tried to marry her, but she refused, protected by her son. Then the king hatched a plot to eliminate Perseus. He ordered the boy to bring him the head of the horrible Medusa (see p. 468), the Gorgon who turned anyone who looked upon her to stone. Perseus succeeded in slaying the monster and returning to Seriphos, where he turned Polydectes to stone by showing him Medusa's head, then delivered the kingdom to Dictys. The myth also mentions that upon returning from his quest, Perseus freed Andromeda, who was threatened by a sea monster, and made her his bride.

☐ Adrift at sea, Danaë and Perseus land on the coast of the island of Seriphos. Behind them, on the water, is Neptune on his chariot: Jupiter had ordered him to lead mother and son to safety on the island.

DANAË AND PERSEUS ON SERIPHOS
Henry Fuseli
c. 1785–90
Yale University Art Gallery, New Haven

Perseus and Medusa

Perseus was aided by Minerva and Mercury in his quest to slay Medusa. The two gods gave him a mirror and a very sharp reaping hook, then instructed him to go to the land of the three Graiae, monsters who lived in the western reaches of the world, in the country of darkness. Since birth they only had one eye and one tooth, which they shared. The three crones knew where to find nymphs who guarded objects useful to Perseus in his quest: a helmet that made the wearer invisible, a magic knapsack, and a pair of winged sandals. Upon reaching the Graiae, the hero stole the eye and the tooth, and the crones revealed their secret to him. After finding the three objects, Perseus moved against the Gorgons and came upon them asleep. He approached Medusa by walking backward and looking in the mirror that Minerva had given him, so as not to be turned to stone, then he sharply cut off her head with Mercury's reaping hook and put it in the magic bag. He escaped the angry sisters by wearing the helmet that gave him invisibility.

PERSEUS PREPARES TO KILL MEDUSA
Gérard de Lairesse
1665
514 | Museum der Bildenden Künste, Leipzig

☐ The artist has freely interpreted the myth of Perseus and depicts him as he gears up for battle: Minerva helps him don the armor, while Mercury ties his winged sandals. Around them, the nine Muses witness the preparations.

Perseus and Medusa

☐ This metope from the Temple at Selinunte depicts Perseus in the act of cutting off Medusa's head. Next to him is Minerva, who assisted him in the endeavor, and to whom the hero will present with the Gorgon's head in gratitude. In turn, the goddess will place the head on her aegis as a further deterrent against her enemies. Medusa holds a horse tight—Pegasus, born from her chopped-off head. The myth also relates that Perseus collected the Gorgon's blood for its magic properties; while the blood spilled from the left vein was a deathly poison, the one from the right vein could revive the dead, and Minerva allegedly presented it to Aesculapius.

PERSEUS AND MEDUSA
Metope from the Temple at Selinunte
6th century BCE
Museo Archeologico Nazionale, Palermo

◄◄

Perseus and Medusa

☐ As Perseus cut off the head of Medusa, the blood of the dreaded monster generated Chrysaor, the giant of the golden sword, and Pegasus, the winged horse that made Hyppocrene, the spring sacred to the Muses, spring forth by striking his hoof on the ground. Here Perseus holds the head he has just cut off while he tries to hold Pegasus back. In the sky, Minerva and Mercury watch over him. On the ground in the back, in addition to Medusa's body, we glimpse the two other Gorgons, Stheno and Euryale, mourning their sister.

BIRTH OF PEGASUS
Filippo Falciatore
1738
Museo Nazionale della Ceramica
| Duca di Martina, Naples

Perseus and Andromeda

Upon returning from his adventure with the Gorgons, Perseus rode through many lands. In Ethiopia, he came upon a lovely maiden who was chained to a rock in the sea—Andromeda, the daughter of Cepheus and Cassiopeia. A beautiful but proud woman, her mother had dared claim that she was more attractive than the Nereids, marine nymphs and grand-daughters of the god Oceanus. Insulted by such arrogance, they asked Neptune to avenge the offense. The sea god then sent a monster to ravage the kingdom. Through an oracle, he made it clear that no relief would be forthcoming until Andromeda was sacrificed to him. While the maiden was waiting for her terrible fate, Perseus saw her and was smitten. He asked Cepheus for her hand in exchange for saving her. The king gave his consent, and Perseus put up a terrible fight against the marine monster, and married Andromeda.

PERSEUS FREES ANDROMEDA
Hans von Aachen
1603–1604
Schloss Ambras, Innsbruck

☐ Riding Pegasus, his winged horse, Perseus battles the dreaded monster to save Andromeda. This popular image of Perseus on the horse is an adaptation of the original myth that does not include this detail, for Perseus could fly thanks to his winged sandals, and did so, crossing the sky to fight the marine monster.

Perseus and Andromeda

☐ Faithful to the written sources, Veronese represents Perseus flying on his winged sandals to do battle with the monster. The iconography of this duel was very popular, perhaps because it was conducive to manifold interpretations. The hero, protected by Minerva and Mercury, perhaps saves beauty from envy and ignorance; or, in a romantic context, he is the lover who faces all sorts of trials for his beloved. Finally, the myth gave painters the opportunity to set a lovely naked woman in the center of the composition.

PERSEUS AND ANDROMEDA
Paolo Veronese
late 16th century
Musée des Beaux-Arts, Rennes

Perseus and Phineus

During the wedding banquet of Perseus and Andromeda, Phineus, the brother of Cepheus and Andromeda's uncle, claimed that he was the rightful groom, since she had been betrothed to him. But the father rejected his argument, reminding him that, unlike Perseus, he had done nothing to save the girl, who would have died without the young hero's providential actions. Angered, Phineus threw a spear at Perseus but missed him; it was the beginning of a huge brawl. Although the enemy had superior forces, Perseus put up a valiant fight until, finding himself cornered, he took out the head of Medusa and turned Phineus and his friends to stone.

☐ The duel between Perseus and Phineus is set in a classical palace. To the left, some of Phineus's comrades have already been turned into stone, while others are still fighting bravely. On the far right, a comrade of Perseus covers his face to escape the Gorgon's spell. In the center is the hero with the head of Medusa. Behind him, Minerva, his guardian deity, looks on. Phineus is on his knees, begging for his life, but he is already being turned to stone.

PERSEUS TURNS PHINEUS INTO STONE
Jean-Marc Nattier
1718
524 Musée des Beaux-Arts, Tours

BELLEROPHON

Bellerophon is the son of Glaucus, king of Corinth, and Eurymede, and the grandchild of Sisyphus. For reasons that are not clear, he was forced to leave Corinth and found hospitality at the court of king Proetus in Tyrins. Stheneboea, the king's wife, fell in love with him, but he rejected her enticements. The queen took revenge by telling her husband that Bellerophon had tried to seduce her. Then Proetus sent the youth to his father-in-law, Iobates, king of Lycia, and in a sealed letter asked the king to kill him.

Because he could not break the rule of hospitality that forbade the killing of a man with whom one had shared the dining table, Iobates decided to send Bellerophon on a quest to slay the frightful Chimera (see p. 474) who was ravaging the land, sure that the youth would perish, but Bellerophon killed the monster with the aid of Pegasus, the winged horse. Returning victorious, the hero was forced to undergo other trials until Iobates, deeply struck by the hero's bravery, reconciled with him and offered him his daughter Philonoe in marriage.

☐ Bellerophon defeats the terrible Chimera by fighting on the winged horse, Pegasus. According to some versions of the myth, the hero had run into the horse as it was drinking at the spring of Pirene near Corinth and had tamed him with the golden bridles Minerva had given him.

BELLEROPHON, RIDING PEGASUS,
SLAYING THE CHIMERA
Giambattista Tiepolo
c. 1723

Palazzo Sandi, Venice

CADMUS

Cadmus is the founder of Thebes. The son of the Phoenician king Agenor and the brother of Europa, he had been sent by his father in search of Europa, who had been carried off by Jupiter (see p. 58). After a futile search all over Earth, Cadmus decided to consult the oracle at Delphi, who advised him to drop the search and found a new city instead. A white cow with crescent-Moon patches on her flanks would show him the place where the new city would rise; he was to follow the cow.

And so it happened: Having reached the site, Cadmus prepared to sacrifice the cow to Jupiter, and asked his companions to fetch water for the libations from a nearby spring, but a dragon consecrated to Mars, the watchman of the spring, killed them. Because his companions did not come back with the water, Cadmus reached the spring and, after a strenuous battle, slew the monster. Minerva, who was protecting him, sowed the dragon's teeth in the ground, from which sprang armed men, who fought each other until the five surviving ones founded the city of Thebes with Cadmus.

□ The dreadful dragon is devouring one of Cadmus's comrades, while the others lie already dead on the ground. In the background, Cadmus confronts the monster. He would atone for the offense of killing him by serving Mars for eight years.

TWO FOLLOWERS OF CADMUS
DEVOURED BY A DRAGON
Cornelis van Haarlem
1588

National Gallery, London

OEDIPUS

The son of Jocasta and Laius, king of Thebes, Oedipus had been abandoned at birth because an oracle predicted that he would slay his father and wed his mother. He was taken in by the king of Corinth, who raised him as his own son. One day, on the road to Thebes, he met his father; not knowing his identity, Oedipus killed him after a futile quarrel. Proceeding on the road, he encountered the famous Sphinx perched on a rock at the city gates. The Sphinx forced all passersby to solve this riddle: "Which animal walks with four legs in the morning, two in the afternoon, and three in the evening?" Those who failed the test were flung into a deep ravine. Oedipus solved the riddle by replying that it was man, who in infancy walks on all fours, as an adult walks on his two legs, and when old helps himself with a cane. Then the Sphinx took her own life by throwing herself from the rock.

Thus Oedipus entered the city a hero, and was given in marriage Queen Jocasta, who unbeknownst to him was his mother, and sired four children with her. Later, when they learned the truth, Jocasta took her own life and Oedipus blinded himself.

OEDIPUS AND THE SPHINX
(detail)
Attic red-figure *kylix*
c. 460 BCE
Musei Vaticani, Vatican City

☐ Dressed as a wayfarer, Oedipus listens to the Sphinx ask him the famous query. The monster, described as having a woman's face and the body of a winged lion, had been sent by Juno to punish Laius for an old offense.

OEDIPUS

☐ A blinded Oedipus leaves Thebes
in the company of his daughter
Antigone. The myth narrates that,
many years after the slaying of the
Sphinx, a terrible plague struck
Thebes. Having questioned the
oracle, Oedipus was told that
it was necessary to drive Laius's
murderer from the city. Oedipus
anxiously looked for the culprit until
he learned that he had killed his
father and wedded his own mother.
Jocasta killed herself, and Oedipus
tore out his eyes. The Thebans then
drove him from the city; a blind old
man, he left with his daughter
Antigone and roamed the world until
he found peace in Colonus, where
he died.

OEDIPUS AND ANTIGONE
Charles François Jalabert
1843
Musée des Beaux-Arts, Marseille

THESEUS

Aegeus, king of Athens, had failed to sire a child, and he turned to the oracle at Delphi for help; the reply was obscure. He then went to the wise king of Troezen, Pittheus, for advice, and there met Aethra, the king's daughter, and begot Theseus with her. When he left, he placed a sword and sandals under a massive boulder, ordering that the son should deliver them to him in Athens when he was old enough to lift the stone. In truth, he was unwilling to return with Theseus to Athens, because he feared the reaction of the numerous sons of Pallas, his brother; believing that the king had no heirs, they were convinced that at his death they would succeed him.

When Theseus came of age and reached Athens, his father immediately recognized him by the sword and the sandals. A fierce struggle ensued, in which the hero defeated his enemies and became the indisputable lord of Athens with his father. Later, Theseus went on many successful quests, including the celebrated battle with the Minotaur (see p. 476) in the Cretan labyrinth. There the hero was assisted by Ariadne, the king's daughter, who gave him a ball of thread that he used to find the exit after slaying the monster.

THESEUS LIFTING THE STONE
Salvator Rosa
17th century
534 | Private collection

☐ Having reached adulthood, Theseus is with his mother, Aethra, who points out to him the rock under which, years before, his father had hidden his things.

Theseus and the Minotaur

Every year—or every nine, according to a different version of the myth—the Athenians were obliged to sacrifice seven youths and seven maidens to the terrifying Minotaur, who was locked up in the labyrinth that Daedalus had built in Crete (see p. 478). On the fateful date, Theseus decided to sail with the victims and free the city from the cruel tribute. Under the protection of Venus, the hero reached the island and the lovely Ariadne, Minos's daughter, helped him, for she had fallen in love with him and wrested from him a promise that he would marry her. She gave him a magic ball of thread so that, after killing the monster, he could retrace his steps and find the way out of the maze. Theseus confronted the Minotaur, slew him, and fled at night with Ariadne and the young Athenians he had saved from the bloody sacrifice. On the way back, the hero put in at Naxos, where he deserted Ariadne; she later wedded Bacchus (see p. 370).

THESEUS KILLS THE MINOTAUR
Mosaic
4th century CE

Kunsthistorisches Museum, Vienna

❑ Upon reaching the eye of the labyrinth, Theseus confronts the Minotaur and kills him. He then exits the labyrinth by retracing his steps along the yarn Ariadne had given him. In another version of the myth, Ariadne gives Theseus a shining crown she had received from Bacchus as an engagement present; thanks to the light radiating from it, the hero finds his way out of the dark maze.

◀◀

Theseus and the Minotaur

☐ In the more popular version of the myth, Theseus made a stop at Naxos one evening. Ariadne fell asleep and, upon awakening, found herself alone as the ship slowly disappeared over the horizon. Scholars differ on the reasons for her desertion. Some claim that Theseus was already in love with another woman; others that Bacchus himself had commanded him to leave the maiden, having fallen in love with her. A third version suggests that either Minerva or Mercury gave him the order; in any case, Ariadne would later marry Bacchus.

ARIADNE ABANDONED BY THESEUS
Angelica Kauffmann
1774

Private collection

HERCULES

Hercules is the most popular and celebrated hero of classical mythology, the son of Alcmene, who was wedded to Amphitryon, and the grandson of Perseus. Jupiter had taken a fancy to lovely Alcmene and had seduced her by disguising himself as her husband, who had left on a military expedition. As Jupiter's illegitimate son, Hercules became the object of Juno's wrath and hate. The queen of the gods tried to suppress him when he was still in the cradle by sending two snakes, which the infant hero strangled.

Later, after he wed Megara, the daughter of Creon, king of Thebes, Hercules sired three children with her, but in a burst of folly brought about by Juno, slew them with his own hands. To atone for the atrocious sacrilege, Eurystheus, king of Mycenae, whose slave Hercules had become by will of the oracle at Delphi, imposed twelve labors on him. After he completed them, Hercules went on many other quests. He married Deianira, who unwittingly caused the hero's death. Raised to Olympus among the gods, he and Juno reconciled, and he was given the gift of immortality.

THE FARNESE HERCULES
3rd century CE
540 | Museo Archeologico Nazionale, Naples

☐ After completing his labors, Hercules rests against a rock on which he has arranged the lionskin and the club. In his right hand, behind his back, he still carries the golden apples stolen from the garden of the Hesperides.

Baby Hercules strangles the snakes

The morning after Jupiter, disguised as Amphitryon, had conceived Hercules with Alcmene, the real Amphitryon returned home from war and begot with her Iphicles, Hercules's twin brother. When the twins were still suckling, Juno sent two terrible snakes with fiery eyes to their room. While Iphicles, terrified, burst into tears, little Hercules fearlessly clutched their throats with his strong hands and killed them. The parents ran to the cries coming from the nursery and were shocked to find baby Hercules holding the snakes' limp bodies in his tiny hands. That morning, Alcmene questioned the soothsayer Tiresias, who confirmed that Hercules was fated to become an indomitable hero.

☐ This statue portrays the child Hercules calmly grabbing a snake by the throat where, according to the ancients, the reptile's deathly poison resided. It was said that even the gods detested this reptile. Some art historians theorize that the statue portrays either Emperor Caracalla as a child or Annius Verus, the son of Emperor Marcus Aurelius.

BABY HERCULES KILLS THE SNAKES
2nd century CE
| Musei Capitolini, Rome

Hercules slays his own children

Megara was the daughter of Creon, king of Thebes. Creon gave her in marriage to Hercules in gratitude for having defeated the ambassadors of his foe Erginus, king of the Minyans in Orchomenus, and freed the city from a heavy yearly tax. After he wed Megara and sired three children with her, Hercules left. In his absence, the tyrant Lycus came to Thebes, scheming to oust Creon and take his place, and threatened Megara and the children. Upon returning, Hercules slew Lycus and freed his wife and children. But while they were performing thanksgiving sacrifices to the gods, by order of Juno, Lyssa, the spirit of madness, took possession of Hercules. His mind altered by madness, he killed his wife and children, whom he had just rescued from death.

HERCULES STRIKES HIS CHILDREN
WITH ARROWS
Antonio Canova
1799

| Museo Civico, Bassano del Grappa

☐ Juno has caused Hercules to go mad, and he stretches the bow to kill his children as a desperate Megara tries to shield them with her body. In another version of the myth, Hercules spares his wife and, after regaining his senses, breaks his marriage vows and gives Megara in marriage to Iolaus, the son of his brother, Iphicles, to atone for the heinous deed.

The labors of Hercules

THE NEMEAN LION

The first labor that Eurystheus imposed on Hercules in atonement for slaying his own children was to rid Nemea of a fearsome lion that ravaged the land, attacking both residents and cattle. After coming upon it, Hercules struck it with arrows, but to no avail. He then wrestled with the horrible beast until he strangled it with his bare hands. Wanting to use its hide, he tried to skin the animal, but neither iron nor flint nor other objects could cut through it. He finally used the lion's own claws. From that day on he wore the lionskin and used the head as a helmet.

□ This Roman cameo depicts Hercules in the traditional image of squeezing the lion's neck in a deathly grip. The lion was the offspring of Echidna and a sibling of the dreaded Sphinx; according to a popular version of the myth, it had been personally raised by Juno.

HERCULES KILLS THE LION
Cameo
1st century BCE
546 | Museo Archeologico Nazionale, Naples

◀◀

The labors of Hercules

▶▶

THE LERNAEAN HYDRA

The Hydra of Lerna (see p. 472), offspring of Echidna and Typhon, was raised by Juno herself, specifically to be used in one of Hercules's labors. It was a many-headed dragon that breathed fetid vapors from its many throats and killed anyone who dared to approach it, even while it slept. The monster devastated crops and fields and cattle; to defeat her, Hercules used flaming arrows.

It is said that his nephew Iolaus, son of his brother Iphicles, helped him in this feat. And because each one of the monster's heads grew back as soon as Hercules slashed them, Hercules had Iolaus set the nearby forest on fire and cauterized the stumps with burning coals to prevent the heads from growing back. Finally, the hero cut off the central head, believed to be immortal, and buried it underground, sealing the grave with a massive rock. Then he dipped the tips of his arrows in the horrid creature's poisoned blood.

☐ In this vase painting, Hercules battles the Hydra; on the opposite side is the figure of Iolaus clutching one of the animal's several heads, about to burn it with a red-hot coal.

HERCULES KILLS THE HYDRA OF LERNA
(detail)
Vase painting
500–475 BCE
Musée du Louvre, Paris

◀◀

The labors of Hercules

☐ Hercules faces the Hydra, clearly challenging her. The dreaded monster raises all its hissing heads; all around, the ground is strewn with the corpses of those who had the misfortune of running into the monster. In the background, a barren, deserted landscape and the setting sun seem to amplify the drama. Hercules is depicted with his characteristic attributes: the lionskin and the club. He had made the latter as he was about to fight the Nemean lion, fashioning it with his own hands from an uprooted olive tree.

HERCULES AND THE LERNAEAN HYDRA
(detail)
Gustave Moreau
1875
| Musée Gustave Moreau, Paris

The labors of Hercules

THE ERYMANTHIAN BOAR

The third labor that Eurystheus requested was to capture and bring home alive a raging wild boar that lived on Mount Erymanthus. Hercules drove it out and pursued it until the animal, exhausted and surrounded by tall banks of snow, let itself be captured. Hercules hoisted the animal on his shoulders and brought it to Mycenae. At the sight of the dreaded creature, Eurystheus hid inside a large jar that he had set aside as a shelter in case of danger.

☐ In this Renaissance sculpture, after catching the monster boar, Hercules hoists it on his shoulders, helping himself with the club, and carries it to Eurystheus.

HERCULES AND THE CALEDONIAN BOAR
Giambologna
Museo Nazionale del Bargello, Florence

◄◄ ◄

The labors of Hercules

THE STYMPHALIAN BIRDS

These birds lived near Lake Stymphalia in Arcadia, and were a true scourge on the land; they ate the fruits of the fields and worked havoc on the crops. To drive them out of the deep woods where they lived, Hercules used bronze clappers forged by Vulcan, which Minerva had given him. The deafening noise frightened the birds and they flew away from their nests; thus, the hero was able to kill them all with his arrows.

☐ Wearing the lionskin on his arms, Hercules kills the terrible lake birds. In his hand he probably holds the clappers received from Minerva. According to another tradition, the horrible birds of prey also ate men and women and had sharp metal feathers that they hurled, arrowlike, at anyone who threatened them.

HERCULES KILLS THE STYMPHALIAN BIRDS
(detail)
Attic red-figure amphora
500–490 BCE
554 | Musée du Louvre, Paris

◀◀◀

The labors of Hercules

THE CRETAN BULL

There are several versions of the identity of the Cretan bull. According to some, it is the same bull that had abducted lovely Europa; in others, it was the white bull that came from the sea, sent by Neptune to Minos and so handsome that the king had kept it with his cattle and sacrificed another bull to the god (see p. 476). Eurystheus asked Hercules to capture the animal and bring it to him alive. Once he landed in Crete, the hero asked Minos for help but the latter refused, though he allowed him to try and capture the bull. Finally, Hercules succeeded and returned to Eurystheus, who decided to sacrifice the animal to Juno. But since the queen of the gods hated Hercules, she refused the sacrifice and set the animal free.

☐ Hercules tries to seize the bull; behind him, a divinity with spear and helmet in her hand, probably Minerva, watches.

HERCULES AND THE BULL
Attic black-figure amphora
520–500 BCE
Musée du Louvre, Paris

The labors of Hercules

THE MARES OF DIOMEDES
Diomedes was king of Thrace. He owned some fierce, uncontrollable mares that ate human flesh; the king fed them the bodies of strangers who passed through his lands. Eurystheus asked Hercules to put an end to such slaughter and bring him the mares. The hero went on the quest and, having found Diomedes, killed him and fed him to the mares, which immediately became tame and let themselves be led to Mycenae. Then Eurystheus freed them.

☐ The animal in this tapestry recalls the episode of the mares of Diomedes captured by Hercules. Here the hero approaches the tamed mare, which has just devoured her own master.

HERCULES TAMES THE MARES
OF DIOMEDES
Tapestry
Audenarde Manufactory
1545–65

Musée du Louvre, Paris

◄◄ ◄

The labors of Hercules

CERBERUS

This, the twelfth labor of Hercules, consisted in traveling to the netherworld and bringing Cerberus back to Earth. The hero was aided by Minerva and Mercury in this task, for he could not have done it alone, his bravery notwithstanding. He descended into Hades through Tenaerum, in Laconia. Once there, he met many other heroes, including Theseus and Pirithous, who had ventured there to bring Proserpina home (see p. 450) but had lost their way. With Proserpina's consent, Hercules freed Theseus. Then he reached Pluto's throne and asked him if he could take Cerberus to Earth.

The lord of the infernals agreed, but only if Hercules could tame him without using weapons. The hero grasped the dog by the throat and held him until Cerberus stopped wrestling, then retuned to Eurystheus, who was mortally afraid of the dog and hid in his storage jar, which had by then become his customary shelter. Not knowing what to do with Cerberus, Hercules returned him to Hades.

HERCULES AND CERBERUS
(detail)
Black-figure hydria from Cerveteri
530–20 BCE
Musée du Louvre, Paris

☐ Depicted with the club and the lionskin, his traditional attributes, Hercules leads Cerberus by the leash to Eurystheus. Upon seeing the terrifying dog, the king of Mycenae raises his hands, terrified, and hides in the large jar.

◀◀ ◀

The labors of Hercules

THE APPLES OF HESPERIDES

For his eleventh labor, Eurystheus ordered Hercules to enter the garden of the Hesperides and fetch him the famous golden apples, a wedding gift from Gaea to Juno when she had married Jupiter. The tree that bore these wondrous fruits grew in a faraway western land in the garden of the Hesperides, who were the evening nymphs; Ladon, a dragon, watched them day and night.

During his journey westward, Hercules met with many other adventures; he crossed Libya, Egypt, and Asia Minor until he reached Caucasus, where he freed Prometheus by killing the eagle that devoured his liver (see p. 500). It was Prometheus who put him on the right track by suggesting that he should not gather the apples himself, but have Atlas do it. Therefore Hercules went to Atlas, the Titan who bore the world on his shoulders, and offered to take his place if he would go and pick the apples from the magic garden. The giant humored him, but when he returned, finally free, he refused to resume bearing the weight of the heavenly vault; Hercules tricked him and convinced him to take up the globe again, then left with the famous apples.

HERCULES AND ATLAS
Metope from the Temple of Zeus at Olympia
5th century BCE
Archaeological Museum, Olympia

☐ On the right side in this metope, we see Atlas returning victorious with the apples of the Hesperides in his hands, while Hercules supports the sky in his stead, assisted by Minerva behind him.

◄◄

The labors of Hercules

☐ This vase painting depicts the famous garden of the Hesperides, with the mythical golden apple tree at the center guarded by the dragon Ladon. Depending on the version of the myth, the Hesperides were either three or seven nymphs, as in this image. Above the tree is Hercules, recognizable by his traditional attributes. He seems to turn toward Atlas, who is holding up the heavenly vault. Atlas is one of the Titans who fought in the War of the Titans against Jupiter (see p. 22). Defeated, he was sentenced to hold up the vault of the sky.

HERCULES IN THE GARDEN
OF THE HESPERIDES
(detail)
Red-figure krater
340–20 BCE
| Museo Archeologico Nazionale, Naples

◀◀

The labors of Hercules

▶▶

☐ Another version of the myth specifies that it was Hercules, not Atlas, who went into the garden to kill the dragon and steal the apples. Dismayed at the theft, the Hesperides were transformed into trees—an elm, a poplar, and a willow. In this work by Rubens, the hero is depicted as he picks the fruits from the fabled tree; the dragon he has just killed lies at his feet.

HERCULES IN THE GARDEN
OF THE HESPERIDES
Pieter Paul Rubens
c. 1638

◄◄

The labors of Hercules

☐ This precious cup topped by a seashell portrays Hercules holding up the sky in place of Atlas, but it is incomplete, since the identifying club that Hercules originally held in his right hand is missing.

CUP WITH HERCULES SUPPORTING
THE TERRESTRIAL GLOBE
1603–1608

Staatliche Kunstsammlungen, Dresden

Hercules and Alcestis

To atone for the offense of having slain Jupiter's Cyclopes, Apollo had been sentenced to serve Admetus, king of Pherae in Thessaly, as his cattle guardian (see p. 122), and had befriended him because the king had treated him fairly. Thus the god helped Admetus win the hand of lovely Alcestis, daughter of Pelias, king of Iolcus.

Apollo also asked the Parcae, who granted his wish (see p. 314), to allow Admetus to live, once the hour of his death came, provided he could find someone willing to sacrifice his life for him. When the hour came, no one was ready to go to the netherworld in his stead, not even his elderly parents. Only Alcestis did not hesitate to accept death in order to prolong the life of her beloved groom. When Hercules, who was passing through Pherae in search of the mares of Diomedes, learned what had transpired, he descended into Hades, and after wrestling long and hard with Death, took Alcestis and escorted her back to Earth to her husband.

☐ Holding Cerberus by the leash, as if to remind the viewer that he is returning from the netherworld, Hercules puts his hand on young Alcestis's shoulder as he leads her to Admetus, who is sitting on the right side of the fresco.

HERCULES LEADS ALCESTIS TO ADMETUS
mid-4th century CE
Catacomba di via Latina, Rome

Hercules and Antaeus

During his long journey in search of the garden of the Hesperides, Hercules passed through Libya, where he met Antaeus, a giant son of Neptune and Gaea who forced all passersby to wrestle with him; he would then offer the lifeless bodies of the defeated strangers to his father. This giant was invincible as long as he touched the ground, from which he drew his gigantic strength. But Hercules grasped him by the hips and held him in the vice of his powerful arms, raising him away from the ground, until Antaeus lost all his strength and died.

☐ In this powerful bronze by Pollaiuolo, Hercules seizes Antaeus by the waist and pulls him to himself. His face grimacing with pain and his legs kicking the air, the giant tries to break free from Hercules's mortal grip by levering himself with his left arm on the hero's head.

HERCULES AND ANTAEUS
Antonio del Pollaiuolo
c. 1475
| Museo Nazionale del Bargello, Florence

Hercules and Omphale

Because he had unjustly killed Iphitus, son of King Eurytus, in a fit of madness, the oracle at Delphi mandated that Hercules sell himself as a slave and live as one for three years. He was bought by Omphale, queen of Lydia, and while he was in her service, he went on further quests. But what mythographers like to recount is that the queen made his slavery less onerous by taking him as her lover.

Living in intimacy with Omphale, Hercules began to wear women's clothes and spin wool, while the queen wore the lionskin and held the club in mockery. It is also said that while Hercules was in the service of the queen, Pan fell in love with her. One night he entered her chamber, but was deceived by Hercules's disguise and slipped into the hero's bed, where he was immediately kicked out.

☐ Omphale embraces Hercules, who sits next to her. The queen is wearing the lionskin and holds the club, while Hercules, covered in damask drapery, holds a distaff in his left hand. Next to them, Cupid reveals the amorous nature of this scene. This episode was popular particularly in Baroque art, as it illustrated woman's power over man.

HERCULES AND OMPHALE
François Le Moyne
1724
Musée du Louvre, Paris

Hercules and Achelous

Having fallen in love with Deianira, daughter of Oeneus, king of Calydon in Aeolia, Hercules asked her hand in marriage, but she had several other suitors, including the river god Achelous, who could take on various forms. Seeing the famous hero and the god, the other suitors withdrew from the contest, leaving Achelous and Hercules to wrestle for the hand of the lovely maiden. After resisting Hercules's attacks, Achelous was exhausted and began to take on various disguises, first becoming a snake, then a bull, but the hero defeated him by grabbing him by the throat, flooring him, and breaking off one of his horns.

☐ Set in a leafy Italian Renaissance landscape, Hercules wrestles with Achelous turned into a bull, and is about to break off his horn. The legend also narrates that the naiads (water nymphs) filled the horn with fruits and scented flowers, turning it into a sacred object, the cornucopia, symbol of abundance. Also, the river that runs through the landscape is probably another representation of Achelous.

LANDSCAPE WITH HERCULES
BATTLING ACHELOUS
Domenico Zampieri, known as Domenichino
1621–22
| Musée du Louvre, Paris

Nessus and Deianira

After their wedding, Hercules traveled to Trachis with his wife, Deianira. Along the way, the couple reached the river Evenus, which had strong, swift currents. The centaur Nessus approached them, offering to carry Deianira to the opposite shore, while Hercules would cross the river alone. Hercules threw his weapons to the opposite shore and crossed the river, but once on the other side, he heard his wife's desperate cries and saw that the centaur was running away with the terrified bride on his back. Hercules grabbed his bow and fired one of his deadly arrows, hitting the centaur, who fell to the ground. Aware that his blood had been poisoned by the Hydra's blood in which Hercules had dipped his arrows (see p. 548), in revenge the dying Nessus gave Deianira his bloodied tunic, falsely telling her to keep it because it would guarantee that Hercules would be true to her forever.

□ This bronze group represents the centaur Nessus trying to abduct Deianira, whose beauty had seduced him, and enraging Hercules. The centaur violently grabs Hercules's bride as she writhes and struggles in vain to get free, her arms raised in a gesture of despair.

NESSUS AND DEIANIRA
Giambologna
c. 1587

| Staatliche Kunstsammlungen, Dresden

Nessus and Deianira

 Hercules embraces a happy, relieved Deianira. Slung on his shoulder is the quiver with the poisoned arrows; the bow lies on top of his club on the ground. At bottom left is the lifeless body of Nessus, the centaur who had attempted to kidnap the hero's young bride and who will nevertheless succeed in his revenge. Hiding behind a tree is Cupid, the god of love, who seems to have just shot one of his arrows.

HERCULES, DEIANIRA, AND NESSUS
Bartholomaeus Spranger
c. 1585
| Kunsthistorisches Museum, Vienna

Death of Hercules

While Hercules was away from home, Fame, who loved to confuse falsehood with truth, let Deianira know that her husband had fallen for another woman. A desperate Deianira then sent their friend Lichas to Hercules with a tunic dipped in Nessus's blood, for according to the centuar's lies, it would strengthen her husband's love for her (see p. 578). As soon as the hero wore the tunic, the poison began to eat away his flesh. Suspecting that the innocent Lichas was guilty of this betrayal, Hercules threw him into the sea; then he climbed Mount Etna and there, still racked with atrocious pain, built a funeral pyre, gave Philoctetes (see p. 694) his bow and arrows, and asked him to light the pyre on which he was lying. Then Jupiter, in agreement with the other gods and even Juno, raised him to Olympus on a cloud.

☐ After laying the Nemean lionskin on the pyre, Hercules throws himself upon it. Kneeling before him is Philoctetes, to whom the hero has donated his bow and arrows in gratitude for setting fire to the pyre. From on high, Jupiter follows the scene.

HERCULES ON THE FUNERAL PYRE
Luca Giordano
1697–1700
San Lorenzo Monastery, El Escorial

Hercules at the crossroads

According to a moralizing tale by Prodicus, a sophist friend of Socrates and Plato, Hercules was wont to stroll reflecting about life, when one day at a crossroads he met two lovely maidens, who represented Virtue and Vice. While the first one expressed purity and dignity, the second one was arrogant and voluptuous. And it was Vice that showed to him the easy path, promising a life filled with joy and pleasure and without pain.

The other maiden, on the contrary, pointed to a steep, rocky path that was difficult to climb but at whose top a large reward awaited, since the gods give nothing without effort, there is neither victory without struggle nor reaping without sowing. When the women disappeared, Hercules, alone once more, chose the steep, difficult path.

HERCULES AT THE CROSSROADS
Pompeo Batoni
c. 1753
Liechtenstein Museum, Vienna

□ Sitting under a tree, Hercules must choose between Vice and Virtue, personified in the two female figures that flank him. Vice is personified as Venus, as indicated by the rose; seated at his side, she offers him the divine flower, while in the other hand she holds a mask to signify that behind lust lies deceit. In front of the hero stands Minerva, who symbolizes Virtue; she points out to him the steep upward path that leads to the Temple of Fame.

ORPHEUS

The son of the river god Oeagrus and the Muse Calliope, Orpheus is the most famous musician and singer of antiquity. The inventor of the kithara, his singing could bewitch wild beasts and soften the hearts of the fiercest man. In this best-known myth, Orpheus descends into Hades to rescue his beloved bride, Eurydice. One day, as she was strolling along a river, she was noticed by a shepherd, Aristaeus, who fell in love with her and tried to abduct her. While running from him, she was bitten by a snake and died.

A desperate Orpheus resolved to journey down to the underworld and rescue his beloved from death. With his mellow songs he bewitched monsters, the souls of the dead, and even the gods of Hades, who were moved to pity and freed Eurydice—on one condition: that Orpheus walk before his wife as they climbed back to Earth, and that he turn to look at her only after reaching sunlight. Almost at the exit of the underworld, the bard could not resist his longing for his beloved bride; he turned around, and Eurydice died a second time.

❑ This Roman mosaic presents the classic image of Orpheus seated under a tree, playing the lyre. Around him farm animals and wild beasts seem spellbound by his song. This subject was very popular in the ancient Roman world; in early Christian art, it was adapted to represent the Messiah.

ORPHEUS AND THE ANIMALS
Mosaic
3rd century CE
586 Museo Archeologico Nazionale, Palermo

ORPHEUS

☐ In the center of the composition, Orpheus holds Eurydice by the hand, having cast a spell with the power of his kithara (the artist has interpreted it as a violin) on the denizens of Hades. He wears a laurel wreath, symbol of his immortal fame as a poet. In the background, Pluto and Proserpina watch the couple leave, while on the left the three Parcae—Nona, Decima, and Morta—spin the thread of human life. In the foreground on the right, we see Tantalus from the back, tormented by eternal thirst and hunger; in the far background is Sisyphus and his famous rock.

ORPHEUS AND EURYDICE
Jean Raoux
1718–20

The J. Paul Getty Museum, Los Angeles

The death of Orpheus

The legend narrates that after he lost Eurydice a second time, Orpheus returned to the underworld to look for her, but was stopped by the incorruptible Charon, who forbade him to enter Hades. After he lost his beloved, the young bard refused all further contact with women. There are different versions of his death. In the most common one, he was dismembered by the women of Thrace, who were seized by a Bacchic frenzy. But even the reasons for murdering the bard differ; perhaps they were angry at him because they felt that his faithfulness to his wife, even after her death, was insulting to them. After the Thracian women tore his body to pieces, they threw it in a river that carried the pieces to the sea. It is said that his head and lips even reached Lesbos, which was later considered the island of lyric poetry.

☐ The women of Thrace, deranged by the wine they drank in honor of Bacchus, kill the poet. The myth recounts that just before killing him, they killed the birds, the wild beasts, and the snakes that had been enchanted by his sweet melody. Then, their hands still dripping blood, they attacked him furiously.

THE DEATH OF ORPHEUS
Albrecht Dürer
1494
Hamburger Kunsthalle, Hamburg

The death of Orpheus

☐ The artist has interpreted the death of Orpheus with originality, imagining a less famous scene. In this adaptation of the myth, a young girl discovers the head and the kithara of the poet. The head seems joined to the musical instrument as one object, underscoring the symbolic union between Orpheus and his art. The myth also recounts that after he died, his lyre was brought up to the heavens, where it became a constellation.

ORPHEUS
Gustave Moreau
1865
592 | Musée d'Orsay, Paris

THE GREAT EXPLOITS

Meleager and the Hunt for the Wild Boar 596
The Expedition of the Argonauts 604

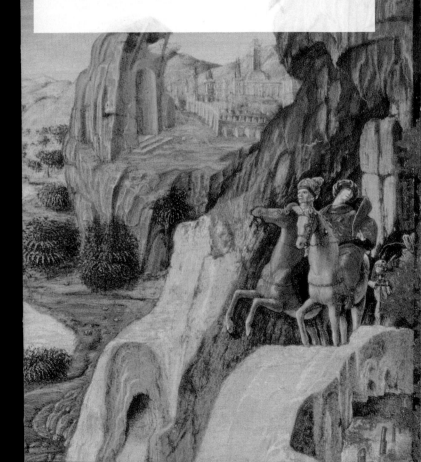

MELEAGER AND THE HUNT FOR THE WILD BOAR

Meleager was a son of Oeneus, king of the Calydon Aetolians, and Althaea. After an unusually bountiful harvest season, Oeneus had offered the customary tributes to all the divinities, but had forgotten Diana. The humiliated goddess sent a ferocious wild boar with flaming eyes that rampaged through the countryside around Calydon, forcing the population to flee for safety inside the city walls. Meleager decided to confront the wild beast and organized an expedition of the bravest heroes, including fair Atalanta (see p. 194), a lovely huntress with whom Meleager immediately fell in love. During the hunt, the furious beast, driven from its den, attacked the hunters, who tried to knock it down but failed. Atalanta was the first to wound the animal with an arrow, and Meleager finished it with a forcefully thrown spear. The youth presented the trophy to Atalanta, angering his companions, especially his two maternal uncles; when they tried to seize the trophy, he killed them.

☐ Meleager wears the chlamys, the mantle of soldiers and hunters. To his right is a dog, an allusion to the hunt, and to the left, the head of the boar he killed.

MELEAGER
Roman copy of an original by Skopas
from *c.* 350 BCE
596 | Musei Vaticani, Vatican City

MELEAGER AND THE HUNT FOR THE WILD BOAR

☐ This scene, in a clearing by a deep forest, shows Meleager about to deal the mortal blow to the boar. The poet Ovid narrates that the young hunter had first thrown a spear that had hit the ground, but a second one had mortally struck the beast. Atalanta, who had wounded the boar, watches the scene and moves back as if threatened by the beast. The hero is assisted by his dogs; the other hunters in the back are about to reach him.

HUNT OF MELEAGER
(detail)
Jacques Raymond Brascassat
1825
Musée des Beaux-Arts, Bordeaux

598

MELEAGER AND THE HUNT FOR THE WILD BOAR

☐ This painting by Jordaens depicts the scene after the hunt, when Meleager presents Atalanta with the trophy of the boar. The maternal uncles, visible behind the couple, have just snatched the trophy from the girl, and Meleager is about to draw his sword to avenge the offense. To the left of the composition are the other hunters, some of whom are identifiable, such as Castor and Pollux (the Dioscuri, see p. 38), who irrupt into the scene; before them in the foreground, two figures point frenetically to the woods where the hunt took place.

MELEAGER AND ATALANTA
Jacob Jordaens
c. 1628

| Museo del Prado, Madrid

The death of Meleager

According to Ovid, when Meleager was born, the Parcae appeared to Althaea, his mother, prophesying that the boy's life would last as long as a coal that was burning in her hearth. After this dire announcement, the three deities left and immediately Althaea removed the burning coal from the fire and doused it with water, then hid it. But when Meleager killed his maternal uncles to punish them for their rudeness to Atalanta, Althaea, enraged, made a great fire and took the fateful coal out of hiding. Torn between her love for her brothers and for her son, four times she was about to throw the branch into the fire and checked herself, but in the end her wrath won. After slaying the Calydon boar, Meleager was returning to the city with a triumphant retinue when he was struck by a mysterious heat and died. His sisters grieved so much for his death that a still-angry Diana metamorphosed them into chickens.

□ Meleager lies on the bed racked by a feverish heat caused by the live coal that his mother has thrown into the fire. His despairing sisters attend to him. Under the bed are the hero's arms, and beside him a dog that recalls the famous hunt.

THE DEATH OF MELEAGER
2nd century BCE
Musée du Louvre, Paris

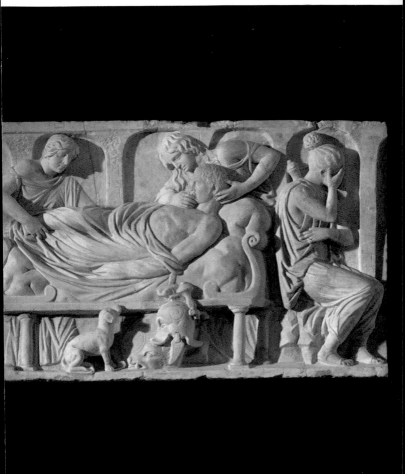

THE EXPEDITION OF THE ARGONAUTS

The origins of the fabled Argonaut expedition are to be sought in Thebes, where king Athamas took as his first wife Nephele, the goddess of clouds, with whom he sired the twins Phrixus and Helle. Later the king repudiated her and wedded Ino, begetting with her Learchus and Melicertes. A wounded Nephele left the city, and soon after the land was hit by a long drought, perhaps sent by an avenging Nephele, or part of a devious plot by Ino, who was bent on suppressing her stepchildren.

To remove this calamity, Athamas consulted an oracle, who commanded the sacrifice of Phrixus and Helle. But Nephele rescued her children by sending a ram with golden fleece that she had received from Mercury. The ram took the young twins on its back and flew them in the sky. During the flight, Helle fell off into the sea, while Phrixus reached Colchis safe and sound; King Aeëtes took him in and gave him his daughter Chalciope in marriage. Then Phrixus sacrificed the ram to Jupiter and made a gift of the Golden Fleece to the king, who nailed it to an oak tree in a grove consecrated to Mars, the god of war, and placed a dragon to guard it.

PHRIXUS AND HELLE
1st century CE
Museo Archeologico Nazionale, Naples

604

□ Riding the ram that Nephele has sent to rescue them, Phrixus tries to help his sister, Helle, but she falls into the sea and drowns. It is from her that the Hellespont took its name.

Jason and Pelias

Jason was a son of Aeson, the legitimate king of Iolcus, who had been overthrown by his half brother Pelias. Aeson was able to save his son from Pelias's persecution by entrusting him to the centaur Chiron, who educated him in all the arts. Having come of age, Jason returned to Iolcus to claim his father's throne. Pelias promised to cede power to him on condition that Jason retrieve the famous Golden Fleece that Phrixus had presented to Aeëtes in Colchis, and which was now guarded in a grove sacred to Mars.

This is how the expedition of the Argonauts originated. Jason ordered the construction of the largest and sturdiest ship ever built and called it *Argo* in honor of its skilled builder, Argus. He then invited the most celebrated heroes of his time to sail with him to Colchis.

☐ Imagined as a fifteenth-century ship, the *Argo* is about to set sail toward Colchis. At the stern is Hercules, identifiable by his club and the lionskin. He is escorting Jason for part of the trip and will disembark in Mysia. The Argonauts (the name given to the heroes that took part in this expedition) were numbered either fifty or fifty-five, depending on the sources, and among them, in addition to Hercules, were Orpheus, Meleager, Theseus, and the Dioscuri.

THE ARGO
Lorenzo Costa
1484–90
606 | Museo Civico degli Eremitani, Padua

Jason and Medea

After meeting with all sorts of adventures, the Argonauts finally set foot in the land of King Aeëtes, where the most difficult challenge awaited them: retrieving the Golden Fleece. Medea, the king's daughter and the grandchild of Sol the Sun god, fell in love with Jason and decided to help him in his difficult quest. Aeëtes promised Jason the Fleece, provided he succeeded in yoking two fire-breathing bulls, plowing a field with them, and sowing the teeth of a dragon killed by Cadmus (see p. 528).

After wresting from Jason a marriage promise, Medea helped him. Still, when Jason overcame these challenges, the king reneged on his promise, claiming that he had been helped. Then Jason decided to act without the king's consent, and he seized the Fleece and sailed away with Medea. He later repudiated Medea in favor of Glauce, daughter of the king of Corinth. Medea avenged the offense by killing the rival and her own children.

□ Medea is usually considered a sorceress. In this painting, she is about the brew her magic potions. Behind her, in the trees, is the famous Golden Fleece, while on the opposite side is the *Argo*, the ship that will carry her away with Jason.

MEDEA
Anthony Frederick Sandys
1868
608 | Museum and Art Gallery, Birmingham

Jason tames the bulls

Medea aided Jason in taming the monstrous bulls that Vulcan had given to Aeëtes by supplying a miraculous ointment that protected him from fire and iron; he spread it on his body and shield before taming the ferocious animals. She also warned Jason that the teeth of the dragon that he was to sow when plowing the field would instantly generate an army of warriors that would attack him. She advised him to throw a rock into their midst. He did as he was told, and the warriors attacked one another, accusing each other of throwing the rock, and died in the fight. Thus Jason succeeded in yoking the bulls, plowing the field, and sowing the dragon's teeth.

☐ Jason stands before the bulls, which are blowing fire from their nostrils. The huge, threatening animals advance towards him, seemingly attracted by a bunch of herbs he holds in his hands, probably an allusion to Medea's magic potion.

JASON TAMING THE BULLS OF AEËTES
(detail)
Jean-François de Troy
1742
The Barber Institute of Fine Arts, Birmingham

The theft of the Golden Fleece

Although Jason had won the challenge, because Medea had lent a hand, Aeëtes refused to hand over the Golden Fleece and even conspired to destroy Jason's ship and its crew. But before he could carry out his plans, Jason captured the Fleece, thanks to Medea. During the night, the two entered the sacred grove, where the sleepless dragon who guarded the Fleece immediately saw them and began chasing them. With a sweet voice, Medea invoked the help of the god of sleep, dipped a juniper branch into a magic potion, and sprayed the monster's eyes with it; the dragon fell asleep. Jason detached the Golden Fleece from the oak tree, and they both reached the ship and sailed away from the Colchian shores.

☐ In the center of the composition is the tree—an oak according to some sources—from which the Golden Fleece hangs. Winding itself around the trunk, the snake-shaped dragon is attracted by Medea's spell as she offers it a cup with a powerful sleeping potion, while Jason steals the Fleece.

THE THEFT OF THE GOLDEN FLEECE
Volute krater
330–10 BCE
612 | Museo Archeologico Nazionale, Naples

Medea rejuvenates Aeson

Returning to Iolcus, Jason found his father greatly advanced in age, as if he only had a short time left to live. Saddened, he asked his wife if she could lengthen his father's life with her magic arts. During a full Moon, Medea climbed on her cart pulled by winged dragons and went in search of herbs for her potions. When she returned, she prepared two altars, prayed to the gods of the netherworld, and offered a sacrifice to them, then asked that Aeson be brought before her. She slashed the old man's throat and replaced his blood with the potion she had prepared; immediately, the king was rejuvenated. Seeing this, the daughters of Pelias—Aeson's brother, who had chased him from the throne—beseeched Medea to do the same for their father, but she deceived them and took revenge by killing Pelias.

☐ In the foreground, Medea performs ablutions in preparation for the rite that will restore Aeson's youth. Behind her is the cauldron in which she is to prepare the magic filter with the herbs she gathered in the countryside for nine days and nine nights on her dragon-pulled cart, which is visible to the right. To the left, the sorceress is about to begin the propitiatory rites at the two altars she built in honor of Hecate (see p. 458), the goddess of youth.

THE SPELL OF MEDEA
Ludovico Carracci
1584
| Palazzo Fava, Bologna

The revenge of Medea

After Pelias's murder, his son Acastus inherited the kingdom. He was determined to avenge his father, so Jason and Medea fled and found shelter in Corinth, where they lived happily for many years with their two children. But one day, Jason deserted Medea to marry Glauce (Creusa), daughter of Creon, king of Corinth. Consumed with jealousy and wrath, Medea decided to punish the offense by presenting Glauce, via her children, with a lovely bridal gown and a diadem dipped in poison. As soon as the bride put them on, the poison set her flesh on fire; she was burned to death, along with her father, who had come to her aid, and the flames destroyed the palace. Still unsatisfied, Medea killed her own children, then fled to Athens on a chariot pulled by winged dragons, which the god Sol had given her.

MEDEA ABOUT TO KILL HER CHILDREN
Eugène Delacroix
1862

Musée du Louvre, Paris

☐ Delacroix has imagined the episode where Medea kills her children in a cave, rather than at home. The sorceress presses the children to her while seizing a sharp dagger. The younger one tries in vain to break free. Medea turns around and looks into the distance, her face covered by a dark shadow.

THE TROJAN WAR

Thetis 620 • Paris 626 • Helen 632 • Agamemnon 636 • Achilles 642
Patroclus 684 • Hector 690 • Philoctetes 694 • The Wooden Horse 696
Laocoön 702 • Cassandra 704

THETIS

The daughter of Nereus and Doris and a grandchild of Oceanus, Thetis is perhaps the most famous of the Nereids, the sea nymphs. Legend has it that Jupiter and Neptune were both enamored of this maiden and wanted to wed her, but a prophecy of Themis, the Law, had warned both gods that the sons they would sire would be more powerful than their fathers.

For this reason, Thetis was given in marriage to Peleus, a mortal, king of Phthia in Thessaly. At the wedding reception held on Mount Pelion, all the gods were invited, with the exception of Eris, the goddess of discord. Offended, she threw to the guests the famous apple that would ultimately provoke the Trojan War (see p. 630). From the union of Thetis and Peleus was born Achilles, the famous hero and protagonist of the *Iliad*. Told by an oracle that her half-mortal son would die in combat, Thetis tried all sorts of stratagems to protect him, but eventually had to yield to what Fate had in store for him.

□ In the center of the composition, Peleus and Thetis are surrounded by the Olympian gods, while Apollo and the Muses play behind them. In the upper right corner, Eris, the goddess of discord, flies toward the gathering and is about to throw the famous apple in the center of the wedding table.

THE WEDDING OF PELEUS AND THETIS
Hendrick de Clerck
1606–1609
620 | Musée du Louvre, Paris

Jupiter and Thetis

Thetis appears primarily in the *Iliad*. During the Trojan War, after the dispute between Achilles and Agamemnon over who should take possession of Briseis (see p. 656), Thetis rose from the sea waves and tried to comfort her son. Then she ascended Olympus and sat by Jupiter, begging him to avenge the offense inflicted on Achilles; she asked him to make the Trojans win on the battlefield, at least until the Greeks paid to her son the tributes to which he was entitled by right. Jupiter acceded to her request with a nod of his head that shook the entire mountain.

☐ The artist has faithfully interpreted the passage of the *Iliad* where Thetis, about to sit beside Jupiter, circles his knees with her right hand and with her left strokes his chin, as if trying to get his attention. The figure of Jupiter enthroned is majestic, hieratical: the image of the supreme ruler. Next to him is the sacred eagle; the base of the throne is carved with scenes from the War of the Giants, in which the father of the gods is depicted fighting on his chariot (see p. 24). In the background, we glimpse Juno, who looks on, unseen.

JUPITER AND THETIS
Jean-Auguste-Dominique Ingres
1811
Musée Granet, Aix en Provence

Thetis asks Vulcan to forge the arms of Achilles

After slaying Patroclus in a duel, Hector undressed the corpse and wore the armor that Achilles had lent to his friend. Upon learning of Patroclus's death (see p. 664), Thetis ran to her grief-stricken son and tried to comfort him, promising him new arms with which to vindicate Patroclus. Then she went to Vulcan's forge; immediately, the god of fire set to work, throwing bronze, tin, gold, and silver into the furnace. Then he sat at the anvil and began to forge the metal to fashion the large, heavy, finely chased shield, armor, helmet, and shin guards of Achilles.

THETIS RECEIVES FROM VULCAN
THE ARMS OF ACHILLES
(detail)
Attic red-figure *kylix* from Vulci
Foundry painter
490–80 BCE
624 | Antikensammlung, Berlin

□ Working in his forge, Vulcan hammers the finishing touches on the helmet of Achilles. Standing before him, Thetis holds the mighty shield and the spear; the greaves hang on the wall behind them. Traditionally, the myth sets Vulcan's forge either on the island of Lemnos or in one of the southern Italian volcanoes; only Homer sets it on Mount Olympus.

PARIS

Also known as Alexander, Paris is the son of Priam and Hecuba, the Trojan sovereigns. According to the tradition, before his birth, Hecuba had dreamed of a flaming torch. She related the dream to her husband, who asked the soothsayers; they prophesied that the child would cause the destruction of Troy. For this reason, as soon as he was born, the child was left to the elements on Mount Ida, where he was found by shepherds, who took him in and raised him.

Once an adult, Paris returned to Troy and was recognized by his sister Cassandra. Happy to have found the son that he had mourned as dead, Priam welcomed him with honors. The most celebrated episode is that of the judgment of Paris (see p. 630), which allegedly caused the Trojan War. According to the legend, Paris slew Achilles by shooting an arrow in his vulnerable heel (see p. 680).

☐ In this Renaissance version of the myth, Hecuba seems to be in a deep sleep; behind her, a genie of sleep—perhaps the personification of a nightmare—shows the queen a lit torch that sends forth snakes. The artist has illustrated a version of the myth reported by Hyginus, a second-century BCE Roman author who wrote the *Fabulae* (Stories).

THE DREAM OF HECUBA
Giulio Romano
c. 1536
Palazzo Ducale, Mantua

PARIS

☐ As soon as Hecuba gave birth to Paris, the infant was delivered to servants with orders to kill him. Moved to pity, they instead left him on Mount Ida, where some shepherds found him and raised him like their own child. In another version of the myth, Priam ordered his servant Agelaus to abandon the child, but a she-bear suckled him for a few days, and, having found him still alive, the servant decided to take him in and raise him as his own son.

THE INFANT PARIS IS DELIVERED
TO THE SHEPHERDS
Vincenzo Camuccini
c. 1850

Accademia Nazionale di San Luca, Rome

The judgment of Paris

At the wedding of Thetis and Peleus (see p. 620) all the gods except Eris, goddess of discord, were invited. Scorned, she threw a golden apple, inscribed "to the fairest of them all," on the banquet table. Juno, Venus, and Minerva all claimed the prize, until Juno asked Mercury to escort them to Mount Ida so that Paris might judge who among the three goddesses deserved the prize.

Once before the prince, each goddess promised him privileges and protection: Juno promised that he would rule the entire world and become the wealthiest of men; Minerva promised that he would be the most valiant, wise, and famous mortal, skilled in all the arts; finally, Venus promised that he would marry Helen, stepdaughter of Tyndareus, the fairest of all women. Paris awarded the apple to Venus; later, driven by the goddess, he abducted Helen, who was the wife of Menelaus, from Sparta and took her to Troy, thus giving rise to the famous war.

☐ Paris pronounces his verdict and is about to award the apple to a naked Venus, escorted by the inseparable Cupid. Next to the goddess of love stands a stern-faced, fully armed Minerva, and behind them, on a cloud, is Juno with a peacock, an animal sacred to her.

THE JUDGMENT OF PARIS
Jean-Antoine Watteau
c. 1718–21
| Musée du Louvre, Paris

HELEN

The daughter of Jupiter and Leda (see p. 38) and the wife of
Menelaus, king of Sparta (with whom she had a daughter,
Hermione), Helen was the fairest of all women. For her
honor, the Greeks fought the Trojan War. After the judgment
of Paris (see p. 630), Venus counseled Paris to sail to Sparta,
where Menelaus welcomed him. Because the king had to
leave suddenly for Crete, Helen entertained the guests. Taking
advantage of Menelaus's absence, Paris kidnapped her and took
her to Troy. Soon, peaceful delegations arrived asking for
Helen's return, but in vain. The abduction of Helen was the
cause for the famous war, and during the conflict she lived in
the royal palace as Paris's wife. Understandably, the Trojans
hated her. After Troy fell, Menelaus and Helen met near the
temple of Venus and the goddess led them to reconcile.

☐ Helen is led away while Paris's
comrades shield the couple, prevent-
ing the Greeks from coming near the
ship. There are several versions of
Helen's abduction; in some, she was
willing; in others it was Tyndareus,
her stepfather, who granted Paris
permission to take her as bride.

THE RAPE OF HELEN
Gavin Hamilton
c. 1770

HELEN

☐ Menelaus seems to threaten Helen, who steps back. Between them is Cupid, the god of love, intent on stopping him. The female figure behind Helen could be Venus, her guardian deity. It is said that when Menelaus saw his wife while Troy was burning, he was overcome with love and forgave her; in any case, several versions exist of this final episode. In one of them, upon the death of Paris, Helen married Deiphobus, a younger brother of Paris and Hector. When Troy was conquered, Ulysses and Menelaus attacked the couple's residence and, thanks to Helen's complicity, Menelaus killed Deiphobus, then pulled his former wife by the hair, determined to kill her, but Ulysses saved her.

HELEN AND MENELAUS ARE REJOINED
Red-figure krater
450–40 BCE

AGAMEMNON

Agamemnon was king of Mycenae and a brother of Menelaus. He was married to Clytemnestra, who was Helen's sister, and had sired three children with her: Electra, Iphigenia, and Orestes. After Helen's abduction, Menelaus asked his brother for help, and the latter led the best Greek princes and their soldiers in the expedition against Troy. On their way, the fleet was blocked in the port of Aulis by a lack of winds. Consulted on the matter, the soothsayer Calchas revealed that Diana was responsible for the contrary winds, for during a hunting party, the king of Mycenae had killed a doe sacred to the goddess. To placate her, he would need to sacrifice his own daughter Iphigenia. Out of ambition, and for the good of all, Agamemnon agreed and the fleet resumed its journey.

In the tenth year of the siege of Troy, the celebrated quarrel between Achilles and Agamemnon broke out (see p. 656); the *Iliad*, Homer's epic poem about the last year of the Trojan War, begins with this episode. After the long, drawn-out war, Agamemnon returned home, where his wife Clytemnestra murdered him to avenge her lost daughter.

THE SACRIFICE OF IPHIGENIA
Giambattista Crosato
1740
636 | Private collection

☐ In this painting, Iphigenia has accepted her tragic fate and is about to be sacrificed, when Diana, moved to pity, sends a young doe to lead her to Tauris, where she would become a priestess of the goddess.

AGAMEMNON

□ This mosaic narrates the episode of Chryses, a priest of Apollo; he kneels before Agamemnon, begging him to release his daughter Chryseis (see p. 656), who had been kidnapped during a raid near Thebes, a city in Mysia. Because the king refused and rudely dismissed him, Chryses turned to Apollo for vengeance. The god answered his prayers and sent a terrible plague to the Achaean camp. When the soothsayer Calchas was questioned, he replied that the Sun god had sent the scourge because he had been deeply offended by the outrageous treatment of his priest, and that his rage would be placated only after Chryseis was freed and returned to her father.

CHRYSEIS AND AGAMEMNON
Mosaic
4th century CE
Archaeological Museum, Nabeul, Tunisia

AGAMEMNON

☐ After his return from the Trojan War, Agamemnon was murdered by his wife, Clytemnestra, who in the meantime had taken as a lover Aegisthus, a cousin of the king. This was her way of avenging the sacrifice of their daughter Iphigenia. There are several versions of Clytemnestra's role in the murder: Homer writes that the killer was Aegisthus, while other versions, those of the tragic playwrights in particular, Clytemnestra is an accomplice at first, but in the end kills her husband herself. In this painting, Clytemnestra, dagger in hand, hesitates while Aegisthus urges her on. Even the accounts of the murder differ: In some versions, Aegisthus murders him during a banquet; in others, the king is slain as he comes out of a bath and dons a shirt, whose neck and sleeves had been sewn up on purpose to hamper his movements, thus making him an easy victim.

THE MURDER OF AGAMEMNON
Pierre Narcisse Guérin
1817

Musée du Louvre, Paris

ACHILLES

The son of Thetis and Peleus, Achilles is the most famous of the Greek heroes and the main character of the *Iliad*. At his birth, Thetis had plunged him in the Styx to make him immortal, but the heel by which she was holding him did not get wet and so remained vulnerable. He was educated by the centaur Chiron and, according to Homer, also by Phoenix who excelled in eloquence and the military arts.

In the flower of his youth and at the height of his power, Achilles joined the Greek army against Troy, even though he knew his fate, for an oracle had predicted to his mother that he would die under the walls of Troy. For this reason, when the war broke out, Thetis had sent him to hide in Scyros, dressed in women's clothes, among the daughters of Lycomedes. But even this failed to keep him from the battlefield, for he was soon unmasked by Ulysses, who took him to Troy (see p. 650). In the tenth year of the war, after a quarrel with Agamemnon over possession of the slave Briseis (see p. 656), Achilles withdrew from combat and returned only after his friend Patroclus was slain by Hector.

THETIS AND ACHILLES
2nd century BCE

| Palazzo Altemps, Rome

☐ Thetis and Achilles sit enthroned. A mantle covers the head of the Nereid and a small Triton is at her feet. Achilles rests his hands on his heavy sword, a foot on the helmet; the shield is partially visible to his right.

The childhood of Achilles

The myth relates that Achilles was the seventh child of Peleus and Thetis, and that his mother, a Nereid, had tried to eliminate all the mortal elements from her children by exposing them to fire, causing their deaths. When Achilles was born, Peleus watched his wife and rescued the baby from the same fate. Angered, Thetis left home and went to live in the depths of the sea with her Nereid sisters. Then Peleus entrusted the child to the centaur Chiron, who educated him.

In another version of the myth that came to prevail, Thetis plunged her young son in the waters of the Styx, the infernal river that gave invulnerability to all those who bathed in it, but as she was holding him by the heel, that part of the body did not get wet, and so remained vulnerable.

□ Before an Arcadian landscape, Thetis kneels by the river and plunges little Achilles in the Styx, holding him by the heel. The Nereid is assisted by women, perhaps her sisters; one of them holds Thetis so she will not lose her balance, while the other women prepare the baby's cradle.

THETIS DIPS ACHILLES INTO THE RIVER STYX
(detail)
Antoine Borel
18th century
644 | Galleria Nazionale, Parma

The childhood of Achilles

☐ This Roman fresco pictures Chiron, the wise centaur who was a friend of man, stringing the lyre Achilles holds in his hands. In so doing, the centaur hugs the student affectionately, as if to protect him. Still a boy, Achilles is dressed with a short mantle and looks trustingly at his teacher. Chiron's human face has horse's ears, because he is a hybrid creature. The two figures are set before a carefully detailed, finely rendered architectural background.

ACHILLES AND CHIRON
1st century CE
Museo Archeologico Nazionale, Naples

◄◄

The childhood of Achilles

☐ The centaur, with Achilles riding on his back, is pointing to the birds in the sky; the boy stretches his bow in the direction where the teacher is pointing. In addition to Achilles, Chiron educated Jason, the hero of the *Argo*, Aesculapius, and even Apollo. In particular, he taught them the arts of hunting, war, music, and medicine.

THE EDUCATION OF ACHILLES
Eugène Delacroix
c. 1862
The J. Paul Getty Museum, Los Angeles

648

Achilles and the daughters of Lycomedes

An oracle had told Thetis that Achilles would die on the battlefield before the walls of Troy, so the Nereid hid her son on Skyros, in the palace of King Lycomedes, who welcomed him under a false name and in a woman's disguise. The king's daughters called him "Pyrrha," which in Greek means red, like the color of the hero's hair. When the Achaeans learned where Achilles was hiding, they sent envoys to Lycomedes. The king denied that Achilles was his guest, even urging the delegates to search the royal palace.

Ulysses devised a stratagem. He offered gifts to the young women, adding a shield and a spear to them. Then, at a signal, he had someone play a trumpet, signaling an enemy attack. Instinctively, Achilles grabbed the weapons and tore off his gown. Finally unmasked, he decided to leave for Troy together with his men, the Myrmidons, even though he knew about the oracle's prediction.

ACHILLES RECOGNIZED BY ULYSSES
Hendrick van Limborch
650 | Museum Boijmans van Beuningen, Rotterdam

☐ Ulysses touches Achilles's shoulder, having finally unmasked him. While the daughters of Lycomedes are attracted by the jewels, the hero, frightened by the sound of the war trumpet, has grabbed a dagger to defend himself, revealing his identity.

◄◄

Achilles and the daughters of Lycomedes

►►

☐ The episode of Achilles and the daughters of Lycomedes is on the left side of the painting; the artist used it as a pretext to describe the interior of a room crammed with all kinds of precious and rare objects. This painting recalls the *cabinets des merveilles* that displayed unusual or surprising objects; these rooms had become popular in the European courts between the fifteenth and the seventeenth centuries, in the wake of several important geographic discoveries.

ULYSSES RECOGNIZING ACHILLES AMONG
THE DAUGHTERS OF LYCOMEDES
School of Frans Francken the Younger
c. 1630

Musée du Louvre, Paris

Achilles and the daughters of Lycomedes

☐ Poussin has set the episode of Achilles and the daughters of Lycomedes before a splendid landscape, dominated by an ancient building whose forms recall the Temple of Fortuna at Palestrina. The girls are trying on the jewels that Ulysses and Diomedes, disguised as merchants, have brought. The men now turn to Achilles, who holds a sword in his right hand, betraying his identity. He is also wearing a feathered helmet and looks at his reflection in the mirror with narcissistic satisfaction. To the right, an isolated figure, Thetis perhaps, watches the scene, frightened by the fate that awaits her son.

ACHILLES ON SKYROS
Nicolas Poussin
1656
Virginia Museum of Fine Arts, Richmond

The wrath of Achilles

The *Iliad* recounts the last year of the Trojan War. The poem opens with a devastating plague that Apollo had sent to the Greek army. After nine days, Achilles called an assembly, at which the soothsayer Calchas announced that it was Apollo's will that Chryseis be returned to her father, Chryses, who was a priest of the god (see p. 638). Hearing this, Agamemnon angrily said that he would return Chryseis only in exchange for Briseis, who was Achilles's slave.

A furious quarrel broke out between the two warriors, and Achilles, deprived of Briseis, withdrew from combat. As a result, the Trojans overwhelmed the Greek army until the hero decided to return to the battlefield to avenge the death of his friend Patroclus.

☐ Assembled in a plenary session, the Greek chiefs are on the right side of the composition; in the middle, the soothsayer Calchas, dressed in white, turns his eyes heavenward. In the center is Agamemnon, gesturing threateningly at Achilles. The enraged hero has been provoked and is about to draw his sword, but Minerva, invisible to the others and hidden by a cloud, stops him by pulling his hair and urges him to put an end to the quarrel.

ACHILLES HAS A DISPUTE
WITH AGAMEMNON
Johann Heinrich Tischbein
18th century
Hamburger Kunsthalle, Hamburg

The wrath of Achilles

☐ In this vase painting, Achilles is portrayed in the center, taking leave of his beloved Briseis; behind him, Agamemnon witnesses the scene as he leans on a stick. The son of Peleus carries a chlamys on his arm, his shield rests against his hip, and he leans on his spear. With one hand, Briseis raises the hem of her tunic; in the other, she carries a pitcher and is about to perform a libation. The hero offers her a *patera*, a flat cup used for rituals. According to the *Iliad*, however, it was Agamemnon's heralds who removed Briseis from Achilles's tent.

ACHILLES TAKES LEAVE OF BRISEIS
BEFORE AGAMEMNON
Red-figure amphora
430–20 BCE
Museo Archeologico Provinciale
S. Castromediano, Lecce

The wrath of Achilles

☐ In this fresco, Briseis appears on the right, her head covered by a veil; she is about to leave Achilles, who is seated in the center and asks his friend Patroclus to take her outside, while behind the hero, Agamemnon's hesitant messenger appears. The armed soldiers in the back are Myrmidons, the Thessalians ruled by Achilles. In the Homeric poem, Achilles reassures the heralds sent by Agamemnon that they are not at fault, being simply the enforcers of the king of Mycenae's orders; then he reiterates in front of witnesses that he is withdrawing from combat.

ACHILLES AND BRISEIS
50–79 CE
Museo Archeologico Nazionale, Naples

The wrath of Achilles

☐ After the reluctant Briseis was taken to Agamemnon's tent, Achilles left his comrades and walked to the seashore. There, he implored his mother to vindicate the offense received at the hands of the king of Mycenae. In this fresco, Tiepolo depicts the scene where Thetis, hearing her son's lament, rises from the waves to comfort him. Achilles begs his mother to travel to Olympus and ask Jupiter to favor the Trojans, at least until the Greeks, including Agamemnon, realize the wrong he has suffered. Thetis accedes to his request; on Mount Olympus, she coaxes the promise from Jupiter (see p. 622).

THETIS CONSOLING ACHILLES
Giambattista Tiepolo
1757
Villa Valmarana, Vicenza

The death of Patroclus

▶ ▶

After Achilles withdrew from combat, the Greeks continued to lose on the battlefield. Agamemnon sent a delegation to convince the hero to pick up his arms again, but promises and enticements did not move him. Because the fighting was getting perilously close to the Greek camp and their ships were in danger of being torched, Patroclus convinced his friend Achilles to lend him his armor and allow him to help their comrades.

After making a massacre of the foe, Patroclus was slain by Hector, who took the armor off his corpse. The following day, when Achilles learned of his friend's death, he was overcome with grief. He donned the new armor that his mother had brought him (see p. 624), convened the army, reconciled with Agamemnon, and returned to the battlefield, killing Hector in a duel.

GRIEVING FOR PATROCLUS
Red-figure krater
490 BCE
Museo Archeologico Regionale, Agrigento

☐ In the center of the composition, two warriors bend as they carry the now-lifeless body of Patroclus. Behind him, Achilles stretches his arm in a final farewell. Near the helmet of the Greek hero is a tiny warrior, an eidolon—the representation of the soul that has left the body of his lifeless friend.

The death of Patroclus

▶▶

□ After killing Hector, Achilles dreams that the ghost of Patroclus longs for a just burial and a final resting place for his roaming spirit. In the dream, Patroclus asks him to bury their bones next to each other. Achilles pledges to comply with his wishes and tries to embrace Patroclus one last time, but the shadow dissolves like fog.

ACHILLES GRASPS AT THE SHADE
OF PATROCLUS
Henry Fuseli
1805

◀◀

The death of Patroclus

☐ The day after Patroclus appeared to Achilles in a dream, Agamemnon invited the Greeks to gather wood for the hero's funeral pyre. In this work, the artist has imagined the scene in which Achilles stands before the burning pyre and cuts the blond tresses that his father, Peleus, had promised as a gift to the river Spercheus if his son returned safely home from Troy. Aware of his fate, the hero knew he would never return home, so he cut his hair and placed it in the hands of his beloved friend.

ACHILLES SACRIFICES HIS HAIR
ON THE PYRE OF PATROCLUS
Henry Fuseli
1800
Kunsthaus, Zurich

The death of Hector

Back on the battlefield after the death of the beloved Patroclus, Achilles made a veritable slaughter of the Trojans, who fled inside the city walls. Heedless of his parents' entreaties, Hector decided to go outside the city gates and face Achilles, but when he saw the great hero, he became deathly afraid and ran three times around the walls. Then Jupiter took the scales of fate and weighed the deaths of the two heroes: Hector's plate was heavier and inclined toward Hades.

Up to then, Apollo had protected the Trojan hero; now he deserted Hector, and Achilles slew the hated foe. He undressed the corpse and, in a gesture of contempt, tied it to his chariot and dragged the body around the city while Priam, Hecuba, and Andromache watched heartbroken from the bastions. Still hungry for revenge, for twelve days Achilles dragged the body, until Priam went to see him and begged to have his son's body back in exchange for a generous reward.

ACHILLES SLAYS HECTOR
Pieter Paul Rubens
1630
670 | Musée des Beaux-Arts, Brussels

☐ Protected by Minerva, here shown hovering over the hero, Achilles is about to strike a cleaving mortal blow against Hector. In the *Iliad*, the Trojan hero, after throwing javelins in vain against his enemy, was left without weapons and drew his sword to fight, but Achilles, full of violent rage, attacked him and killed him mercilessly.

Achilles drags Hector's corpse

▶▶

Just before dying, Hector begged Achilles to return his body to his father, Priam, but the hero angrily refused; then he predicted that Achilles too would soon die. Still thirsty for revenge, Achilles took the armor off Hector's lifeless body, pierced the tendons between the ankle and the heel, threaded two leather strips through them, tied them to his chariot, jumped on it, and whipped the horses into a frenzied race around the walls of Troy.

☐ This vase painting depicts the dramatic scene in which Achilles drags Hector's body after tying it to his chariot. To the left, Priam and Hecuba, Hector's parents, desperately mourn their son. Armed with his round shield, Achilles is about to step on his chariot, and he turns to them. To the far right is the mound that marks the grave of Patroclus, with the small figure of a warrior representing his soul. In the center, the winged deity is Isis: A messenger of the gods, she is sent by Jupiter to advise Priam that he should go to Achilles to ask the return of his son's body.

ACHILLES DRAGS HECTOR'S CORPSE
Attic black-figure amphora
520–10 BCE
672 | Museum of Fine Arts, Boston

Achilles drags Hector's corpse

☐ On his chariot, Achilles spurs the horses dragging Hector's body, while behind him some armed warriors seem about to attack him. From a cloud, the gods witness the slaughter. In the background, Achilles stands victorious before the walls of Troy, with the dead body of Hector at his feet.

ACHILLES DRAGGING THE BODY OF HECTOR AROUND THE WALLS OF TROY
Donato Creti
late 17th–early 18th century
Musée Massey, Tarbes

674

Priam visits Achilles

Even after burying Patroclus and slaying Hector, Achilles could not resign himself. Every morning, he tied the horses to his chariot and dragged the corpse of the hated foe around the grave of his dead friend. Then the gods took action in an attempt to save the Trojan warrior's body: On the twelfth day, no longer willing to suffer the sight of that desecration, Jupiter ordered Thetis to persuade her son to deliver Hector's body to his father. At the same time, he sent Isis to Priam, instructing him to visit Achilles and offer a generous ransom for his son's body.

Protected by Mercury, Priam reached the tent of Achilles, who gave in to the old king's entreaties and allowed him to return to Troy with the corpse. Thus Hector was finally given a honorable burial. The *Iliad* ends with this episode.

PRIAM BEGS ACHILLES TO RETURN HEC-
TOR'S BODY
(DETAIL)
Attic red-figure *skiphos*
490–80 BCE
676 | Kunsthistorisches Museum, Vienna

☐ Priam enters Achilles's tent followed by his retinue, carrying gifts
for the ransom. The hero is dining
reclined on his couch and turns
around, as if refusing the old king's
visit. In the *Iliad*, Homer writes that
Achilles gave in to Priam's tears and
returned to him Hector's body washed
and scented, promising to suspend
warfare for the time necessary to
celebrate a proper funeral.

Achilles and Penthesilea

The tales written after the *Iliad* complete the story of the Trojan War. One of them recounts the duel between Achilles and Penthesilea, queen of the Amazons, the legendary tribe of women warriors descended from the god Mars. After Hector's funeral, the discouraged Trojan army received unexpected assistance from Penthesilea. At first, the queen overwhelmed the Greeks, driving them back toward their camp; then, face to face with Achilles, she dueled with him. The hero inflicted a lethal wound, but in the very instant that he removed the helmet that covered her face, he was deeply struck by her beauty and fell in love with her. The queen's body was returned to the Trojans for burial.

❏ This scene depicts the duel's supreme moment, when the hero pierces the Amazon's throat with his spear. Achilles's helmet is pulled down to shield his face, while Penthesilea's is raised, as if to heighten her vulnerability. Her spear brushes against Achilles's armor without striking him, while the hero strikes her in the throat. According to a later version of the myth, the love between the two warriors sprung up when their eyes crossed, but it was, alas, too late.

ACHILLES KILLS PENTHESILEA,
QUEEN OF THE AMAZONS
Black-figure amphora from Vulci
540–30 BCE
| British Museum, London

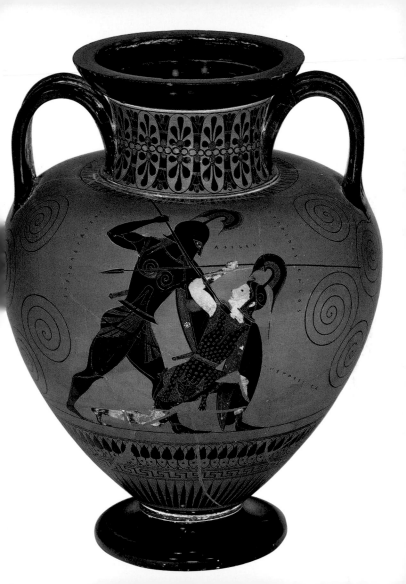

The death of Achilles

Several versions survive of the death of Achilles. After the death of Patroclus, Achilles could not contain his wrath. He led the Greeks several times in attacks against Troy. Apollo stopped him just as he was about to knock down the city's gates. Undaunted by the god, the hero was about to raise his arm to throw the javelin, when Apollo, faster than the hero, struck his heel with an arrow, killing him. In another version of the myth, it was Paris who killed Achilles before the gates of Troy, with an arrow that Apollo deflected to hit the heel, a fatal wound.

☐ Rubens narrates a version of the myth where Achilles is drawn into a trap by Priam, who had promised him the hand of his daughter Polixena in exchange for lifting the siege of Troy. In this scene, Achilles is about to perform a sacrifice to Apollo as the maiden had requested, but as he kneels before the altar, Paris strikes him with an arrow guided by the Sun god, who drives it into the heel, his only vulnerable spot, killing him.

DEATH OF ACHILLES
Pieter Paul Rubens
1630–35
| Courtauld Institute of Art, London

The battle over the arms of Achilles

After Achilles died, a fierce fight for his corpse took place in front of the gates of Troy, until Ajax and Ulysses rescued the body from the enemy and took him back to the camp, where a solemn funeral was readied. Then a bitter dispute broke out between Ulysses and Ajax over the arms of the slain hero. Agamemnon refused to make a decision and invited the Greeks commanders to meet, remanding the judgment to the assembly.

Ajax and Ulysses took turns extolling their virtues. At the end, the assembly voted to give the arms to Ulysses. Deeply angered, Ajax drew his sword and plunged it in his chest. From the blood that spilled on the ground, a carnation was born. (see p. 434).

❑ An earlier version of the myth recounts how the arms of Achilles were delivered to Ulysses, although it was Ajax who had rescued the hero's body. Enraged, Ajax decided to take revenge on the Achaeans, but the goddess Minerva caused him to go mad, and he unleashed his violence on harmless cattle, thinking they were his enemies. Once back to his senses, Ajax realized what had transpired and, deeply humiliated, decided to end his life.

DISPUTE OVER THE ARMS OF ACHILLES
(detail)
White-background *lekythos*
5th century BCE
682 | Museo Nazionale Archeologico, Taranto

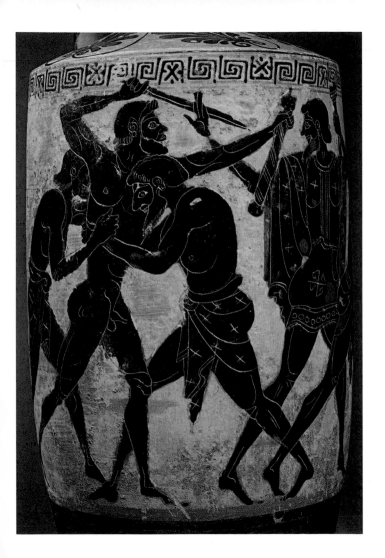

PATROCLUS

Patroclus was the son of Menoetius and lived in Opus in Locris. Because as a boy he had accidentally killed a friend while playing dice, his father had sent him to Thessaly to live with King Peleus. There he was raised with Achilles and became his closest friend; they fought in the Trojan War together.

When Agamemnon's envoys entered the tent of Achilles to take away Briseis, it was Patroclus who escorted the young woman. Also, when Achilles withdrew from combat and the military situation became dire for the Greeks, Patroclus borrowed the hero's armor and led the Myrmidon troops, driving back the Trojans from the Greek camp and killing a great many of them, until he was slain by Hector, who stripped the corpse of his armor. Heartbroken over his friend's death, an enraged Achilles avenged his friend by slaying Hector and recovering the armor. After Achilles died, his ashes were interred together with those of Patroclus, as the latter had requested in a dream.

PATROCLUS
Jacques-Louis David
c. 1780
Musée d'Art Thomas-Henry,
Cherbourg-Octeville

□ Seen from the back and seated on a red cloth, the bow and arrows lying on the ground, Patroclus hides his face in a reticent pose, almost underscoring the loneliness of human suffering and the extraordinary virtue of overcoming one's passions.

PATROCLUS

☐ Keeping his promise to Thetis (see p. 622), for some time Jupiter favored the Trojans in the war. Therefore, Agamemnon decided to send ambassadors to Achilles to persuade him to resume fighting. He offered several gifts in exchange, including Briseis, but the hero was immovable. In this painting, Ingres portrays Achilles holding a lyre; next to him is the ever trustworthy, quiet friend Patroclus. Before them are the ambassadors Phoenix (Europa's father), Ajax, and Ulysses.

ACHILLES RECEIVING THE AMBASSADORS OF AGAMEMNON
Jean-Auguste-Dominique Ingres
1801
École Nationale Supérieure des Beaux-Arts, Paris

The battle for the body of Patroclus

After slaying Patroclus, Hector removed the armor and wanted to seize the corpse, but Ajax and Menelaus stopped him, calling to other comrades for help. Many Achaeans came, and a bitter fight ensued between them and the Trojans led by Hector. After a day of fighting, the Greeks prevailed and drove the foe back. Then Menelaus ran to Antilocus, a friend of Achilles, to give him the terrible news, and raced back to protect the body of Patroclus. When Achilles learned of the death, he went mad and ran onto the battlefield. When they saw him, the Trojans fled terrified, and the Achaeans finally took the body of Patroclus to safety and mourned him the entire night.

☐ Greeks and Trojans face each other on the battlefield with raised weapons. On the ground is the dead body of Patroclus, his weapons already removed. Although the figures are almost still, they are very tense, heightening the intense drama of this scene.

BATTLE FOR THE BODY OF PATROCLUS
(detail)
Black-figure krater
c. 530 BCE

National Archaeological Museum, Athens

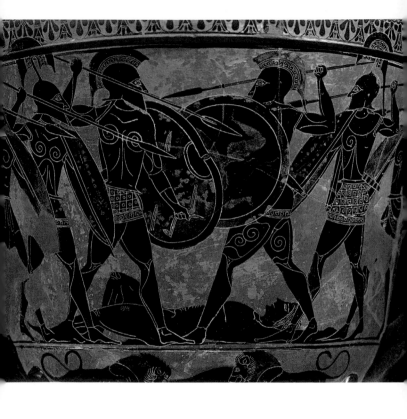

HECTOR

The son of the Trojan king Priam and Hecuba and the brother of Paris, Hector is the famed hero and commander of the Trojan army. Although Priam was king, Hector was loved by his people, and he made all the decisions. He was married to Andromache, and they had a son, Astyanax. After Achilles refused to fight, with Mars's protection Hector slew a great number of Greeks, including Patroclus, who had borrowed his friend's armor and was trying to repel the Trojans' dangerous advance.

Achilles's revenge was swift: the Greek hero met Hector before the walls of Troy and, after killing him in a duel, dragged his body around the city walls (see p. 670); for many days, he left the body to the elements in the Greek camp, until even the gods were moved to pity and ordered Thetis to make Achilles return Hector's body to his father (see p. 676). The war was then suspended to allow the Trojans to pay funeral honors to their slain hero.

☐ On the eve of his last duel, Hector takes leave of his wife, Andromache, and son, Astyanax, at the city's famous Scaean gates. In this image, the child is frightened by the father's feathered helmet and retreats into the nurse's arms, while Hector and Andromache lovingly bid farewell to each other.

HECTOR AND ANDROMACHE
Angelica Kauffmann
1768
The Morley Collection, Saltram

HECTOR

☐ Overcome with grief, Andromache mourns her husband. Hector's
body lies on the thalamus, his head
wreathed with laurel, the symbol of
glory. The carving on the left side of
the bed portrays the couple's farewell at the Scaean gates, and on
the right, the hero's death at the
hand of Achilles.

ANDROMACHE MOURNING HECTOR
Jacques-Louis David
1783
Musée du Louvre, Paris

PHILOCTETES

Born in Thessaly, Philoctetes is one of the Greek princes who fought in the Trojan War. A skilled archer and a faithful friend of Hercules, he received the hero's bow and arrows in gratitude for lighting his funeral pyre (see p. 582). But Philoctetes did not reach Troy with the rest of the Greek fleet, for according to the myth, during a stop at the island of Chryses, a snake bit his foot and the wound would not heal, but became infected and foul-smelling. Thus his comrades resolved to leave him on the island of Lemnos, where he survived for ten years.

In the meantime the Greeks still had not defeated Troy; an oracle counseled that victory would be theirs only if they fought with Hercules's arms. Thus they decided to send Ulysses and Neoptolemus (the son of Achilles and Deidamea) to Lemnos to bring Philoctetes to Troy. Once there, the archer was treated by Aesculapius (or Macaon, according to another version). In the end, he slew a great many Trojans and made an important contribution to the defeat of the city.

LANDSCAPE WITH PHILOCTETES
ON THE ISLAND OF LEMNOS
Achille-Etna Michallon
1822
Musée Fabre, Montpellier

694

☐ The island of Lemnos, where Philoctetes had been left, was deserted. The archer survived by killing birds with the arrows he had received from Hercules. The hero is traditionally pictured, as he is here, with a bandaged foot and Hercules's weapons in his hands.

THE WOODEN HORSE

The construction of the Trojan horse is treated cursorily in the *Odyssey*; it is, however, covered at length in Virgil's *Aeneid*. After years of setting sieges and making raids on Troy, the Greeks were tired and disheartened. Counseled by Ulysses, who was their wisest commander, they decided to build an enormous wooden horse, as big as a mountain, and hide the boldest Greek warriors inside its empty belly.

Epeus, a Greek leader from Phocis, built the horse with the help of Minerva. The construction was left on the beach, and the Greeks pretended to have given up on their endeavor and hid on a nearby island. At first uncertain about what to do, and notwithstanding the many warnings of Laocoön (see p. 702), the Trojans decided to bring the horse inside the city. The following night, at a given signal, the Greeks again came ashore while the warriors inside the horse came out and opened the city gates; this done, the city of Troy was theirs.

☐ In this bas-relief, the Trojan horse is shown with the Greek warriors hiding inside. Some are about to jump out, like the warrior who throws his weapons outside with the help of his comrades.

THE TROJAN HORSE
(detail)
Amphora
7th century BCE
696 | Archaeological Museum, Mykonos

◄◄

THE WOODEN HORSE

►►

☐ The Trojans looked curiously at the horse and were deceived by Sinon, a Greek soldier who pretended to have deserted his army to escape Ulysses's murderous rage. Questioned about the horse, Sinon replied that it was a votive gift for Minerva and had been built so large on purpose, to prevent the Trojans from carrying it inside the city and earning Minerva's favors. As soon as Sinon stopped speaking, Laocoön was killed by two snakes (see p. 702); the Trojans interpreted the event as a divine punishment of the Apollonian priest for giving mendacious advice, and as a confirmation of Sinon's sincerity. They therefore resolved to bring the horse into the city.

THE WOODEN HORSE IS BROUGHT
INTO THE CITY
(detail)
Miniature
1490
British Library, London

◄◄

THE WOODEN HORSE

☐ Once inside the city, the Greek army surprised the Trojans in their sleep. They sacked and looted viciously, and a veritable slaughter followed. The surviving inhabitants tried in vain to resist. King Priam, his wife, Hecuba, and their daughters were all killed; the other Trojan warriors died in combat, and only a handful escaped the fury of the Greeks. Aeneas fled Troy with his child, Ascanius, and carried his father, Anchises, on his shoulders.

This painting shows the city on fire in the background and the fleeing Trojans in the foreground. Among them, his father on his shoulders, is Aeneas, the Trojan hero, son of Venus, and legendary ancestor of Rome.

THE BURNING OF TROY
Jan Brueghel the Elder
1595
Alte Pinakothek, Munich

LAOCOÖN

A son of Capys and a brother of Anchises, Laocoön was an Apollonian priest. He drew the contempt of the god for having desecrated the temple by lying with his wife before a statue sacred to Apollo. When the Trojans saw the huge horse on the beach, Laocoön, who was preparing a sacrifice for Neptune, warned them that it was a new ruse prepared by the Greeks.

As he said this, he threw a spear at the animal's body, which gave forth a dull metallic noise, but the Trojans did not hear, because Sinon arrived just then, telling his story (see p. 698). Suddenly, two horrible serpents rose from the seafoam and with fiery, angry eyes moved threateningly ashore, crushing Laocoön's two young children in their coils. The priest attempted to save them by attacking the monsters, but they crushed him as well.

☐ In the center of the canvas, we see Laocoön attacked by a serpent, while behind him one of his sons lies lifeless on the ground. The other son is still alive and in vain tries to defend himself from the second monster. In the background is the Trojan horse that would be carried into the city.

LAOCOÖN
Doménikos Theotokópoulos,
known as El Greco
1610–14

National Gallery of Art, Washington, D.C.

CASSANDRA

A daughter of Priam and Hecuba, Cassandra was loved by
Apollo, who promised to teach her the arts of divination
in exchange for her love; but after the maiden learned, she
refused his love. Angered by this treatment, he gave her the
gift of divination but withheld that of persuasion, sentencing
her to be always disbelieved.

   She recognized Paris, the brother who had been left to
die on Mount Ida (see p. 626); after he abducted Helen, she
predicted that the city would be destroyed for the offense,
but no one ever believed her words. When the Trojans led
the famous horse into the city, Cassandra tried in vain to
warn them, shouting that the horse hid armed warriors.
When Troy fell and the Greeks divided the spoils, Cassandra
was given to Agamemnon, who took her back home to
Mycenae, where she was apparently murdered with him
by Clytemnestra.

☐ Cassandra lies inside the temple
of Minerva, a lit fire on the altar,
her hands bound, her eyes turned
upward, while outside the city is
on fire and the battle rages.

CASSANDRA IMPLORING THE
VENGEANCE OF MINERVA
Jérôme-Martin Langlois
1810
Musée des Beaux-Arts, Chambéry

THE RETURN
AFTER THE WAR

Ulysses 708 • Aeneas 736

ULYSSES

The son of Laertes, lord of Ithaca, and of Anticlea, Ulysses received the throne from his father once he reached adulthood. Famous for his courage, eloquence, and cunning, he was one of the commanders who waged war against Troy. His adventures are narrated primarily in the *Odyssey*, and a vast iconographic repertoire illustrates them. After the war, the nymph Calypso held him captive for seven years on Ogygia, until the gods allowed him to return home.

After sailing from Ogygia, a storm drove him to the island of the Phaeacians, where Nausicaa, daughter of king Alcinous, took him to the royal palace. The king welcomed him with great honors, and during the banquet, Ulysses recounted his many adventures. Alcinous was moved and gave him a ship so he could return to his kingdom. When he finally landed in Ithaca, Ulysses decided to appear at the palace disguised as a beggar. After slaying all the suitors, he took again his place next to his faithful wife, Penelope.

Greek name: Odysseus

☐ This carving portrays a pensive, sad Ulysses. Homesickness for his country and family is a recurring theme of the *Odyssey*, as is Ulysses's destiny, which subjects him to trials and suffering. After leaving Troy with twelve ships, he was to return to Ithaca alone.

THE SADNESS OF ULYSSES
2nd century BCE
British Museum, London

Ulysses and Calypso

Homer's *Odyssey* narrates Ulysses's return trip from Troy to Ithaca. The poem opens with an assembly of the gods, where Jupiter informs them that the time has come for Ulysses to return home. At the time, the king of Ithaca was on the island of Ogygia, where he had been shipwrecked. Here lived Calypso, the fair daughter of Atlas who had taken a fancy to him and had welcomed him warmly, holding him for seven years and even offering him immortality in hopes of keeping him there.

Jupiter instructed Mercury to visit Calypso and order her to allow Ulysses to leave. Unwillingly, the nymph complied and even helped the hero build a raft. After seventeen days at sea, the god Neptune, who hated Ulysses for having blinded Polyphemus (see p. 714), unleashed a violent storm, but Ino, a sea deity, helped Ulysses reach Scheria, where the Phaeacians lived.

ULYSSES AND CALYPSO
Arnold Böcklin
1883
710 | Kunstmuseum, Basel

□ Deep in thought, Ulysses scans the sea while Calypso watches him. The entire composition evokes a sense of anxious expectation. Although Ulysses lay with the goddess at night, during the day he sat and looked at the sea, his heart full of longing for his fatherland and his wife, Penelope.

Ulysses and Nausicaa

Shipwrecked on Scheria, an exhausted Ulysses fell asleep under the trees. Nausicaa, daughter of Alcinous, the king of the island, used to go to the shore to wash the linens in the river with her maids. Ulysses was awakened by the chatter of the girls playing on the beach and asked Nausicaa where he was. After reassuring him that he had reached a peaceful land, the princess asked her handmaids to attend to the stranger, feeding him and giving him new clothes, then invited him to her father's palace; they asked him to walk separately for the last stretch of road toward the city, to avoid gossip. The hero was welcomed respectfully, and in his honor the king arranged a splendid banquet, during which, pressed by Alcinous, Ulysses revealed his identity and told of the misadventures that had befallen him during his long return trip.

ULYSSES AND NAUSICAA
Lucas van Uden
1635

The Bowes Museum, County Durham

□ This scene is set before an expansive landscape with the city of the Phaeacians in the middle ground. Ulysses turns to Nausicaa, while her frightened maidservants withdraw, for the shipwrecked hero is naked and covers himself with a branch. On the left is a cart on which Nausicaa and the handmaids carried the linens to be washed in the river.

Ulysses in the cave of Polyphemus

At the banquet in the palace of King Alcinous (see p. 712), Ulysses told of the perilous adventures he had faced after leaving Troy with twelve ships. Sailing toward his fatherland, the wind brought him to the island of the Ciconians, against whom he fought a fierce battle; leaving that island, a storm took him to the land of the Lotus-Eaters, near Libya; then he reached the island of the Cyclopes—the wild, one-eyed giants who live by raising sheep. With some of his men, Ulysses ended up in the cave of Polyphemus, a son of Neptune, who imprisoned them, intending to eat them one by one. The shrewd hero offered some wine to the Cyclops; not being used to it, he became drunk and Ulysses blinded him. The following morning, Ulysses escaped by hiding with his men under the fleece of the sheep that were going out of the cave to pasture.

ULYSSES BLINDING POLYPHEMUS
Pellegrino Tibaldi
1554
Palazzo Poggi, Bologna

☐ Here Ulysses is shown as he blinds Polyphemus with a large, sharpened olive-tree trunk made red-hot on the fire. The Cyclops is racked by pain. Before him are the bones of Ulysses's devoured comrades and the giant's walking stick and flute. In the back, hidden in a niche in the cave, Ulysses's men watch.

Ulysses in the cave of Polyphemus

☐ To escape from the cave of Polyphemus, the *Odyssey* narrates that Ulysses tied the thick-fleeced sheep three by three and hid one man under each group. He himself hid under a ram. The following day, as the flock was going out to pasture, Polyphemus felt the back of all the animals, to make sure that his prisoners were not escaping. In this painting by Fuseli, Polyphemus is checking the ram under which the cunning hero, who is leaving the cave last, has hidden. The Cyclops is shielding his wounded eye with one hand, his lips wincing in pain.

ULYSSES ESCAPING FROM POLYPHEMUS
THE CYCLOPS
Henry Fuseli
1803
Private collection

Circe the enchantress

Continuing his journey, Ulysses and his men reached the land of Aeolus, god of the winds, then the land of the Laestrygonians, man-eating giants, who destroyed all their ships except one. From there they landed on the island of Aeaea, the abode of Circe, daughter of the Sun god and an enchantress who could transform men into animals. Ulysses asked some of his men, including Eurylochus, to go inland to explore. After crossing a forest, the sailors reached a valley where they glimpsed Circe's house; she invited them inside. Only Eurylochus hid, suspecting treachery; the witch had them sit down, offered them a drink—and turned them into swine. Eurylochus immediately returned to the ship and reported what had transpired. Ulysses decided to visit the witch to free his men. Along the way he met Mercury, who gave him a magic herb, thanks to which Circe's spell had no effect on him. Overwhelmed by Ulysses's personality, the sorceress freed the sailors and became his mistress. After a year, the men asked their leader to resume the journey home.

CIRCE
Giovanni Benedetto Castiglione
1653
Private collection

❏ Circe dominates the scene: The animals surrounding her are men that she transformed; theirs are the arms lying about. The sorceress holds the magic wand with which she casts her magic spells, but thanks to the herb he received from Mercury, Ulysses resists the spell.

Ulysses in the netherworld

Pressed by his comrades, Ulysses told Circe that they wanted to leave, but before sailing away, the witch advised him to travel to the netherworld and consult with Tiresias, the sooth-sayer. After performing the ritual sacrifices, Ulysses descended into Hades. The first soul he met was that of his friend Elpenor; then he saw the soul of his mother, Anticlea, whom he had thought was still alive, and felt a great sorrow. He met Tiresias, who told him that his return home would not be simple, because Neptune was angry with him for blinding his son Polyphemus. In any case, he would return alone on a foreign ship, and would have to eliminate his wife's suitors. Then he would leave again in search of a people who did not know the art of navigation, and would need to make sacri-fices to Neptune to atone for his offenses. Finally, Tiresias predicted that Ulysses would die old and happy.

❑ In the center of the composition, old Tiresias speaks to Ulysses. In the background at left, a shadow wanders through Hades, while on the right are Tityus, Sisyphus, and Tantalus. In the foreground at right, Ulysses is with his mother, Anticlea, next to the rams that he slaughtered in sacrifice, for the only way to talk with the shadows of the dead was to have them drink the blood of the sacrificed animals.

ULYSSES AND TIRESIAS
Alessandro Allori
1560
720 | Banca Toscana, Florence

Ulysses and the Sirens

Before taking leave of Ulysses upon his return from Hades, Circe revealed the new adventures that were in store for him; she gave him useful suggestions on how to prevail, then disappeared. Ulysses and his men resumed their journey and reached the island of the Sirens (see p. 464). Following Circe's suggestion, he sealed his sailors' ears with wax and had them bind him tightly and securely, hands and feet, to the ship's mast. When they saw the ship, the Sirens immediately broke into a lovely song, calling to Ulysses with their tempting voices; spellbound, Ulysses tried to break his bonds and jump into the sea after them, but two sailors got up and bound him even tighter. After they left the island behind, the sailors removed their wax plugs and freed Ulysses. In another version of this myth, deeply upset because they had not been listened to, the Sirens took their own lives by jumping into the sea.

ULYSSES AND THE SIRENS
1st century CE
British Museum, London

☐ This Roman fresco depicts Ulysses's ship sailing through a narrow passage near the island of the Sirens—half-woman, half-bird marine creatures. One Siren plays the flute, another the lyre, and a third sings. On the right are the skeletons of the unlucky sailors who were charmed by their song and whose ships were smashed against the rocks.

Scylla and Charybdis

After passing the Sirens, Ulysses and his comrades sailed through the "wandering rocks" inhabited by Scylla and Charybdis, the terrible sea monsters from whom no ship had ever escaped, except for the fabled *Argo* (see p. 606), which had Juno's protection. Scylla was a monster with twelve legs and six very long necks with terrifying heads who lived in a deep grotto, from which she extended her heads and mangled whatever came her way with her multiple jaws. On the opposite side of the strait was Charybdis, who absorbed a great quantity of seawater, attracting in her whirlpool whatever floated by; three times a day she threw water back into the sea, and three times she reabsorbed it.

Circe had cautioned Ulysses that instead of challenging the monsters, which were invincible and immortal, he should try to escape as fast as possible from that deathly trap. When they reached the abode of the monsters, Ulysses forgot the witch's words, put on his armor, and stood on the deck trying to put up a defense against the monsters; the ship passed through the straits, but lost six sailors.

ODYSSEUS IN FRONT OF SCYLLA
AND CHARYBDIS
Henry Fuseli
1794–96

Aargauer Kunsthaus, Aarau

□ Ulysses is on the ship's prow, trying in vain to shield himself from the monster. In her jaws, Scylla holds some of his comrades, exactly as Circe had predicted.

Penelope at the loom

After the trial of Scylla and Charybdis, Ulysses landed on the island of the Sun, where his comrades killed some oxen from the god's herds, taking advantage of the fact that Ulysses had fallen asleep after cautioning them precisely about that. To punish them, Jupiter struck the ship with a thunderbolt, and Ulysses alone escaped and shipwrecked at Ogygia, the island inhabited by the nymph Calypso.

In the meantime, in Ithaca, the descendants of the island's aristocracy had moved into Ulysses's palace, squandering his goods and demanding that Penelope choose a new husband. But the woman tried to gain time, promising that she would choose only after she finished weaving a funeral shroud for her father-in-law, Laertes. But while she did weave during the day, at night she undid her work. Thus she was able to delay the decision for three years, until a maid revealed her deception. Defeated, Penelope promised to set a day on which to make her choice. But at just about this time, Ulysses was landing in Ithaca from the land of the Phaeacians.

TELEMACHUS AND PENELOPE
AT THE LOOM
(detail)
Attic red-figure *skiphos*
440 BCE
Museo Archeologico Nazionale, Chiusi

□ An afflicted Penelope sits at the loom, with Telemachus, her son, at her side. When his father returned to Ithaca, the latter devised with him a plan to eliminate the suitors.

Ulysses and Euryclea

After Ulysses landed in Ithaca, Mercury, his guardian god, suggested that he dress as a beggar and ask for shelter at the hut of Eumaeus the swineherd, who updated him on the palace situation. There Ulysses revealed his identity to Telemachus and decided with him on a course of action. The following day, the fake beggar arrived at the palace; notified by Eumaeus, Penelope asked to meet him. At dusk, after the suitors were dismissed, the queen visited the stranger. At her questions, the beggar replied correctly, proving that he had indeed known Ulysses, and when he spoke, the queen began to weep. She then asked Ulysses's old nurse, Euryclea, to wash the stranger's feet. The woman recognized her master from a deep leg scar, but Ulysses ordered her to keep his identity secret.

☐ Euryclea recognizes Ulysses by a scar on his leg: Shocked, she turns to Penelope and in so doing drops her master's leg, which in turn spills some water from the basin. But the queen does not notice because Minerva, whose effigy is at the top of the column, distracts her. Ulysses covers Euryclea's mouth with his hand, enjoining her not to speak.

ULYSSES RECOGNIZED BY EURYCLEA
Gustave Boulanger
c. 1849
École Nationale Supérieure des Beaux-Arts, Paris

Penelope challenges the suitors

After consulting with Ulysses, still disguised as a beggar, about a dream that predicted the return of her beloved husband, Penelope decided to challenge the suitors to an archery contest. The following day, during a banquet organized in honor of Apollo, Penelope asked that Ulysses's heavy bow be brought in, and told the suitors that she would marry the man who could string the bow and shoot an arrow through twelve ax handles.

Telemachus made preparations for the contest, then tried to draw his father's bow, but failed. Because none of the suitors could string it, they decided to postpone the contest to the following day, but the fake beggar asked permission to try; heedless of the suitors' opposition and scorn, Penelope and Telemachus gave Ulysses the bow, and he easily strung it, shooting the arrow and winning the contest.

ULYSSES WINNING THE ARCHERY CONTE-
ST IN THE PRESENCE OF
PENELOPE'S SUITORS
Francesco Primaticcio
late 16th century
Musée National du Château, Fontainebleau

☐ This scene unfolds in the throne room, where the suitors are banqueting. Bent forward from the effort of stretching the bow, Ulysses shoots the arrow, which goes through all the rings of the twelve ax handles. Behind Ulysses is the goddess Minerva, recognizable by the helmet and the shield, watching over him.

The slaying of the suitors

While the bow contest was taking place, Ulysses revealed his identity to two faithful servants, Eumaeus and Philoetius, asking them to shut all the palace doors and not enter the throne room, even if they heard wails and lamentations. After Ulysses won the contest, an armed Telemachus joined his father. The king of Ithaca killed Antinous, the leader of the suitors; the latter begged for his life, offering riches in exchange, then tried to fight back with weapons supplied by Melantius, an unfaithful servant of Ulysses, but with Mercury's aid, Ulysses and his son slew all the suitors. Then Ulysses ordered that some unfaithful servants, whom Euryclea had pointed out to him, remove the corpses and wash the room of the blood. After purifying the palace with fire and sulphur, Ulysses ordered that the queen be brought in.

☐ In the palace, Ulysses is joined by Telemachus and Eumaeus on the far right, attacking the suitors. Telemachus is below on the right behind a large shield; behind him, Ulysses shoots his arrows, and above them, Eumaeus holds a sort of club. Most of the scene is filled with the young unarmed princes trying to resist the attack.

THE MASSACRE OF THE SUITORS
Red-figure krater
330 BCE
Musée du Louvre, Paris

Ulysses and Penelope

Even after Ulysses had won the bow contest and slain all the suitors, a shocked and unbelieving Penelope still had not recognized her groom under the beggar's garments. In the meantime, Ulysses urged Telemachus to organize a fake wedding feast so that no one might understand what had transpired. Then, after washing and putting on fine clothes, he appeared before Penelope, who was still confused and at a loss for words.

She tested him by ordering the wet-nurse to move the bed to another chamber. But Ulysses protested that a mortal could not move the bed, since he had built it himself from a living olive tree, a detail that only the couple knew. Hearing these words, Penelope began to weep, embracing her beloved husband and asking forgiveness for having tested him, fearful that someone might usurp his throne.

☐ His gaze lost in his wife's eyes, Ulysses gently holds her face, and she returns a sweet look. Thus embraced, husband and wife spend the night recounting to each other their trials in the twenty long years of separation. In the meantime, Minerva holds the dawn and her horses in check over the ocean, to make the night last longer.

ULYSSES AND PENELOPE
Francesco Primaticcio
c. 1552
Museum of Art, Toledo (Ohio)

AENEAS

The adventures of Aeneas, the son of Venus and Anchises, and a valiant Trojan commander, are the subject of Virgil's *Aeneid*. After fleeing Troy with his father and son, the hero roamed for a long time in the Mediterranean. Leaving Epirus and Sicily, he was caught in a fierce storm and shipwrecked on the Libyan coast. There he was taken in by Dido, queen of Carthage, who fell in love with him, and he returned her love. But the hero was compelled by Mercury to continue on his journey and leave a heartbroken Dido, who took her own life.

Having finally reached the Italian coast, near Cumae, he consulted the famous Sibyl, who led him into Hades, where his father showed him his future: He was destined to found a new Troy in Latium, the future Rome. From Cumae, he reached the mouth of the river Tiber, where King Latinus welcomed him with great honors and gave him the hand of his daughter, Lavinia. There the hero had to face the hostility of the native Italic populations, led by Turnus, king of the Rutuli, whom Aeneas killed in a duel.

VENUS AS A HUNTRESS
APPEARS TO AENEAS
Pietro da Cortona
1630–35
736 | Musée du Louvre, Paris

❏ After being shipwrecked on the Libyan coast, Aeneas inspects those unknown shores with his comrade Acates. In the forest he meets his mother, Venus, disguised as a huntress, who informs him that he has landed in Carthage, a city ruled by Queen Dido.

The founding of Carthage

Venus recounted to Aeneas the story of Carthage (see p. 736).
Queen Dido was originally from Tyre, where her merciless
brother Pygmalion ruled; to seize her property, he had
treacherously slain her husband, Sychaeus. But Dido had a
dream in which her husband's ghost revealed what had
happened and urged her to flee, showing her a secret place
where a treasure was buried, which she would need during
her exile.

   With a small, faithful group, Dido organized her escape
and reached the coast of Libya. There she asked Iarbas, the
powerful king of the Gaetuli, for some land on which to
found a new city. The king mocked her, promising that he
would grant her a lot as large as what could be enclosed in
a cowhide. Undaunted, Dido took a hide and cut it into
extremely thin strips, which she sewed into a very long strip;
she then occupied all the land within the borders marked by
the strips and the sea.

□ A servant brings Dido the cowhide and the shears with which to cut
it, to mark the area where Carthage
would rise. The queen turns to her
handmaids, pointing out the objects
to them.

DIDO FOUNDS CARTHAGE
Giambattista Pittoni
late 17th–early 18th century
Hermitage Museum, Saint Petersburg

Dido's banquet

Enveloped by Venus in a cloud that made them invisible, Aeneas and Acates reached Carthage and entered the temple of Juno. Here, to their great surprise, they saw the great deeds of the Trojan War carved on a wall. In the meantime, Dido entered, followed by the nobility and other Carthaginians, including some Trojans whom Aeneas had believed perished in the storm. They asked the queen for hospitality, and she generously invited them to settle in Carthage. At these reassuring words, the cloud dissolved and Aeneas and his friend became visible. Dido knew of the hero's fame and invited him to the palace. To ensure that Aeneas would run no risk while he stayed in Carthage, Venus caused Dido to fall in love with him; thus on the night of the banquet, the queen was spellbound by Aeneas and spoke only to him, asking him to recount Troy's tragic end.

AENEAS TELLS DIDO ABOUT THE DISASTERS OF TROY
Pierre Narcisse Guérin
1815
Musée du Louvre, Paris

☐ Aeneas sits on a chair, while Dido, reclining on a couch, embraces little Ascanius. In truth, the child is Cupid disguised as Aeneas's son, something that Venus has asked him to do in order to more easily strike Dido with one of his arrows, making her fall in love with the Trojan hero.

The flight from Troy

At Dido's banquet (see p. 740), Aeneas recounted his city's tragic end. The wooden horse, Laocoön, Sinon's lies, the blindness of the Trojans, and the fatal night when Aeneas dreamed that Hector was urging him to flee with the Penates—the guardian deities of family and hearth—and the sacred fillets. He had suddenly awakened to see Troy engulfed by flames, and had armed himself, trying to resist the Greeks' murderous frenzy. But seeing that all was lost, he had taken shelter on Mount Ida, carrying his old father on his shoulders. During the flight he had lost his wife, Creusa.

He then armed a fleet and left with other exiles, sailing toward Thrace, then the island of Delos, where the famous oracle of Apollo exhorted him to seek an ancient land, his family's original birthplace. Then Aeneas sailed toward Crete, the fatherland of Teucrus, an ancient Trojan king, but the Penates appeared to him in a dream and suggested that the land of his ancestors was Italy, and so the Trojan hero again took to the sea.

□ Carrying his old father on his shoulders, with little Ascanius behind, Aeneas flees Troy. Anchises holds in his hands the Penates—the guardian deities of hearth and family. Reluctant to desert his home and fatherland, he was convinced when a star raced through the sky in the direction of Mount Ida, fulfilling a prediction.

AENEAS, ANCHISES, AND ASCANIUS
Gian Lorenzo Bernini
1618–19
| Galleria Borghese, Rome

The flight from Troy

☐ Carrying Anchises on his shoulders, Aeneas fled Troy with his wife and son. After stepping through the city gates, he realized that he had lost his wife. He desperately retraced his steps to look for her, but saw his house consumed by the flames and grief and desolation everywhere. Suddenly, as he was desperately calling to her, her shadow appeared. Petrified and terrified, Aeneas could not speak, but Creusa comforted him, saying that such was the will of the gods, for her presence would have hindered the mission to which he had been called in a distant land, Italy, where a new kingdom and a new bride awaited him. Aeneas was about to reply, but the shadow vanished.

AENEAS'S FLIGHT FROM TROY
Federico Barocci
1598
Galleria Borghese, Rome

The island of the Harpies

Aeneas again put out to sea, sailing toward the West. His ships were caught in a sea storm that caused them to crash on the Strophades Islands. Here the hero and his men killed some cattle and goats that were grazing in a meadow and prepared the tables. Suddenly they heard a frightening noise; then the Harpies (see p. 466) plunged down from the mountain and devoured the food, fouling the tables. Then the Trojans moved to a place sheltered by trees, made a fire, and again set the tables, but once again they were attacked by the terrible monsters. Then Aeneas decided to fight the Harpies, but in vain; they were invulnerable. As the monsters were flying away, one of them, Celaeno, perched on a high rock and told the Trojans that even in Italy they would meet with a hostile fate and would be forced to eat the very tables for food.

AENEAS AND HIS COMPANIONS
FIGHTING THE HARPIES
François Perrier
1646–47
746 | Musée du Louvre, Paris

❐ The Harpies were half-woman and half-bird monsters with frightful claws. Aeneas's men in vain used their weapons to repel them. His sword drawn, the Trojan leader seems to issue an order to the woman holding the child. On the ground next to him, a Harpy is attacking one of his soldiers.

Aeneas and Dido go hunting

Spellbound by the story of Aeneas, Dido fell in love with the Trojan commander. Afraid of her feelings, she confided in her sister, Anna, who urged her to break her vow of faithfulness to her husband's memory (see p. 738). She suggested that the dead did not care for such things, and that she should consider this marriage that would give stability to the kingdom. Aeneas reciprocated her passion, also because both Venus and Juno favored it. One day during a hunting party, the two goddesses caused a violent storm that forced the party to seek shelter in the countryside. Aeneas and Dido ran to the same cave, where they celebrated a secret marriage. Indifferent to the gossip, the couple lived their passionate love story, to the point of forgetting their respective obligations.

☐ Dido and Aeneas set out for a hunting party with their court. Juno and Venus follow them from atop a cloud. The queen of the gods is angry at first when Venus causes the couple to fall in love, but later feels that she might profit from the situation, for should their love continue into a stable union, the Trojans might very well give up Italy.

AENEAS AND DIDO HUNTING
Jan Miel
1650
748 | Musée des Beaux-Arts, Chambéry

Mercury compels Aeneas to leave Dido

Dido always appeared in public with Aeneas at her side and publicly referred to him as her husband. Now Fame quickly spread the news of Dido's new love, deforming it, as was her custom. King Iarbas, who had helped Dido when she first arrived, even presenting her with the land on which she built Carthage (see p. 738), had been rejected, and he was offended. He asked Jupiter for justice, and the king of the gods sent Mercury to remind Aeneas of his duties. The divine messenger found Aeneas busy helping the Carthaginians build the city and immediately confronted him, reminding him of the task that Fate had set in store for him. With a heavy, saddened heart, Aeneas resolved to leave.

☐ This fresco by Tiepolo depicts Mercury's second warning to Aeneas: While Dido makes her tragic plans (see p. 754), Mercury appears to Aeneas, this time in a dream, and warns him of the dangers he is facing, exhorting him to sail at dawn without any further delay.

MERCURY APPEARING TO AENEAS
Giambattista Tiepolo
1757
750 Villa Valmarana, Vicenza

Aeneas takes leave of Dido

After Mercury's apparition, Aeneas stood briefly undecided, then resolved to leave and asked his men to make secret preparations for departure; he would tell Dido of his decision at the right time, but the queen had a presentiment and openly confronted him, reproaching him for the secret preparations and reminding him that she had sacrificed her all for him. She begged him to reconsider, and not leave her at the mercy of Fame, who had caused her to be hated by the neighboring populations.

But a resolute Aeneas reminded her that he had never promised marriage; while he would forever be grateful and never forget her, a higher will was forcing him to leave for Italy, where he was fated to found a new fatherland. Hearing these words, the heartbroken queen understood that her love was powerless and accused him of being cold and ungrateful.

AENEAS'S FAREWELL TO DIDO
IN CARTHAGE
Claude Lorrain
1675–76
Hamburger Kunsthalle, Hamburg

☐ With classical architecture in the background, Dido stands with Aeneas; next to him is Ascanius, holding the helmet. Reacting to Aeneas's cold demeanor, an angry Dido reproaches him for his ingratitude, then curses him, wishing he might die in a storm; as he leaves, she faints and falls to the ground.

Dido's suicide

Dido's repeated entreaties were futile, as was her sister Anna's appeal that he postpone the departure. Aeneas had resolved to leave, and the heartbroken queen decided to kill herself. She deceived her sister, claiming that a priestess had suggested that powerful spells could dispel her insane passion. Her sister should make a pyre inside the royal palace and throw all the belongings of her beloved—arms and clothing—on it, that they might be turned into ashes and his memory dissipate. The sister did as she was told and the sorceress performed the rituals, invoking the infernal deities. In the meantime, Aeneas, pressed by Mercury, decided to set sail at dawn. From the top of her tower, the queen saw the Trojan ship leave and threw herself on the burning pyre, piercing her heart with Aeneas's sword.

☐ Dido lies on the funeral pyre with Aeneas's sword in her chest. On the left, her desperate sister rushes to her, while in the background Aeneas's ship leaves Carthage behind. Before dying, Dido curses the Trojans, exhorting her people to hate Aeneas and his progeny for all eternity.

DEATH OF DIDO
Giovanni Francesco Barbieri,
known as Guercino
c. 1631

| Galleria Spada, Rome

Aeneas and the Sibyl at Avernus

After leaving Carthage, Aeneas landed near Cumae, where he consulted the Sibyl; she led him into the netherworld, where he saw his father, Anchises, who had died in Sicily before the Trojans reached Carthage and in dreams had begged his son to visit him. After warning Aeneas of the dangers of the netherworld, the Sibyl told him that he needed a golden bough in order to enter Hades, for Queen Proserpina demanded it as gift; it was hidden among the branches of a tree in a nearby forest. His finding it would be a confirmation that the visit was fated to take place.

Venus helped Aeneas find the bough, and he descended into Hades escorted by the Sybil. There he met the shadows of his comrades and his ancient enemies, and of Dido, who haughtily turned away. He reached his father; from a hill, Anchises showed Aeneas a long, moving line of people in which he pointed out several of his descendants who would make Rome great. Then he revealed that he would have to wage war in Latium.

□ Aeneas stands with the Cumaean Sibyl near Lake Avernus, inside a crater, which was believed to be one of the doors to the underworld. The Sibyl holds the golden bough Aeneas has found.

AENEAS AND THE SIBYL, LAKE AVERNUS
J.M.W. Turner
c. 1798

Tate Gallery, London

Aeneas and the Sibyl at Avernus

☐ Aeneas and the Sibyl have just ventured into Hades when horrible figures materialize before them: the personifications of the evils that afflict humankind and terrifying monsters such as the Harpies, the Gorgons, and the Hydra of Lerna. Frightened, Aeneas is about to draw his sword when the Sibyl reminds him that they are bodiless shadows. They then reach Charon the ferryman, here seen in the center of the composition as he raises an oar; the old man addresses them harshly and reminds them of the woeful consequences that befell those who ventured before them into Hades. But the Sibyl reassures him and shows him the golden bough. Appeased, Charon allows them to step into his boat and ferries them to the opposite shore.

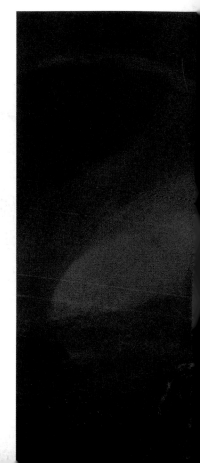

AENEAS AND THE SIBYL IN HADES
John Martin
c. 1820
Yale Center for British Art,
Paul Mellon Collection, New Haven

Venus in Vulcan's forge

Returning to Earth, Aeneas took leave of the Sybil and resumed his voyage, reaching the mouth of the river Tiber in Laurentum. There, a benevolent King Latinus welcomed him, for an oracle had predicted that Fate had arranged for his daughter Lavinia to marry a stranger coming from afar, whose progeny would one day rule the world.

But Juno, who still hated the Trojans because Paris had not awarded the famous golden apple to her (see p. 630), caused Turnus, king of the Rutuli and a suitor of Lavinia, to wage war against them. In the meantime, Venus had become worried by the sudden turn of events and the dangers to her son, and she visited Vulcan, asking him to make a new armor and weapons for him, as he had done for Achilles (see p. 624). The god went into his forge and ordered his assistants, the Cyclopes, the interrupt their chores and make the weapons.

☐ Behind Vulcan, busy forging the arms of Aeneas, we see his assistants, the Cyclopes. Around the couple are three little cupids; one of them is about to shoot an arrow, as if underscoring Vulcan's love for his bride.

VENUS ASKING VULCAN FOR ARMS
FOR AENEAS
Anton van Dyck
1630–32
| Musée du Louvre, Paris

The duel of Aeneas and Turnus

The war alternated between battles and funerals, until the decisive duel between Aeneas and Turnus. The latter seemed about to lose from the outset, not so much because of inferior strength, but because Fate was against him. The two threw their spears at each other and missed, then drew their swords. Turnus struck a downward blow, but broke his sword and started to run; his sister, Juturna, a nymph allied with Juno, threw him a new one and the duel resumed.

Then Jupiter turned to Juno, who was supporting Turnus, and ordered her to stop, for Fate had already decided. Realizing that she had lost, the goddess asked her husband that he allow the Etruscans to retain their original language and customs and that the race that would issue from the Etruscans and the Trojans be called Roman. At this point, the father of the gods sent a Fury in the guise of a night bird, who began to fly around Turnus. Juturna understood that death was approaching and left in despair, just as Aeneas was triumphing over her brother.

❑ Aeneas is about to thrust his sword into Turnus's chest, while Jupiter and Venus follow the duel from atop a cloud. Hovering in the center, above the enemies, is the night bird that hides a Fury. To the right, Juturna, Turnus's sister, has seen the dark omen and desperately flees from her brother.

AENEAS AND TURNUS
Luca Giordano
17th century
Collezione Corsini, Florence

The apotheosis of Aeneas

VENUS AND AENEAS

Other mythological tales written after the *Aeneid* recount how, after Aeneas prevailed over Turnus, Venus asked Jupiter to welcome her son among the sky gods. All the deities, including Juno, whose anger was now spent, gave their consent, and the father of the gods moved his head, granting her wish. Venus thanked them, then had her doves fly her to the mouth of the river Numicius in Laurentum, where she ordered the river god to wash away all mortal elements from Aeneas. She then spread a divine salve over her son's purified body and, lightly touching his lips with ambrosia and nectar, made him divine.

☐ Aeneas kneels before his mother, who spreads the divine salve over his body. Next to her are the doves, her attributes, which led her to the river. The old man with the bamboo wreath, resting near an amphora that spills water, is the personification of the spirit of the river Numicius, which carries the mortal remains of Aeneas in its slow flowing current, down into the depths of the sea.

VENUS AND AENEAS
Nicolas Poussin
17th century

PRIMARY SOURCES

This section contains a short list of the main authors and works with mythological themes that have inspired artists through the centuries. It is important to remember that artists did not literally follow the primary mythological sources, but often used contemporary compendia or poetic adaptations. Especially in the Baroque era, Greco-Roman historical and mythological themes were extensively reworked in poetry and music, as well as paintings and sculptures.

Anonymous

Ovide moralisé (Ovid Moralized) is an early fourteenth-century poem attributed to either Philippe de Vitry, bishop of Meaux, or Chrétien Legouais de Sainte-More. This poem gives a moralistic interpretation of Ovid within a Christian context.

Apollodorus of Athens

(*c.* 180–15 BCE) A Greek philologist, some of his most important works are the *Catalogue of Ships*, a commentary on the second book of the *Iliad*; *On the Gods*, a compilation of information about myths; and *Chronicle*, which reports on events in the period from the conquest of Troy to 199 BCE.

Apollonius Rhodius

(*c.* 295–15 BCE) A Greek epic poet and a student of Callimachus, he was the director of the famous library of Alexandria in Egypt from 260 to 247 BCE. Among his works is the *Argonautica*, a poem in four books that tells of the journey of Jason on the ship *Argo*, his capture of the Golden Fleece with the help of Medea, and the heroes' return home. A very popular poem during antiquity, Valerius Flaccus later reworked it in Latin.

Apuleius (Lucius Apuleius Platonicus)

(Madaurus, Algeria, *c.* 125–*c.* 180 CE) An author famous for his *Metamorphoses* (Transformations), an eleven-book novel that relates the adventures of young Lucius, who was transformed into an ass and then changed back into a man thanks to the intercession of the goddess Isis. In Book IV, Apuleius narrates the famous story of Love and Psyche.

Boccaccio, Giovanni

(Florence, 1313–Certaldo, 1357) In addition to the celebrated *Decameron*, around 1350 he wrote *Genealogia deorum gentilium* (Genealogy of the Gods of the Gentiles), an extensive fifteen-volume treatise on classical mythology that was an important reference work until the mid-sixteenth century.

Cartari, Vincenzo

(Reggio Emilia, *c.* 1531–71) An Italian author who lived at the Este Court, he wrote *Le imagini colla sposizione degli dei degli antichi* (Images of the Gods of the Ancients), first published in Venice in 1556 and one of the most popular books on mythology, a true iconographic catalogue with commentary that inspired many a Renaissance artist.

Diodorus Siculus

(Agira, Sicily c. 90–20 BCE) A Greek historian, he is the author of the *Bibliotheca historica* (Historical Library), a forty-volume document, only parts of which have survived, and the first universal history.

Aeschylus

(Eleusis, 525–Gela, Sicily, c. 456 BCE) Greek playwright, to whom about eighty tragedies are attributed; of these, only seven survive: *The Suppliants*, *Prometheus Bound*, the *Oresteia* (a trilogy: *Agamemnon*, *The Libation Bearers*, and *The Eumenides*), *The Seven Against Thebes*, and *The Persians*.

Hesiod

(7th–6th century BCE) A Greek poet whose *Theogony* is the first attempt at a rational collection of the existing myths and religions and a description of the origins of the universe and the gods. In *Works and Days*, he illustrates farming and navigation techniques, interspersed with many mythological tales.

Aesop

(7th–6th century BCE) Greek author of fables. The popularity of his work is documented by Aristotle and Plato. His short fables, with mostly animals as characters, all have moral messages.

Euripides

(Salamis, c. 480–Pella, 406 BCE) Greek playwright. The following plays survive from about a total of ninety-two that he authored: *Alcestis*, *Medea*, *Hyppolitus*, *Hecuba*, *Andromache*, *The Heracleidae*, *The Suppliants*, *Heracles*, *The Trojan Women*, *Electra*, *Helen*, *Iphigenia in Tauris*, *Ion*, *The Phoenician Women*, *Orestes*, *Iphigenia in Aulis*, *The Bacchae*, and a satirical play, *The Cyclops*.

Phaedrus

(c. 15 BCE–c. 50 CE) A slave freed by Augustus, he wrote fifteen volumes of fables inspired directly by Aesop and Hellenistic tales, only parts of which survive. Some fables were transmitted in Medieval codices, while others were discovered by Renaissance scholars. In particular, *Romulus*, a work popular in the Middle Ages, contains several fables by Phaedrus paraphrased in prose.

Hyginus (Gaius Julius Hyginus)

(c. 64 BCE–17 CE) Another a slave freed by Augustus, he was the director of the Palatine Library and the author of two mythological works, *Fabulae* (Stories) and *Poeticon astronomicon* (Poetical Astronomy).

Homer

(8th–6th century BCE ?) Greek epic poet. He is the author of the *Iliad*, a poem that narrates the final year of the Trojan War, and the *Odyssey*, which recounts the meandering journey home of Ulysses, king of Ithaca.

Ovid (Publius Ovidius Naso)

(Sulmona, 43 BCE–Tomis, Black Sea, 17 CE) Latin poet. He is the celebrated author of the *Metamorphoses*, the fifteen-book poem narrating the transformations of human beings and gods that became extremely popular in the Middle Ages. In his *Fasti* (Festivals), Ovid describes the festivals of the Roman calendar month by month, recounting legends, rituals, and related events. *Heroides* (The Heroines) is a collection of letters that several real and mythical heroines of antiquity wrote to their lovers.

Petrarch (Francesco Petrarca)

(Arezzo, 1304–Arquà, 1374) An Italian poet and scholar, famous for his *Canzoniere* (Sonnets). He also wrote *Africa*, a poem inspired by the Roman historian Livius in which he recounts the Second Punic War, exalting Rome's virtues. *De viris illustribus* (Of Illustrious Men) discusses ancient heroes and their exemplary deeds. He also wrote the *Trionfi* (Triumphs), from which the iconography of the triumphal cart developed with allegorical and mythological figures.

Pindar

(Cynoscephalae, Boeotia, 522–Argos, 443 BCE) Greek poet. In his *Epinikia* (Victory Odes), he celebrated the skill of the winning athletes of the various sports competitions, interlacing his verses with mythical anecdotes linked to the family of the athlete or the place where the games took place.

Pliny the Elder (Caius Plinius Secundus)

(Como, 23–Stabia, 79 CE) An author and natural scientist, his fame is principally due to his encyclopedic work, *Naturalis historia* (Natural History), in thirty-seven volumes, one of the most important in ancient and medieval culture. He recounts many mythological anecdotes and writes about astronomy, medicine, botany, metallurgy, art, and architecture.

Plutarch

(Chaeronea, *c.* 46–Delphi, *c.* 120 CE) A Greek philosopher and scholar, famous especially for his *Parallel Lives*, in which he compares the lives of famous Greek and Roman generals and statesmen.

Sophocles

(Colonus Hippius, 495–Athens, *c.* 406 BCE) Greek playwright. Of his vast literary production, only eight survive: the tragedies of *Antigone*, *Philoctetes*, *Ajax*, *Oedipus Rex*, *The Trachiniae*, *Electra*, and *Oedipus at Colonus*, and fragments of a satirical drama, *The Tracking Satyrs*.

Virgil (Publius Vergilius Maro)

(Andes, Mantua, 70–Brindisi, 19 BCE). Roman poet. Between 42 and 39 BCE, he wrote the *Bucolics*, a collection of pastoral poems, followed by the *Georgics*, a four-book poem about agriculture. He is famous above all for the *Aeneid*, the twelve-book epic poem that recounts the mythical origins of Rome.

INDEX OF EPISODES

Achilles
    and the daughters of Lycomedes, 650–55
    and Penthesilea, 678
    drags Hector's corpse, 672, 674
Acis and Galatea, 382
Aeneas
    and Dido go hunting, 748
    and the Sibyl at Avernus, 756–59
    takes leave of Dido, 752
Apollo
    and Coronis, 120
    and Daphne, 114–19
    and Hyacinth, 124
    and the cattle of Admetus, 122
    and the Cumaean Sibyl, 210
    and the serpent Python, 110
    flays Marsyas, 112
The apotheosis of Aeneas, 764
Atalanta and Hippomenes, 194
Augustus and the Tiburtine Sibyl, 212
Aurora and Tithonus, 232
The bacchanal of the Andrians, 378
Bacchus
    and Ariadne, 370–73
    and his court, 360–369
The battle for the body of Patroclus, 688
The battle of the Lapiths and the centaurs,
    416–21
The battle over the arms of Achilles, 682
The birth of Bacchus, 356–59
The birth of Minerva, 96
The birth of the Centaurs, 414
The blinding of Orion, 222
Ceres
    and Stellion, 338
    and Triptolemus, 340
    Sine Cerere et Baccho friget Venus, 342
The childhood of Achilles, 644–49

The childhood of Jupiter, 36
Claudia Quinta, 200
Clytia and Leucothea, 224
Coresus and Callirhoe, 376
The creation of the Milky Way, 84
Cupid
    blinded, 286–89
    and the honeycomb, 290
Cupid and Psyche, 292–11
    Psyche asleep, 308
    Psyche discovers Cupid asleep, 298
    Psyche and her sisters, 296
    Psyche in the netherworld, 306
    Psyche is led to Cupid's palace, 294
    The trial of the seeds, 300
    The trial of the Stygian water, 302
Daedalus and Icarus, 478–81
The death of Achilles, 670
The death of Hector, 670
The death of Hercules, 582
The death of Meleager, 602
The death of Orpheus, 590
The death of Patroclus, 664–69
Diana
    and Actaeon, 136–39
    and Callisto, 140–43
Dido's banquet, 740
Dido's suicide, 754
The duel of Aeneas and Turnus, 762
Echo and Narcissus, 386
The fall of the kingdom of Saturn, 20
The fall of the Titans, 22
The flight from Troy, 742, 744
The founding of Carthage, 738
Glaucus and Scylla, 384
Hercules
    and Achelous, 576
    and Alcestis, 570

and Antaeus, 572
at the crossroads, 584
and Deianira, 578, 580
and Omphale, 574
slays his own children, 544
strangles the snakes, 542
Jason
  and Medea, 608
  and Pelias, 606
  tames the bulls, 610
The judgment of Midas, 406–409
The judgment of Paris, 630
Juno in Hades, 86
Jupiter
  and Antiope, 70–73
  and Danaë, 66–69
  and Semele, 64
  and Thetis, 622
Jupiter and Io, 48–57
  Juno and the eyes of Argus, 56
  Mercury and Argus, 52
Jupiter and Latona, 42–47
  The birth of Apollo and Diana, 42
  The death of the children of Niobe, 46
  The peasants transformed into frogs, 44
The labors of Hercules, 550–69
  Cerberus, 560
  The apples of the Hesperides, 562
  The Cretan bull, 556
  The Erymanthian boar, 552
  The Lernaean Hydra, 548
  The mares of Diomedes, 558
  The Nemean Lion, 546
  The Stymphalian birds, 554
The labors of Sisyphus, 442
Leda and the Swan, 38
Luna and Endymion, 228
Mars, Venus, and Vulcan, 146–49
Medea rejuvenates Aeson, 614
Mercury
  and the herd of Apollo, 160
  and Herse, 162–65
  compels Aeneas to leave Dido, 750
The metamorphosis of Cyparissus, 126

Midas's wish, 374
Minerva and Arachne, 100
Pan and Syrinx, 404
Penelope
  at the loom, 726
  challenges the suitors, 730
Perseus
  and Andromeda, 520–23
  and Medusa, 514–19
  and Phineus, 524
Phaeton, 216–21
Philemon and Baucis, 74–77
Picus and Canens, 388
Priam visits Achilles, 676
The punishment of Ixion, 444
The punishment of Tantalus, 440
The punishment of Tityus, 446
The quarrel between Minerva and Neptune, 98
The rape of Europa, 58–63
The rape of the daughters of Leucippus, 40
The revenge of Medea, 616
Saturn devours his children, 18
The satyr and the peasant, 396
Scylla and Charybdis, 724
The slaying of the suitors, 732
The stones of Deucalion and Pyrrha, 508
The theft of the Golden Fleece, 612
Theseus and the Minotaur, 536–39
Thetis asks Vulcan to forge the arms of Achilles, 624
Tuccia, 198
Ulysses
  and Calypso, 710
  in the cave of Polyphemus, 714–17
  and Euryclea, 728
  and Nausicaa, 712
  in the netherworld, 720
  and Penelope, 734
  and the Sirens, 722
Venus and Adonis, 184–93
  The death of Adonis, 186
The War of the Giants, 24–27
The wrath of Achilles, 656–63

INDEX OF NAMES

Acastus, 616
Acates, 736, 740
Achelous, 576
Achilles, 232, 328, 422, 434, 620–27, 636, 642–95, 760
Acis, 382
Acrisius, 66, 512
Actaeon, 136–39
Admetus, 122, 160, 570
Adonis, 166, 184–92, 434
Aeacus, 438
Aeëtes, 604–13
Aegeus, 378, 466, 476, 534
Aegina, 442
Aegisthus, 456, 640
Aello, *see* Harpies
Aeneas, 166, 208, 258, 470, 700, 736–65
Aeolus, 234, 506, 718
Aesculapius, 120–23, 422, 516, 648, 694
Aeson, 606, 614
Aethlius, 228
Aethra, 322, 534
Agamemnon, 440, 456, 622, 636–43, 656–65, 668, 682–87, 704
Agave, 352
Agelaus, 628
Agenor, 58, 528
Aglaia, *see* Graces
Aglauros, 162, 164
Ajax, 434, 682, 686–89, 704
Alcestis, 570
Alcinous, 708, 712, 714
Alcmene, 84, 540, 542
Alecto, *see* Furies
Althaea, 596, 602
Amalthaea, 36
Amazons, 130, 144, 678
Amisodarus, 474

Amor, *see* Cupid
Amphion, 46, 70
Amphitrite, *see* Nereids
Amphitryon, 540–43
Anchises, 166, 700–703, 736, 742–45, 756
Andromache, 670, 690–93
Andromeda, 512, 520–25
Anna, 748, 754
Antaeus, *see* Giants
Anteros, 270
Anticlea, 708, 720
Antigone, 532
Antilocus, 688
Antinous, 732
Antiope, 70, 72
Aphrodite, *see* Venus
Apollo, 16, 42–47, 102–29, 140, 146, 154, 160, 206–11, 214–17, 226, 236–39, 254, 262, 372, 406–409, 422, 434, 446, 570, 620, 638, 648, 656, 670, 680, 698, 702–705, 730, 742
Aquilo, *see* Winds
Arachne, 100
Arcas, 140
Ares, *see* Mars
Argo, 40, 48–57, 88
Argonauts, 88, 466, 604–17
Ariadne, 368–73, 476, 478, 534–39
Aristaeus, 586
Artemis, *see* Diana
Ascanius, 700, 736, 740–45, 752
Asopus, 442, 464
Asteria, 458
Asterion, 58
Astraea, 488, 490
Astraeus, *see* Titans
Astyanax, 690
Atalanta, 194, 596–603

Athamus, 86, 356, 604
Athena, *see* Minerva
Atlas, *see* Titans
Atropos, *see* Parcae
Attis, 344
Aura, 176, 324
Aurora, 16, 190, 214, 226, 230–35, 734

bacchants, *see* maenads
Bacchus, 64, 86, 150, 208, 342, 346–81,
    390, 398, 402, 410, 536–39, 590
Baucis, 74, 76
Bellerophon, 474, 526
Beroe, 64
Boreas, *see* Winds
Briseis, 622, 642, 656–63, 684–87

Cadmus, 64, 528, 608
Calais, 234
Calchas, 636–39, 656
Calliope, *see* Muses
Callirhoe, 264, 376
Callisto, 140–43
Calyce, 228, 262
Calydon, 576, 596–603
Calypso, *see* nymphs
Canens, *see* nymphs
Capys, 656, 702
Cassandra, 626, 704
Cassiopeia, 520
Castor, *see* Dioscuri
Cecrops, 162
Cedalion, 222
Celaeno, *see* Harpies
Celeus, 340
centaurs, 328, 410–23, 444
    Chiron, 120, 136, 410, 422, 492, 606,
    642–49
Centimani, *see* Hecatonchires
Cephalus, 230
Cepheus, 520, 524
Cerberus, 306, 438, 448, 452, 470–73,
    560, 570
Ceres, 18, 334–45, 450, 464

Ceto, 468
Charites, *see* Graces
Charon, 306, 438, 470, 590, 758
Charybdis, 724–27
Chimera, 474, 526
Chiron, *see* centaurs
Chloris, 428
Chrysaor, *see* Giants
Chryseis, 638, 656
Chryses, 638, 656, 694
Ciconians, 714
Cinyras, 184
Circe, 384, 388, 458, 718–25
Claudia Quinta, *see* Vestals
Clio, *see* Muses
Clotho, *see* Parcae
Clymene, 216, 220, 492
Clytemnestra, 38, 456, 636, 640, 704
Clytia, 224, 434
Coeus, *see* Titans
Coresus, 376
Coronis, 120–23
Creon, 540, 544, 616
Creusa, 616, 742–45
Crius, 22
Crocus, 434
Cronus, *see* Saturn
Cupid, 30, 38, 50, 68, 70, 82, 114, 124,
    152, 172, 178, 182, 186–91, 228,
    268–311, 318, 342, 376, 412, 426–29,
    448, 574, 580, 630, 634, 704, 740
Cyane, *see* nymphs
Cybele, 194, 200, 344–47
Cyclopes, 22, 32, 122, 150, 154, 570, 714,
    760
Cyparissus, 126

Daedalus, 476–81, 536
Danae, 66–69, 512
Daphne, 114–19
Dardanus, 206
Dawn, *see* Aurora
Deianira, 540, 576–83
Deidamea, 694

Deioneus, 414
Deiphobus, 634
Demeter, *see* Ceres
Deucalion, 506–509
Dia, 414
Diana, 42–47, 102, 110, 128–43, 148,
    188, 222, 226–29, 380, 404, 446, 458,
    596, 602, 636
Dictys, 512
Dido, 736–43, 748–57
Diomedes, 558, 570, 654
Dion, 166
Dionysus, *see* Bacchus
Dioscuri, 10, 38–41, 600, 606
    Castor, 38–41, 600
    Pollux, 38–41, 600
Doris, 328, 620
dryads, 380

Echidna, 470–75, 546–49
Echo, *see* nymphs
Elara, 446
Electra, 456, 636
Elpenor, 720
Endymion, 228
Envy, 162
Eos, *see* Aurora
Epeus, 696
Epimetheus, 492, 502–505, 508
Epopeus, 70
Erato, *see* Muses
Erechtheus, 234
Erginus, 544
Erinyes, *see* Furies
Eris, 620, 630
Eros, see Cupid
Eumaeus, 728, 732
Eumenides, *see* Furies
Euphrosyne, *see* Graces
Euridyce, 470, 586–91
Euritos, 416, 574
Europa, 58–63, 330, 476, 528, 556, 686
Eurus, *see* Winds
Euryale, *see* Gorgons

Euryclea, 728, 732
Eurylochus, 718
Eurymede, 526
Eurynome, 254
Eurystheus, 470, 540, 546, 552, 556–63
Eurythemis, 38
Euterpe, *see* Muses

Fates, *see* Parcae
Flora, 428–35
Fortuna, 318, 466, 654
Furies, 86, 316, 456
    Alaetto, 456
    Megaera, 456
    Tisiphone, 86, 456

Gaea, 18–25, 96, 166, 334, 562, 572
Galatea, *see* Nereids 774
Ganymedes, 262–67
Giants, 22–27, 622
    Antaeus, 322, 572
    Chrysaor, 468, 518
    Lestrigons, 718
    Orion, 222
    Tityus, 86, 446, 720
Glauce, 608, 616
Glaucus, 384, 526
Gorgons, 468, 514, 520, 758
    Euryale, 222, 468, 518
    Medusa, 88, 94, 144, 468, 512–19, 524
    Stheno, 468, 518
Graces, 176, 254–57
    Aglaia, 254
    Euphrosyne, 254
    Thalia, 254
Graiae, 514

Hades, *see* Pluto
hamadryads, *see* dryads
Harmonia, 64
Harpies, 466, 746, 758
    Aello, 466
    Celaeno, 466, 746
    Ocypete, 466

Hebe, 262–65, 358
Hecate, 458–61, 614
Hecatonchires, 22
Hector, 624, 634, 642, 664–67, 670–79, 684, 688–93, 742
Hecuba, 626–29, 670–73, 690, 700, 704
Helen, 38, 630–37, 704
Helios, see Sol
Helle, 604
Hephaestus, see Vulcan
Hera, see Juno
Heracles, see Hercules
Hercules, 24, 84, 144, 262, 422, 470–73, 492, 500, 540–85, 606, 694
Hermes, see Mercury
Hermione, 632
Herse, 162–65
Hesperides, 194, 540, 562–67, 572
Hestia, see Vesta
Hippocrates, 422
Hippodamia, 416–21
Hippomenes, 194
Hours, 16, 30, 176, 216, 230, 262, 504
Hyacinth, 124, 434
Hydra of Lerna, 472, 548–51, 758
Hyperion, 22, 214, 230

Iapetus, see Titans
Iarbas, 738, 750
Icarus, 478–81
Idas, 40
Inachus, 48
Infernals, 20, 86, 306, 308, 322, 334, 436–61, 470, 560, 570, 586, 588, 614, 722, 736, 758
Ino, 86, 356, 604, 710
Io, see nymphs
Iobates 474, 526
Iolaus, 544, 548
Iphicles, 542–45, 548
Iphigenia, 636, 640
Iphitus, 574
Iris, 34, 56, 672, 676
Ixion, 86, 410, 414–17, 444

Janus, 16, 202–205, 388
Jason, 422, 606–17, 648
Jocasta, 530–33
Jove, see Jupiter
Juno, 18, 26, 34, 38–45, 48–53, 56–59, 64–67, 78–87, 100, 112, 116, 120–27, 132, 136, 140, 144, 150, 160, 194–97, 200–205, 210, 214, 218, 228, 234, 248, 262–67, 290–95, 302, 308, 316, 334–41, 356, 362–65, 368–71, 376–79, 382, 386, 396, 404–407, 414–17, 442–51, 472–77, 488, 492, 498–503, 516, 520, 524–27, 530–33, 538–51, 556, 562, 570–75, 578, 582–85, 590, 598–603, 606–609, 612, 622, 630–33, 636–41, 680, 690, 694, 698, 712–15, 720–27, 736–45, 748–53, 756, 760–65
Jupiter, 10–13, 18–27, 30–89, 96–99, 102, 122, 128, 140, 144, 148–51, 156, 160, 166, 196, 202, 206, 216–21, 228, 232, 236, 254, 258, 262–69, 278, 292, 302–305, 308, 314, 322, 334, 344–47, 356–61, 368, 386, 414, 440–51, 476, 486–93, 496–503, 506–509, 512, 528, 540–43, 562–65, 570, 582, 604, 620–23, 630–33, 662, 670–73, 676, 686, 710, 726, 750, 762–65
Juturna, see nymphs

Lachesis, see Parcae
Ladon, 404, 562, 564
Laertes, 708, 726
Laius, 530–33
Laocöon, 69–99, 702, 742
Laomedon, 232
Lapiths, 120, 410, 414–22, 444
Latinus, 736, 760
Latona, 42–47, 102, 128, 446
Lavinia, 92, 736, 760
Learchus, 86, 604
Leda, 38–41, 632
Lestrigons, see Giants
Leucippides, 40
Leucippus, 40

Leucothea, 86
Leucothoe, 224
Lichas, 582
Liseros, 270
Lotus-Eaters, 714
Love, see Cupid
Lucina, 184
Luna, 214, 226–31
Lycaon, 140
Lycomedes, 642, 650–55
Lycus, 70, 544
Lynceus, 40
Lyncus, 340
Lyssa, 544

Macaon, 694
maenads, 362–69, 372–75, 390, 402
Mars, 88, 144–51, 154, 166, 178–83, 224,
    230, 268, 276–79, 444, 528, 604–607,
    678, 690
Marsyas, 112
Medea, 458, 608–17
Medusa, see Gorgons
Megaera, see Furies
Megara, 540, 544
Melantius, 732
Meleager, 596–603, 606
Melicertes, 86, 604
Melpomene, see Muses
Memnon, 232
Menelaus, 440, 630–36, 688
Menoetius, 684
Mercury, 30, 48, 52–57, 74–77, 84, 110,
    122, 148, 156–65, 308, 356–61, 390,
    398, 402, 450, 496, 502, 514, 518, 522,
    538, 560, 604, 630, 676, 710, 718, 736,
    750–55
Merope, 222
Metis, 88, 96
Midas, 374, 406–409
Minerva, 88–101, 110–13, 144, 148, 162,
    258, 468, 492, 502, 514–19, 522–29,
    538, 548, 554–57, 560–63, 584, 630,
    656, 670, 682, 696–99, 704, 728–35

Minos, 58, 370, 438, 476–79, 534–37,
    556
Minotaur, 322, 370, 476–81, 534–39
Mnemosyne, 22, 236
Modesty, 490
Moerae, see Parcae
Moon, see Luna
Muses, 102, 106, 112, 236–55, 262, 464,
    514, 518, 620
    Calliope, 236–39, 244, 250, 464, 586
    Clio, 236–39
    Erato, 236–39
    Euterpe, 236–39
    Melpomene, 236–39, 464
    Polyhymnia, 236–39, 246–49
    Thalia, 236–39, 252
    Terpsichore, 236–39, 464
    Urania, 236–39, 242
Myrmidon, 650, 660, 684
Myrrha, 184

naiads, 380, 390, 576
Narcissus, 358, 386, 434
Nausicaa, 708, 712
Nemesis, 38, 316, 386
Neoptolemus, 694
Nephele, 604
Neptune, 18, 42, 86, 98, 146, 222,
    322–31, 448, 476, 506, 512, 520, 556,
    572, 620, 702, 710, 714, 720
Nereids, 328–31, 380, 520, 620
    Amphitrite, 324–31
    Galatea, 328, 382
    Thetis, 22, 78, 150, 318, 328, 620–25,
        630, 642–45, 650, 654, 662, 676,
        686, 690
Nereus, 328, 620
Neso, 206
Nessus, 578–83
Nessus, see Centaurs
Nike, see Victoria
Niobe, 46
Notus, see Winds
Nycteus, 70

nymphs, 360, 380–91, 402
    Calypso, 708–11, 726
    Canens, 388
    Cyane, 450
    Echo, 358, 386
    Juturna, 762
    Io, 48–57
    Scylla, 384, 724–27
    Syrinx, 404

Oceanus, 22, 78, 254, 318, 328, 422, 520
Ocypete, *see* Harpies
Odysseus, *see* Ulysses
Oeagrus, 586
Oedipus, 530–33
Oenopion, 222
Oeneus, 576, 596
Olympus, 10, 20, 26, 30, 40, 88, 98, 150,
    254, 262–67, 292, 308–11, 402, 416,
    470, 494, 504, 620–25, 662
Omphale, 574
oreads, 380
Oreithyia, 234
Orestes, 456, 636
Orion, *see* Giants
Orpheus, 470, 586–93, 600, 606
Orynoe, 230

Palaemon, 86
Pallas, *see* Titans
Pan, 136, 358, 382, 398–409, 434, 574
Pandora, 492, 502–505
Parcae, 32, 314, 456, 570, 588, 602
    Atropos, 314, 588
    Clotho, 314, 588
    Lachesis, 314, 588
Paris, 626–37, 680, 690, 704, 760
Pasiphaë, 476
Patroclus, 624, 642, 656, 660, 664–71,
    612, 676, 680, 684–91
Pegasus, 468, 474, 516–21, 526
Peleus, 620, 630, 642–45, 658–61, 668,
    682, 684
Pelias, 570, 606, 614, 616

Pelops, 440
Penelope, 708–11, 726–31, 734
Peneus, 114–17
Penthesilea, 678
Persephone, *see* Proserpina
Perseus, 66, 88, 94, 458, 468, 512–25,
    540
Phaeton, 216–21
Philemon, 74–77
Philoctetes, 582, 694
Philoetius, 732
Philonoe, 526
Phineus, 466, 524
Phlegyas, 120
Phoebe, 22, 40–43
Phoenix, 642, 686
Pholus, 410
Phorcys, 468
Phosphorus, 230
Phrixus, 604–607
Picus, 388
Pirithous, 416, 560
Pittheus, 534
Pluto, 18–21, 322, 334, 438, 442, 448–55,
    464, 470, 560, 588
Polixena, 680
Pollux, *see* Dioscuri
Polydectes, 512
Polyhymnia, *see* Muses
Polyphemus, 322, 328, 382, 710, 714–21
Polyphemus, *see* Cyclopes
Pomona, 424–27
Poseidon, *see* Neptune
Priamus, 232, 626–29, 670, 612, 676, 680,
    690, 700, 704
Proetus, 526
Prometheus, *see* Titans
Proserpina, 306, 334–37, 340, 448–55,
    464, 470, 560, 588, 756
Psyche, 30, 292–311, 470
Pygmalion, 738
Pyrrha, 506–509, 650
Python, 108–11, 114

Rhadamantus, 58, 438
Rhea, 18–23, 32, 78, 196, 322, 334, 344, 422, 448

Sarpedon, 58
Saturn, 10–27, 32, 36, 78, 148, 166, 196, 216, 322, 334, 344, 388, 422, 448, 456, 484–87
satyrs, 328, 362, 368, 312, 374, 390–99, 402, 410
   Silenus 356, 360, 368, 374, 398–401
Scylla, see nymphs
Scyros, 194, 642, 650
Selene, see Luna
Semele, 64, 86, 346, 356
Sibyls, 206–13
   Cimmerian Sibyl, 206
   Cumaean Sibyl, 206–11, 756
   Delphic Sibyl, 206
   Hellespontine Sibyl, 206
   Erythraean Sibyl, 206
   Phrygian Sibyl, 206
   Libyan Sibyl, 206
   Persian Sibyl, 206
   Samian Sibyl, 206
   Tiburtine Sibyl, 206, 212
sileni, 362, 398, 410
Silenus, see satyrs
Sinon, 698, 702, 742
Sirens, 464, 722–25
Sisyphus, 442, 526, 588, 720
Smilax, 434
Sol, 108, 154, 160, 214–27, 230, 450, 608, 616, 718, 726
Stellion, 338
Stheneboea, 526
Stheno, see Gorgons
Styx, 258
Sun, see Sol
Sychaeus, 738
Syrinx, see nymphs

Tantalus, 46, 86, 440, 588, 720
Telemachus, 726, 728, 730, 732, 734

Terpsichore, see Muses
Teucrus, 742
Thalia, see Graces or Muses
Thaumas, 466
Theia, 22, 214, 230
Themis, 22, 110, 314, 490, 508, 620
Theseus, 322, 370, 372, 476, 478, 534, 536, 538, 560, 606
Thestius, 38
Thetys, see Nereids
Tiresias, 542, 720
Tisiphone, see Furies
Titans, 22, 30, 36, 78, 214, 322, 448, 498, 564
   Astraeus, 234
   Atlas, 498, 562–65, 568, 710
   Ceo, 22, 42, 126
   Iapetus, 22, 492
   Pallas, 258, 534
   Prometheus, 422, 492–503, 506–509, 562
Tithonus, 230–33
Tityus, see Giants
Triptolemus, 340
Tritons, 328–31
   Triton, 328, 642
Trojan Horse, 696–701, 742
Tros, 264
Tuccia, see Vestals
Turnus, 736, 760–63
Tyche, see Fortuna
Tyndareus, 38, 40, 630, 632
Typhon, 470, 472, 474, 548

Ulysses, 634, 642, 650, 654, 682, 686, 694–99, 708–35
Urania, see Muses
Uranus, 10, 18, 22–25, 96, 166, 456

Venus, 12, 60, 144–55, 166, 168–95, 224, 230, 254, 268, 274–85, 290–93, 300–303, 306–11, 342, 380, 448, 470, 502, 536, 584, 630–35, 700, 736–41, 748, 756, 760–65

Vertumnus, 424–27
Vesta, 18, 196–201
Vestals, 196
    Claudia Quinta, 200
    Tuccia, 198
Victoria, 88, 258–61, 276
Voluptas, 310
Vulcan, 30, 96, 122, 144–55, 166,
    222–25, 264, 444, 492, 496, 502, 554,
    610, 624, 760

Winds, 234
    Aquilo, 506
    Boreas, 234
    Eurus, 234
    Notus, 234, 506
    Zephyrus, 10, 124, 176, 234, 294–97,
    428

Zephyrus, *see* Winds
Zetes, 234
Zethus, 70
Zeus, *see* Jupiter

PHOTO CREDITS